SHAWN O'BRIEN, TOWN TAMER

Shawn O'Brien, Town Tamer

William W. Johnstone
with J. A. Johnstone

PINNACLE BOOKS
Kensington Publishing Corp.
www.kensingtonbooks.com

PINNACLE BOOKS are published by

Kensington Publishing Corp.
119 West 40th Street
New York, NY 10018

PUBLISHER'S NOTE
Following the death of William W. Johnstone, the Johnstone family is working with a carefully selected writer to organize and complete Mr. Johnstone's outlines and many unfinished manuscripts to create additional novels in all of his series like The Last Gunfighter, Mountain Man, and Eagles, among others. This novel was inspired by Mr. Johnstone's superb storytelling.

All Kensington titles, imprints, and distributed lines are available at special quantity discounts for bulk purchases for sales promotions, premiums, fund-raising, educational, or institutional use. Special book excerpts or customized printings can also be created to fit specific needs. For details, write or phone the office of the Kensington special sales manager: Kensington Publishing Corp., 119 West 40th Street, New York, NY 10018, attn: Special Sales Department; phone 1-800-221-2647.

PINNACLE BOOKS and the Pinnacle logo are Reg. U.S. Pat. & TM Off.
The WWJ steer head logo is a trademark of Kensington Publishing Corp.

ISBN-13: 978-0-7860-3263-1
ISBN-10: 0-7860-3263-4

First printing: March 2014

10 9 8 7 6 5 4 3 2 1

Printed in the United States of America

First electronic edition: March 2014

ISBN-13: 978-0-7860-3264-8
ISBN-10: 0-7860-3264-2

CHAPTER ONE

Hours of jolting, swaying misery ended suddenly as the stage came to a harness-jangling halt. It remained still until the following dust cloud caught up and covered the four passengers inside with a coat of fine, mustard-colored grit.

The driver climbed down, stepped to the window and stuck his shaggy head inside. A patch made from a scrap of tanned leather covered his right eye.

"Town coming up, folks, but this stage don't stop there," the man said. "Fact is no stage stops there. We go on through Holy Rood at a gallop, so hold on tight an' say your prayers if you got 'em."

Shawn O'Brien had been lost in thought, deep in heartbreaks of the past, but now he stirred himself enough to say, "Why is that? Why all the hurry?"

"Because Holy Rood is a downright dangerous place to be, young feller," the driver said. "Especially if you got a sin to hide."

"Hell, we've all got a sin to hide," a passenger said.

He was a pleasant-faced man who wore the broadcloth finery and string tie of the frontier gambler, his black frockcoat now a uniform tan from trail dust.

"Then repent for yer sins an' hold on like I told you," the driver said. "This here stage is barrelin' through that damned town like a deadheading express."

"Oh, dear," said a small man with the timid, downtrodden look of a henpecked husband. "When we left Silver Reef, Wells Fargo didn't inform me that my life would be in such peril."

"Hell, they never do." The driver grinned. "Holy Rood ain't on the map as far as Wells Fargo is concerned."

The gambler grinned at the little man. "What sin are you hiding, mister?" The humor reached his eyes. "Looking at you, I'd say whiskey and women are your downfall."

"Good heavens no," the man said. "My lady wife would never allow it. She bade me promise on our wedding eve that my lips would ne'er touch ardent spirits nor my loins join in unholy union with those of another woman." The little man seemed to shrink into his seat. "She's a stern, unbending woman, my wife, much given to the virtues of Holy Scripture and liberal doses of prune juice."

"Then I guess you've nothing to fear," the gambler said. "Hell, man, you're a shining example to all of us."

His eyes moved to the girl sitting next to the little man. She'd seemed pretty in the Silver Reef boomtown, but hours in the stage had taken its toll. Now she looked weary, hot and uncomfortable and smelled musky of perspiration and stale perfume.

"What about you, missy?" the gambler said. "You got a little sin to confess?"

A hot breeze gusted through the stage window, carrying dust and a faint odor of sage and mesquite.

"I don't think that's an appropriate question to ask a lady," Shawn O'Brien said. "I reckon you should guard your tongue, mister."

The gambler had to crane his head to look at Shawn. And when he did, he wished he hadn't.

The young man's handsome, well-bred face bore a mild, almost amused expression, but the gambler read a hundred different kinds of hell in his blue eyes. He'd seen eyes like that before across a lot of card tables, the I-don't-give-a-damn look of the seasoned gunfighter.

By the nature of his profession the gambler was a cautious man and he tacked on to a more favorable course.

To the girl, he said, "The gentleman is correct, of course. I'm sorry if I said anything to offend you, ma'am. That was far from my intention."

The girl had a beautiful smile, white teeth in a pink mouth. "No offense taken," she said. "You asked a most singular question, sir, and my answer to it is that I cuss sometimes."

"I rather fancy that any cuss from lips as sweet as yours must be mild indeed," Shawn said.

"Well, I do say hell and damn when the occasion demands it," the girl said.

"And I say a hell of a lot worse than that, young lady," the stage driver said. "And you'll probably hear it when we hit the main street through Holy Rood. So hang on, everybody, and let's git this here rig rolling."

He rubbed a gnarled hand across his mouth. "You see a poor soul with his head on the chopping block, don't look no further, huh? It ain't a sight fer good Christian folks."

Without another word the driver disappeared and the stage creaked and lurched as he climbed into the box. A whip cracked and the six-mule team shambled into motion.

"Yeeeeah!"

The whip snapped again and the mules took the hint and stretched into a gallop.

"What did he mean about a poor soul's head on a chopping block?" the little man said. "That was a most distressing thing to hear."

His voice hiccuped with every jolt of the stage and his knuckles were white on the carpetbag he held on his lap.

"I wouldn't worry about it," the gambler said. "Stage drivers are like ferrymen, crazy as bullbats. I ain't never met a sane one yet."

"It was a strange thing to say, all the same," Shawn said.

"I'll allow you that, mister," the gambler said. "'Twas a strange thing to say. . . ."

A couple of minutes later it was the girl who first saw them . . . the yellowed skulls that grinned atop tall, timber posts bordering both sides of the wagon road.

The girl opened her mouth to say something, but the words bunched up in her throat and wouldn't come.

The timid little man spoke for her.

"My God, what kind of town is this?" he said, his voice breaking. "It's signposted by the devil himself."

Shawn stuck his head out the window.

Skull after skull flashed past, most yellow, a few still red and raw, a macabre march of the mutilated dead.

The driver stood in the box, his whip cracking over the backs of the straining mules, and the stage rocked and pitched like a barque in a storm.

Shawn tried to count the skulls, but soon gave up. There were just too many of them.

Gunshots slammed beside him and the girl let out a high-pitched shriek of surprise and fear.

The gambler leaned out the window and cut loose with a short-barreled Colt. After the hammer clicked on the empty chamber, he sat back in the seat and said, "That isn't decent, the skulls of dead men lining the road. I tried to shoot some of them off."

"Hit any?" Shawn said.

"Not a one."

Above the rumble of the wheels and the pound of the mules' hooves, the driver yelled, "Town comin' up! Hang on, folks!"

Shawn looked out the window again. A dozen yards in front of him a large, painted sign read:

WELCOME TO HOLY ROOD
A Blessed Place
~
Come Worship with Us

Then the stage hammered into the town's main drag, its attendant dust cloud rolling along behind, trying desperately to catch up.

Shawn was aware of a wide street lined on both sides with timber buildings, all of them painted white, and the strange fact that there was not a soul around.

Then disaster struck . . . an unforeseen incident that would soon plunge Shawn O'Brien and the other passengers into a living nightmare.

CHAPTER TWO

As the thundering stage took Holy Rood's main street at a gallop, the cussing driver stood in the box and frantically cracked his snaking whip, urging the mules to go faster . . . and faster. . . .

The town's buildings flickered past like runaway slides at a demented magic lantern show . . . and then catastrophe.

Fleeing a butcher, the big meat hog that charged out of an alley weighed a little over three hundred pounds. It was solid enough and fast enough to slam into the left lead mule with the force of an out-of-control freight train.

The mule went down, screaming, like a puppet that just had its strings cut. Panicked, the rest of the team swerved to their right. Too late! The following mules crashed into the downed animal and then hit the ground in a tangle of kicking legs and jangling traces.

Rocking violently, the stage couldn't right itself,

tipped over on two wheels and then crashed onto
its side.

The driver was thrown clear, but his neck broke
when the back of his head slammed into the boardwalk. He died within seconds, soundlessly and without movement.

But the scene inside the stage was as chaotic as
the tangle of kicking, screaming mules.

As the stage filled with dust, Shawn was thrown
on top of the gambler and the timid man was lost
under a flurry of the girl's white petticoats.

"Hell, mister, you're crushing me to death," the
gambler said, gasping for breath. "Git off me!"

"Sorry," Shawn said. "I'm going to move and get
the door open."

"Then move carefully, for God's sake," the gambler said. "I'm dying here."

"I'll try," Shawn said.

The girl had managed to squirm into a sitting
position on the little man's chest, and he wailed in
protest.

"Are you all right?" Shawn said to her. "No
broken bones?"

The girl nodded. "I don't think so."

"I can't breathe," the little man wailed. "I'm getting crushed to death. Oh, my poor wife."

"Hold on. I'll get you out of there," Shawn said.

But before he could make a move, the stage door
was thrown open and a man's head appeared.

"Is anybody hurt?" he said.

"I don't think so," Shawn said.

"Then praise the Lord," the man said. "His sweet mercy has spared you."

A moment later two sets of hands reached into the stage and Shawn said, "Get the girl first."

"Grab my hands, young woman," the rescuer said.

The girl was hauled out and then the little man, who staggered a little and declared that this entire experience was an "outrage," and that Wells Fargo and this benighted town would "pay for his terrible injuries."

"I need to stand on you," Shawn said to the gambler. "I'll try not to step on your face."

"Just . . . do it," the gambler growled, his distorted cheek jammed against the other door. "And be damned to ye for weighing more than my ex-mother-in-law."

Using the gambler as a step, Shawn clambered though the open door and onto the street. The gambler got out a few moments later, bleeding from a cut on his forehead, his eyes blazing and some sharp words for Shawn on the tip of his tongue.

But then, like the intended target of his wrath, he could only stand openmouthed and silent, stunned by what he saw. . . .

Five men wearing monkish black robes and flat-brimmed, low-crowned hats of the same color, stood around the stage. All wore belted Colts and carried Winchesters. Nowhere was a smile to be seen.

Shawn pegged them as hard cases in monks' clothing, and a couple of them had the look and arrogant attitude of Texan hired guns.

A couple of shots rang out as someone killed the injured mules, and then one of the five men spoke. He had ice-blue eyes and a black, spade-shaped beard.

"Your driver is dead," he said. "You will stay here in town until your fate is decided."

"Now see here," the little passenger said, puffing up a little. "My name is Ernest J. Pettwood the Third and I'm a senior representative of the Miles and Anderson Ladies Corset Company of St. Louis. I demand that you arrange transportation to my original destination. And I mean—instanter!"

The bearded man stared at Pettwood as though he was a slimy thing that had just crawled out from under a rock.

His face like stone, he raised his rifle and shot the little drummer in the chest.

Pettwood staggered back and fell on his butt. He glanced down at the scarlet flower blossoming on his chest with a mix of surprise and shock, then keeled over onto his side and lay still.

The girl ran to the dead man and took his head in her arms. Her hands bloodstained, she glared at the drummer's killer and said, "You damned animal!"

"Anybody else got a demand they want solved 'instanter'?" the bearded man asked.

"Damn you for a murdering rogue," Shawn said. "I'll see you hang for this."

He took a step toward the bearded man, then stopped as four rifles rattled as they swung in his direction.

"His was an obscene profession," the bearded man said. "Such as he can't be allowed to live and pollute the very air we breathe in this fair town."

"I've seen you before, mister," Shawn said, his anger barely under control. "I can't remember where, but I'll swear it was on a wanted poster."

The man made no answer, but he turned to one of the others with him.

"Brother Melchizedeck, search the men for firearms," he said.

The gambler opened his coat with his left hand. "Take it," he said. "In the shoulder holster."

Brother Melchizedeck took the gambler's Colt, then said to Shawn, "Where is your gun?"

"I don't have one," Shawn said.

"Search him, brother," the bearded man said. "He has a dishonest face and a mocker's tongue."

Shawn opened his coat and the man named Melchizedeck patted him down. "He has no gun, Brother Uzziah."

The bearded man nodded. Then, to the gambler he said, "By what name do you call yourself?"

"I call myself by the name my parents gave me. What misbegotten son of a whore gave you yours?"

"You wear the garb of a professional cardplayer, and are thus already suspect," Uzziah said. "Best you keep a civil tongue in your head."

"Or what? You'll murder me like you did the drummer?" the gambler said, anger flaring his cheeks.

"I must tell you that I believe that your fate may already be sealed," Uzziah said. "Look to the church and tell me what you see?"

The gambler eyes shifted to the steepled church at the end of the street. Even at a distance the preacher could be heard roaring at the faithful inside.

"Damn you, it's a gallows," the gambler said. "What kind of people puts an obscenity like that at the door of a church?"

The man called Uzziah smiled without humor. "It's a guillotine," he said. He tucked the butt of his rifle under his arm and bladed his right hand into the open palm of his left. "It removes the heads of the sinful and dispatches them to hell. 'Instanter,' as the drummer said."

"Mister," the gambler said, "you're a sick man and this is a sick town."

"No, it's a peaceful town, and prosperous," Uzziah said.

A dust devil reeled in the street, then collapsed in a yellow cloud.

"He's not a sick man, he's a hired gun and a woman killer," Shawn said. He stared at Uzziah, a hard blue light in his eyes, "As I recollect, his name is Sheldon Shannon from down Nogales way with time out for a five-year spell in Yuma. I reckon he was spawned with a price on his head. A far piece off your home range, aren't you, Shel? I never knew you to operate north of the Red."

"And who might you be?" Shannon said. "Or do you know?"

"Name's Shawn O'Brien from the Glorieta Mesa country in the New Mexico Territory."

Recognition dawned in Shannon's eyes. "Your pa's the bull o' the woods down that way an' you got a brother, Jacob. Big man, plays the piano real good."

"My father, Colonel Shamus O'Brien, is the biggest rancher in the territory," Shawn said, his face stiff. "As for my brother, Jake, he plays the piano among other things."

"He's a rum one, all right, is Jacob," Shannon said. "I was there the night he killed Everett Wilson down Austin way. You heard of him?"

"Yes. I've heard of him."

"Wilson was no bargain."

"So Jake told me."

"Judging by your kin, I reckon you're gun slick,

O'Brien. Strange thing in a man who doesn't carry a pistol."

"You should be in Yuma, Shel. But I don't see you carrying chains."

Shannon nodded. "You have a quick wit, O'Brien. Well, I don't know how long you'll live, but you call me Shel Shannon just one more time and your life ends right here."

"So what do I call you, besides son-of-a—"

"You call me Brother Uzziah. Get it right next time, O'Brien, or I'll kill you."

"What do we do with them?" Brother Melchizedeck said.

His eyes still burning into Shawn's face like branding irons, Shannon said, "Take O'Brien and the gambler to the prison. They'll be put to the question later."

"And the girl?"

"The hotel. Once the church service is over two holy and righteous women of the town will examine her for the witch's mark."

"Brother Uzziah, look!" one of the other men yelled. He pointed to a rock ridge above the town where a man sat a white horse in front of a stand of aspen.

Shannon scanned the ridge, then screamed, "Damn him! Damn him to hell!"

He threw his Winchester to his shoulder and

levered off several shots at the rider on the ridge. The man didn't flinch.

"Is it him?" Shannon yelled, lowering the rifle. "Is it the shifter?"

"It's him all right," Melchizedeck said, a strange, stricken fear in his eyes. "It's Jasper Wolfden as ever was. He's come back from the grave." Then, "My God, Uzziah, look at that!"

The rider leaned from the saddle and hefted a long pole that seemed heavy for him because of the human head stuck on the axe-shaved point.

"Who is it?" Shannon shrieked. "Damn you, whose head is that?"

"It's Mordecai," a young, towheaded brother said.

"Are you sure?" Shannon said, his voice ragged with near hysteria. "Damn you, are you sure?"

"Yes, it's Brother Mordecai. I can make out the black powder burn over his left eye."

Shawn studied Shel Shannon. The gunman was a cold-blooded killer, lightning fast on the draw and shoot, but his hands trembled and he continually swallowed as though his mouth was filled with saliva.

"He's a shifter," Shannon said. "You can't kill a shifter."

His eyes keen, Shawn directed his attention to the horseman on the ridge.

The man held his macabre trophy high. By the

look of the head, its late owner had died recently. Shawn guessed within the past couple of hours.

He had no idea who Jasper Wolfden was, but dead men don't sweat. Dark arcs showed in the armpits of the man's shirt and his hat had a salt-crusted stain around the crown.

Wolfden had not returned from the grave, but spook or not, shifter or not, he'd put the fear of God into Sheldon Shannon . . .

. . . a man who didn't scare worth a damn.

CHAPTER THREE

The doors of the church swung open and the congregation of about a hundred men, women and children spilled onto the street. They had obviously turned out in their best, the men in go-to-prayer-meeting broadcloth, the women in silk afternoon dresses that boasted much lace.

All eyes turned to the wrecked stage and then to the passengers who stood under guard.

It seemed no one had noticed the dead men.

At least not yet.

Shawn watched a man stand in the church doorway for a few moments before he too stepped into the street.

He was very tall; at least five inches over six feet, and his shoulders under the monk's robes were an axe handle wide. His black hair was cropped close and his clean-shaven face was long, lean and hard, the mouth thin, touched by a hint of cruelty.

The townspeople bowed their heads as the man

walked through them, his stride purposeful, like a soldier crossing a parade ground.

"Why all the shooting, Brother Uzziah?" the big man said. "I had to cut my sermon short and a mere two hours isn't nearly enough to drive mortal sin from these people."

"Jasper Wolfden was on the ridge, Brother Matthias," Shel said.

"He's dead," Matthias said. His face was like stone and his eyes slid from Shannon's face to conceal his emotions.

"He's back," Melchizedeck said. "Look on the ridge, Brother Matthias."

The man called Matthias shaded his eyes against the sun and studied the ridge. The rider was gone, but the pole with the head was stuck into the ground.

"Who is it?" he said. Then louder for the sake of the gathering crowd, "Who is the holy martyr?"

"Brother Mordecai," Shannon said.

"But . . . he was good with a gun," Matthias said.

"Yeah, but he wasn't a patch on Wolfden, boss," Melchizedeck said. "And Wolfden is a shifter. He may have killed Brother Mordecai as a wolf or a cougar."

Matthias looked like a man who'd just been slapped. His nostrils flaring, he said, "I told you never to call me 'boss.' In this town I'm Brother Matthias."

"Sorry, it just slipped out," Melchizedeck said. He looked scared.

"Don't let it slip out again or I'll make you eat it, washed down with hot lead," Matthias said. "Do you understand?"

Melchizedeck swallowed hard, his Adam's apple bobbing.

"I won't forget, Brother Matthias."

The big man ignored him and said to Shannon, "Only the heathen Navajo believe in shifters. Wolfden is only a man, a washed-up actor for God's sake, and like any man he can be killed. We must have shot and buried the wrong feller is all."

Matthias's eyes moved to the two dead men sprawled in the street.

Who are they?" he said.

"A nobody. A ladies' corsets drummer," Shannon said. "And the stage driver who broke his damned fool neck when the stage went over."

"The drummer was shot. Why did you kill him?"

"He made demands," Shannon said.

Matthias nodded, only half-interested. His eyes ranged over Shawn, the gambler and the girl, then back to Shawn.

"Do I know you?" he said to Shawn.

"Maybe. I'm Shawn O'Brien of Dromore in the New Mexico Territory."

"Old Shamus's son?"

"One of them."

Matthias looked like a man who'd just gotten bad news. And the skin of his face stiffened tight to the skull when Shannon said, "He recognized me, Brother Matthias. He knows who I am."

Shawn said, "As I recall, a couple of years back good ol' Shel here took to running with a hard crowd ramrodded by a feller by the name of Hank Cobb. Seems this Cobb feller got his start in life as a small-time, dark alley crook who'd stick the shiv into any man, woman or child for fifty dollars. That's what I heard, anyway."

Matthias was silent for a long time, then he said, "Brother Uzziah, take these men to the prison. They will face the Grand Council tonight. The girl goes to the hotel. Have the women search her for the witch's mark. If such is found, she'll burn."

Panic flashed in the girl's face and she turned and ran toward the church.

She didn't get far.

A couple of men stepped away from the rest of the congregation and grabbed her by the arms.

"Take her to the hotel, brethren," Matthias said. "A couple of you righteous women go with her and put her to the test."

Shawn O'Brien, made reckless by recent grief that continued to hurt like a knife blade twisting in his belly, said, "Damn you, you're Hank Cobb all right. Only a lowlife like you would treat a woman that way."

Cobb smiled. "Yeah, I'm Cobb, the man who'll sign your death warrant, O'Brien. Your pa and your gunslinging brothers ain't here to protect you now, pretty boy."

It looked as though Cobb was prepared to say more, but Shawn's hard fist crashing into his mouth discouraged any further attempt at speech.

Cobb hit the ground flat on his back, but the big man made no effort to rise again. He back-handed a trickle of blood from the corner of his mouth, smearing red across his chin. His eyes were murderous.

"Want me to gun him, Matthias?" Shannon said.

"No. I want a different death for him." Cobb got to his feet, helped by members of his congregation. "Take him to the prison, and the gambler with him."

Cobb pushed his face close to Shawn's.

"Before this day is done, you'll regret the day you were spawned and you'll curse the mother that bore you."

Shawn spat in the man's face . . . and paid the price.

Something hard crashed into the side of his head and suddenly he saw the ground cartwheeling up to meet him.

And then he saw nothing at all. . . .

CHAPTER FOUR

"How you feeling, pardner?"

Shawn O'Brien opened his eyes, saw the gambler's face solidify from an angular, concerned blur. He groped for words through the fog of a headache.

"All right, I reckon."

"You took a hard bump. Rifle butt."

"Seems like."

"Name's Hamp Sedley. I know yours. Shawn O'Brien of Dromore. Hell, you sound like royalty."

Shawn struggled to a sitting position and heard an iron cot creak under him. Late afternoon sunlight angled through a high window and bladed into his eyes. He smelled vomit, man sweat and ancient piss.

"Where are we, Hamp?" he said.

"In what them fellers in robes call a prison," Sedley said. "They say we won't be here much longer on account they plan to hang us."

"Cut our heads off, you mean," Shawn said.

"I was going to break that to you gently," Sedley said. "You having a misery an' all."

Shawn looked around, studying the jail and Sedley said, "Don't even think about it. This place is built like the National Bank of Texas."

"No way out, huh?" Shawn said.

"Not that I can see. And I sure looked."

Shawn rose from the cot's filthy cornhusk mattress and waited for the expected wave of pain to crash through his head. He wasn't disappointed.

"Take it easy, O'Brien," Sedley said. "You ain't hardly yourself yet. That was quite a bump you took."

Unsteady on his feet though he was, Shawn ignored that and explored the room.

Rats rustled in the shadowed corners where the spiders lived and the walls felt dank, as though their coating of winter frost had just melted. The single window, barred with iron, was high on one wall and allowed a narrow beam of light to splash a pale rectangle onto the muddy floor.

There was an exit, a heavy iron gate, and behind that a heavy timber door that was shut and probably bolted from the other side.

The only furnishings in the room were a row of six cots and an overflowing bucket that stank to high heaven. The Holy Rood jail was an annex of hell.

"I don't want to say I told you so, but I told you

so," Sedley said. "Unless you have the keys, there's no way out of this place."

Shawn nodded. "I'd say that's a one-way door," he said. "Prisoners who leave by that portal don't ever come back."

"I reckon that's about the size of it," Sedley said. He managed a bleak smile. "And me too young and good-looking to die."

"Any age is too young to die," Shawn said.

Sedley was quiet for a while, then said, "You're hurting, O'Brien."

"Yeah, I took some bruises when the stage tipped."

"Not that kind of hurt."

Sedley reached into his coat and produced a silver flask. "Here, take a swig. It's good Kentucky bourbon."

"Real lawmen would've taken that from you," Shawn said, reaching for the flask.

The gambler nodded. "A natural fact as ever was. But we're dealing with amateurs, not real lawmen."

"They're not amateurs when it comes to killing," Shawn said. "Cobb and Shannon are experts at that."

"Is the whiskey to your taste?" Sedley asked.

"Real good." He passed the flask back to the gambler. "Here, take it, before I drink it all."

"Man needs whiskey in a place like this," Sedley said, looking around him. "Man needs whiskey when he's hurting."

Shawn smiled. "Hamp, you're like a dog with a bone."

"I make a living from reading other men's eyes, and I see a world of hurt in yours. A woman, huh?"

"My wife. She died."

"That's the whole story?"

"She was murdered. Yes, and that's where the story ends."

Sedley shook his head. "Sorry to hear that, O'Brien. Was she a good woman?"

"The best that ever was."

"I reckon we're dead men and they say dead men don't tell tales," the gambler said. "But I've got a tale to tell if you're willing to hear it. It's short, bitter and to the point and now is a good time to get it off my chest."

"I can read a man's eyes too, Hamp," Shawn said. "So talk away."

Sedley thought for a while, and then said, "I had me a wife once. She was real pretty and I guess I loved her, but she never liked me. I made her pregnant, or so she said, and I did the decent thing."

The gambler passed the flask to Shawn.

"For a spell it went all right, I guess, but we were never alone, even when it was just the two of us. Always in the background there was the shadow of another man. The man she really loved, but didn't marry. You catch my drift?"

"I reckon," Shawn said. "I guess it happens more often than people think."

"I was working the riverboats back then and got back to my hotel one afternoon and found"— Sedley reached into the pocket of his frockcoat and pulled out an envelope—"this. It was lying on my pillow. I've kept it ever since."

He took a piece of folded notepaper from the envelope and passed it to Shawn. "Read 'em and weep," he said.

The note was indeed short and to the point.

> I'VE LEFT YOU, HAMP.
> YOU DON'T UNDERSTAND
> WHAT LOVE MEANS AND I
> FOUND A MAN WHO DOES.
> DON'T COME AFTER ME.

And it was signed, *Doris.*

Shawn passed the paper back to Sedley.

"And after that you never saw her again?" he said.

"No, but a few years later I heard she'd been working the line up Ellsworth way and had died of the cholera, Doris and three hundred other people."

"Bad way to go," Shawn said.

"Will ours be any better?" Sedley said.

"Quicker, I reckon. Everything I've read about the guillotine said it's real sudden."

Sedley took a swig of whiskey and talked again.

"Going back to what I said, I didn't shed a tear

for Doris, but I felt bad, like I'd lost a small part of me. Funny that, ain't it?"

"I can understand how you feel," Shawn said.

"Yeah, of course you can," Sedley said.

He was quiet for a few moments, then said, "I been thinking about what you were saying about a blade being sudden, an' all. One time I read a book about them old-time English kings and the folks they chopped, and it said that if you cut off a man's head his brain will keep working for a while afterward. He'll know what's happened to him and feel the pain."

"You got any more good news, Hamp?" Shawn said.

"Gallows humor, O'Brien. I think that's what it's called."

"I'm not laughing," Shawn said.

The timber door creaked open and then a key clanked in an iron lock.

In the dim half-light, Shawn watched a man carrying a zinc bucket shuffle inside. He looked like a great, shortsighted mole as he glanced around, blinking through thick, round glasses.

Shel Shannon came in behind him, a Greener scattergun in his hands. Beside Shannon stood a stocky, muscular blacksmith, his face sooty from the forge, shackles in both hands.

"Water," Shannon said.

"Get him to take the other bucket out of here, Shannon," Shawn said. "It stinks."

"Your problem," Shannon said. To the mole he said, "Leave the water bucket where you're at and get the hell out of here. I can't stand to look at you."

The man seemed bewildered and Shannon said, "Put the bucket down, you idiot. Down, understand me? Down!"

The man did as he was told, water slopping over the bucket rim.

"Now beat it afore I take a stick to you," Shannon said.

He looked at Shawn. "He's tetched in the head. You have to tell him to do a thing at least two or three times. I don't know why Cobb keeps him."

The mole man looked terrified as he walked wide of Shannon and shuffled rapidly out the door.

The gunman watched the man leave, then said, "He knows I'll beat him to death the day Cobb decides he don't want him around no more." He shook his head. "Seems like two retarded dimwits got together for a roll in the hay and that creature was the result."

"What is Cobb going to do with us?" Sedley asked.

Shannon said, putting emphasis on the first two words out of his mouth, "Brother Matthias has extended, to both of you, an invitation to an execution."

"Who's getting executed? Us?" Shawn said.

If Shannon answered yes, Shawn had made up

his mind to rush the man and take his chances with the shotgun.

But Shannon shook his head. "No, not you two, at least not yet. The condemned is a Texas cowboy who rode into Holy Rood with a lump in his pants looking for fancy women."

"That's all?" Shawn said. "Punchers look for women all the time."

"It's enough," Shannon said. "Besides, he had a money belt around his waist that contained a thousand dollars in cash. The drover swore on the Bible that his employer gave it to him to buy a Hereford bull from a ranch down in the Sand Mountain country."

Shannon stared at Shawn. "You know what that was? It was sacrilege to tell a lie with your hand on the Good Book. Yet another reason why the man was condemned."

The Greener leveled on Shawn and to the blacksmith Shannon said, "Put the irons on him. Try any fancy moves, O'Brien, and I'll cut you in half."

Shawn's puzzled expression framed the question he was about to ask. "What's in this for you, Shannon? And what's a human outhouse like Hank Cobb doing here?"

"We got religion," Shannon said. "Now shut your damned trap or I'll shut it permanently with two barrels of buckshot."

The blacksmith, clanking the wrist and ankle shackles on Sedley, said nothing, his rugged, bearded face like stone.

CHAPTER FIVE

It's hard for any man to be brave when he faces death by execution.

Still, most try, and many succeed.

But the freckled, eighteen-year-old cowboy called Sandy Worth didn't try.

He died like a dog.

And watching him, Shawn O'Brien died a small death of his own.

Screaming, the young puncher was tied face-down onto a timber bench. A couple of Cobb's men in robes pushed the bench forward until Worth's neck was in line with the guillotine and grinned at the cowboy's wild shrieks for mercy.

Cobb held the knotted end of the rope that was threaded through a pulley on the crossbeam of the frame to keep the triangular blade, black with a honed steel edge, in place. He wore a bright scarlet mask with devil horns that covered his head and eyes and thick leather gloves.

Shawn's shackles clanked as he looked around him.

Of the hundred-strong crowd, more than half looked on eagerly at the proceedings, their eyes aglow and lips wet, hungry for blood. Some had children in their arms and held them high to watch the fun. But others, especially a knot of dignified businessmen in broadcloth, stood expressionless and showed no emotion.

Did they disapprove?

Shawn couldn't tell. It sure didn't look like it.

But he made up his mind right there and then that this hell town needed to die . . . and its inhabitants with it.

Cobb's voice rose in song and the crowd enthusiastically joined him.

> *"Shall we gather at the river,*
> *Where bright angel feet have trod,*
> *With its crystal tide forever*
> *Flowing by the throne of God?"*

The cowboy screamed for mercy and called loudly for his mother to help him.

> *"Yes, we'll gather at the river,*
> *The beautiful, the beautiful river.*
> *Gather with the saints at the river*
> *That flows by the throne of God."*

As though suddenly bored by the proceedings, Cobb abruptly stopped singing and let go of the rope.

The heavy, angled blade fell with such speed that Shawn later realized that if he'd blinked he would've missed the decapitation.

The guillotine cut clean and, since there was no basket, the cowboy's head flew onto the timber boards of the platform and bounced once before landing on its side, the blue eyes wide open.

To Shawn's horror, the eyes looked right at him, blinked, once, twice, three times, and the lips stretched in a grimace. He estimated that after his head was struck off, Sandy Worth was conscious for three or four seconds before merciful death finally took him.

Cobb stepped through a spreading pool of blood and lifted the head by its shock of corn-silk yellow hair. He grinned and held his gory burden high, skeletal fingers of scarlet trickling down his forearm, and the townspeople of Holy Rood cheered.

Beside Shawn, Hamp Sedley's face sharpened and a hot red flush burned across his cheekbones. "That's a hell of a way to kill a man," he whispered.

Shawn was numb. Unable to speak. He felt like a man who goes to sleep in his own bed at night and wakes up in an insane asylum.

A woman with the glowing amber eyes of a snake smiled at him and said, "What a lark."

Beyond her, the molelike man who'd brought

the water into the cell stared at the cowboy's dripping head as it was plunged into a cauldron of boiling water to separate flesh and brain from the bones.

"No!" he yelled. "Not right!"

He pushed his way through the crowd toward the bubbling pot.

"Stop that idiot!" Shannon yelled, up on tiptoe to see the man better.

"Not right!" the mole said, shoving irritated gawkers aside.

Cobb said, "You men there, get him."

A big-bellied man wearing black broadcloth stepped into the mole's path and crashed a huge, meaty fist into his face.

The retarded man went down as though pole-axed . . . and then the boots started to go in.

Half a dozen men surrounded the mole, kicking him so hard Shawn heard the *thud* . . . *thud* . . . *thud* of leather on ribs.

After a while Cobb grinned and said, "That's enough. Don't kill him. He makes me laugh."

The mole's tormentors stepped back, their faces flushed, and behind him Shawn heard a grinning Shannon say, "Show's over, O'Brien. Back to your cell."

Shawn wanted to cry out, tell Cobb that he planned to kill him. Warn the citizens of Holy Rood that he'd burn down their damned town about their ears.

But he'd be like a mariner shouting into a nor'easter, mouthing empty noise.

A shackled, unarmed man does not make threats. At least threats that people heed.

Shawn and Hamp Sedley clanked to their cell and the iron door slammed shut behind them.

Neither of them felt like talking and they sat in silence on their bunks and stared down at their hands.

In the distance, coyotes yipped and a rising wind rustled restlessly around the jail and sang through the frame of the guillotine.

CHAPTER SIX

The day had shaded into night and the cell was shadowed by darkness when the cell door opened and Shel Shannon and another robed man stepped inside.

Both carried shotguns, but Shannon held a cast-iron skillet in his right hand and the second man an oil lamp.

"Grub," Shannon said.

"Get these chains off us, Shannon," Shawn said.

"Sure, when Brother Matthias gives the word."

The gunman handed the skillet to Shawn, two spoons crossed on top of the food.

"Share," he said. "If you don't want the grub, I'll throw it to the hogs."

To Shawn's surprise, the skillet was almost filled to the brim with half a dozen fried eggs, bacon, chunks of sausage and cubed pieces of yellow cornbread.

"Cobb always feed his prisoners this good?" he said.

"Yeah, he does. Says it's his Christian duty."

"Pious of him," Sedley said.

"So eat. When you've finished, Brother Bernard will take the skillet and eating irons away." Then, almost as an afterthought, Shannon said, "He'll also be on guard on t'other side of the door tonight, and he's not a man to mess with. He won't take sass, understand?"

Despite the events of the day, Shawn rediscovered his appetite. He and Sedley spooned food into their mouths, and the gambler said, egg yolk clinging to his mustache, "Who were you, Brother Bernard, before you got religion?"

"Ah, maybe it's just as well you asked that, keep you honest, like," Shannon said. "You recollect Crazy Clay Trevett an' that hard crowd?"

"From the San Bernardino country down Arizona way," Sedley said.

"As ever was," Shannon said, "except when Brother Bernard ran with Crazy Clay he called himself Jack Fendy." Shannon turned his head. "Didn't you, Jackie, boy?"

"I'm not your boy, Shannon," Fendy said. "And don't call me Jackie."

He was a man of medium height with cold, dead eyes and he wore two guns, butt forward in plain, black holsters.

Shawn dismissed Fendy as just another Bill

Hickok wannabe, but Sedley seemed fascinated by the man.

"Here, were you in on the Silver Lode massacree, back in the summer of '84, Jack, huh?" he asked.

Fendy spat and said nothing.

"You bet he was," Shannon said. "He helped wipe out that whole town. Ol' Crazy Clay offered a bonus of ten dollars for every ear his men brung in, and Jack laid ten pair at his feet. Ain't that so, Jack?"

Fendy spat again, then said, his strange, high-pitched voice echoing in the barren cell, "They was all cut from men, not from women and children like some I could mention done."

"Yeah, you done good, Jack," Shannon said. "Only men it was, gambling man, you can lay to that."

"Hank Cobb was there and he done more than his share o' cuttin'," Fendy said. "You know that, Shannon, without me needin' to tell you. It was him that collected High Timber Tess McNeil's ears, her that owned the Pink Pussy cathouse in Silver Lode."

"I mind her fine," Shannon said. "That gal must've stood six foot tall, if she stood an inch."

"I heard eighty people died in that massacree, men, women and children," Sedley said. "And all because Clay Trevett spent three days in the town jail for vagrancy the year before."

"That's a damned lie," Fendy said. "And the man saying it is a damned liar."

"It's nothing personal, Jack," Sedley said.

As though he hadn't heard, Fendy said, "Clay

hoorawed that town because them respectable citizens hung his brother on Christmas Eve the year afore. An' we kilt five score, not eighty."

"Sorry, Jack, my mistake," Sedley said. "I guess I didn't study up my ciphers enough."

"An' hung the mayor and his fat wife and then the town marshal," Fendy said. "By God, we done it right, we did."

"You're a hard, unforgiving man, ain't you, Brother Bernard?" Shannon said.

"Kiss my ass," Fendy said.

Shannon grinned. "As you can tell, Brother Bernard is a mighty fierce man. You wouldn't want him to step in here and see you doing anything but sleeping in your bunks."

The gunman slapped his hands together. "Now for some good news, boys—your date with the Grand Council has been postponed for a couple of days. It means two extry days of life fer you fellers."

"Thank Brother Matthias fer that," Shannon said. "Tomorrow bein' the Sabbath, we got the tithes to collect and it's always a chore to wring money out of folks that don't want to part with it."

Shannon beamed as though a thought had just pleased him.

"On Monday we're burning the witch, and the day after is when you'll be questioned by the Council," he said. "Brother Matthias penciled in your executions for Tuesday."

"If you got any more good news, Cobb, keep it to yourself," Sedley said.

"Why are you killing the girl?" Shawn said. "She didn't do anything."

"Didn't I just tell you? She's a witch. The women found a cat-shaped mole on her left shoulder an' that's a sure sign of witchcraft, they say. She'll burn in the evening. Fire looks better in the dark, like."

Shannon smiled. "Next week's tithe will be increased threefold, since Brother Matthias, in addition to all his other parochial duties, must protect the town from the witches who'll surely come seeking terrible revenge."

Those last sounded like Cobb's words and Shannon was obviously repeating them by rote.

Overcoming a feeling of utter helplessness, Shawn sought to give death a human face and a name he would remember. "What does the girl call herself?" he said.

"Name's Sally Bailey, or so she claims. But she's probably called fer a witch of some kind."

"Like Hecate, maybe," Shawn said.

"Huh?"

"Hecate was the Greek goddess of witchcraft, magic, the night and the moon," Shawn said. "But an ignoramus like you wouldn't know anything about that, would you, Shannon?"

Realizing that Shawn was making fun of him, Shannon's face stiffened and he said, "Maybe I don't have book learnin' or a rich pa, but I know this, O'Brien. I'll be standing in the crowd the day your head rolls. Now give me the skillet back. You two have eaten enough."

He turned to Fendy. "Jack, these two get up to any fancy moves or give you back talk, shoot them in the belly."

"Depend on it," Fendy said.

In the lamp-streaked darkness the gunman looked like a grinning reptile.

CHAPTER SEVEN

A north wind that smelled of rain sighed like a spurned lover around the eaves of the jailhouse and tugged at the roof, sending down drifts of dust that dropped silently to the floor. From beyond the cell doors a railroad clock ticked slow, stately seconds into the quiet.

Wandering, drowsy, in that misty, opalescent twilight between wakefulness and sleep, Shawn O'Brien returned to another time and place and again looked out on the terrible moor that surrounded Lovell Manor. . . .

Built in 1550 by the then lord of the manor, Sir Henry Lovell, the house had been set down in the midst of the moor, as though to defy the devil and his pack of red-eyed hounds that were said to stalk the place and haul the unwary, screaming, into Hades.

Dartmoor was a twenty-by-thirty mile wasteland, dominated by dizzying cliffs and bare flat-topped hills of raw granite called tors that rose out of the ground like columns holding up the roof of hell.

The brutal moor was unfit for human habitation, a land of treacherous swamps surrounding rocky islands of gorse and heather, and its harsh, chaotic weather spawned bitingly cold winds and ghostly fogs.

Dartmoor crouched like a dark, savage beast among the fair, green fields and peacefully grazing cattle of southern Devon, England, a wild, harsh and haunted spot to be avoided at all costs.

Nevertheless Shawn tolerated the moor, but only because his wife loved it with a passion.

Lady Judith Lovell's smile made Dartmoor a less somber, less godforsaken place, and she moved through the gloom of the manor like a candle flame, shedding her inner light into the darkest corners.

And then, suddenly, violently, all that died.

Shawn saw again . . . the day . . . the hoarfrost on the hawthorn tree . . . the red, jolly face of Inspector Giles Fortescue of Scotland Yard, his breath smoking in the December air.

"I fear she's been taken by the escaped convicts, like the girls from the village," the big detective said, his face turned away as he stared out at the low mist clinging to the moor. "We found her horse, but not milady."

Sir James Lovell, Judith's father, said, "You've made a search, inspector?"

"Not an adequate one, I'm afraid, Sir James. I've asked for an 'undred mounted policemen and they should be here within a couple of days."

His skin crawling with anxiety, Shawn said, "Damn it, man, a couple of days could be too late."

Fortescue jumped like a jovial Santa Claus pricked with a pin.

"I'm doing my best, sir," he said, his tone defensive. "The moor is a big place and exceedingly dangerous and at the moment I only have half a dozen officers."

Sir James turned to his son-in-law. He was obviously trying to hide his worry, but the lines had deepened in his face and his lips were bloodless.

"Shawn, Judith has been gone only since this morning," he said. "Her horse may have thrown her and she could be making her way home this very minute."

"Then I'm going to search for her," Shawn said.

"Oh, please, sir, there is a fog on the moor and night is coming down," Fortescue said, his concerned face topped by a bowler hat and framed by huge muttonchop whiskers. "You may perish out there yourself."

Realizing he'd made a mistake, the inspector quickly added, "I mean—"

"I know what you mean," Shawn said. "And that's why I aim to find my wife before it's too late."

Fortescue shook his head. "Mr. O'Brien, she's been taken. I'm sure of it. And by the same three men who took the girls from the village and they're probably armed. What you plan, though of the greatest moment, is a singularly dangerous undertaking. Wait until the horsemen arrive."

"He's right you know, Shawn. . . ."

The mist parted and his older brother, Patrick O'Brien, booted, spurred, wearing shotgun chaps and a sheepskin coat, stepped under the frosted hawthorn tree.

He pushed his glasses higher on his nose and smiled. "You must get away from here, Shawn. The Roman soldiers used the hawthorn tree to make the crown of thorns for the crucified Christ. It is an unlucky tree. . . ."

"Indeed," Inspector Fortescue said, shaking his head, "the hawthorn is a harbinger of doom. It has always been thus, Mr. O'Brien."

"And never, I charge you, bring a hawthorn branch into the house, Shawn," Sir James said. "It is damned bad luck."

"Bad luck . . . bad luck . . ." Shawn said. "It's bad luck . . . damned . . . damned . . ."

"For God's sake wake up, O'Brien," Hamp Sedley said in a hoarse whisper as he shook Shawn by the shoulders. "You'll bring Jack Fendy in here and he'll come a-shooting."

Shawn blinked, then focused on Sedley's face. "I . . . I was dreaming," he said. "And my brother was there . . . but he wasn't there when Judith was taken . . . and he stood under the hawthorn tree and told me about the Crown of Thorns and the crucified Christ and then Detective Inspector Fortescue said—"

"Damn it, O'Brien, come back from where you're at!" Sedley said, shaking Shawn by the shoulders so hard his chains clanked. "Leave that damned awful place and return to one that's just as bad, but quieter!"

Shawn looked into the gambler's eyes that gleamed like chipped flints in the darkness.

He shook his head. "I'm back, Hamp. I know where I am." Then, after a pause he reached out and grabbed Sedley by the front of his coat. "Am I losing my mind? Sometimes my brother Jake does that, goes away into a dark place and maybe one day he won't come back from it."

"No, you're not losing your mind," the gambler said. "Men deal with grief in different ways. There's no telling how a man will handle his hurt."

"It was all so real, Hamp. It all came back to me, like I was living it again."

The mists of sleep finally cleared, Shawn smiled. "Except I saw my brother Patrick, and he wasn't there. I mean, he wasn't on the moor when Judith . . . died."

"A man's dreams mix up what's real and what

isn't," Sedley said. "For a spell there, you were in a bad place."

"Dartmoor. I was in Dartmoor in England."

"Yeah, like I said, a bad place."

Shawn swung his legs off the bed. "And now I'm in another bad place. What time is it?" he said.

"I don't know," Sedley said. "Early in the morning, I reckon. Two or three o'clock."

"I'm surprised I could sleep on this stinking cot."

"Yeah, well, don't sleep on it again. You'll get us shot."

"They're going to kill us, Hamp," Shawn said. "Kill us for nothing. Damn it all, that's hard to take."

"Dying is never easy," the gambler said. "Mind you, I came close one time. Got shot in the chest by Lucas Selfert. You ever hear of him?"

"Can't say as I have," Shawn said. He didn't want to listen to Sedley. He was again enduring the pain of Judith's passing and he needed quiet. But he made the effort.

"Lucas was a gambling man out of New Orleans. Nice enough feller when he was sober, but a sore loser when he was drinking, and mean with it. A pint of whiskey in him and ol' Lucas would piss on a widow woman's kindling. Anyhow, one night in the Crystal Palace sporting house in N'Orleans—I recollect it well because, aside from getting shot, I'd had me a crawfish boil earlier in the evening that was the best I ever ate. Well anyhoo, Lucas accuses me of stacking the cards and he says, 'You're a damned cheat, Sedley, and low down.'"

The gambler passed his depleted whiskey flask to Shawn. "Now, you don't call a professional gambler a cheat. It's bad for business, you understand. So, says I, 'Be damned to you for a sore loser, a rotten poker player and no kind of gentleman, Lucas.'"

Sedley accepted the flask from Shawn and took a swig. He wiped his mustache with the back of his hand and said, "Next thing I know, Lucas draws down on me with a .32 sneaky gun and cuts loose. Now, as a general rule, on account of the card table, a gambler gets shot either in the balls or in the chest. Well, Lucas, doin' me a favor, like, plugs me just under the diamond stickpin in my cravat. I was prospering in those days."

"Nice of him to do that," Shawn said.

"Yeah, that's what them as saw the shooting scrape said."

"So what happened?"

"Well, I skinned my own .32 and fired back. Shot a bunch of feathers off a sporting woman's head and put another bullet into the chandelier. Some feller yelled, 'Here, that won't do!' and took my gun."

Sedley shook his head, then said, "What happened next was they carried me out of the sporting house to a doctor. And the doc says, 'Mr. Sedley, there's nothing I can do for you. The bullet ranged downward and is too close to your heart to remove.

All you can do now is to take your medicine and make your peace with God.'"

"But you're still here," Shawn said.

"Yup, I got better and surprised the hell out of everybody, especially Lucas Selfert. The law wrote the whole thing off as a misunderstanding and Lucas served five days in jail for the unlawful discharge of a firearm and then lit a shuck."

"You ever see him again?"

"Sure I did, up Denver way a couple of years back. He was down on his luck, lying in the gutter, a pitiful sight."

"So what did you do?"

"Nothing. I just walked past him. Served him right for plugging me."

Shawn smiled. "You're an unforgiving man, Hamp. I reckon the very least you—"

The inner wooden door swung open and then a key clanked in an iron lock. . . .

CHAPTER EIGHT

The cell's iron gate clanged open and a figure out of a nightmare stood silhouetted in the doorway.

Holding a massive wooden club in his right hand, the mole shuffled inside, dressed in a shabby shirt and pants, carpet slippers on his feet. The man's face was splattered with blood and the club, a knotted limb cut from the white skeleton of a dead tree, dripped scarlet and gray gore. . . .

"My God, man," Hamp Sedley said, "what have you done?"

"I set you free," the mole said. There were specks of blood on his slicked-back black hair. "Come. No time to be lost." He held up a key. "I take the shackles off."

Shawn, his chains clanking, crossed the floor. "Where is Jack Fendy?" he said.

"Dead. He beat me many times." The mole

brandished the club. "I kill him real good. Scatter his brains all over the sheriff's office."

A rat scuttled between the man's feet, then scurried into a corner.

Shawn shivered. "Get the chains off," he said. "What's your name, mister?"

The mole shrugged his round shoulders, a strange lost look on his face. His eyes were the color of spilled molasses. "No name. I have no name."

A fat, soft man with no discernible human shape, he got down on one knee and unlocked the padlock that held the shackles binding Shawn's feet and hands.

"What name would you like to have?" Shawn said, as his chinking chains fell around him.

"No name," the mole said. He rose heavily and turned to Sedley.

"What if I call you Sammy?" Shawn said. "I've always been partial to that name."

The mole said nothing. He worked the key into Sedley's padlock.

"Then Sammy it is," Shawn said, rubbing his wrists. "It's a crackerjack name for a man who doesn't have one."

Sedley was free, and the man newly christened Sammy put a finger to his lips, then motioned for the gambler and Shawn to follow him.

They walked behind Sammy into the next room,

a typical lawman's office with a desk, chairs, gun rack and yellowed wanted dodgers on the walls.

Jack Fendy was propped up in a sitting position in the chair behind the desk, as dead as a man could ever be.

A man hit fatally on the head with a heavy club will normally show only blood-matted hair, the lethal damage hidden. But very occasionally the skull will reveal a crack, the splintered edges of bone visible through the scalp. Brain matter oozes to the surface through this fracture, like oatmeal overflowing a pot.

But Fendy's head was smashed to a pulp, like the top of a soft-boiled egg after a hungry breakfaster has tapped it all over with a spoon. There was little left of his features and the shoulders of his shirt were glistening with blood and bone.

"My God, Sammy," Sedley said, "when you kill a man, you kill him all the way, don't you?"

"He beat me many, many times," Sammy said. "I hated him."

"No surprise there," Sedley said. "You got to hate a man real bad to do damage like that to him."

Shawn crossed the floor quickly. He'd spotted his carpetbag, which had been tossed carelessly into a corner. The buckles of the leather straps hadn't been undone and it looked like the bag hadn't been opened and searched.

His heart thumping in his ears, Shawn fervently hoped that was the case.

Yes! Everything was still intact, including a cartridge belt and holster and a short-barreled Colt revolver.

He strapped on the Colt, then took a box of ammunition out of the bag. "Forty-five?" he said to Sedley as he watched the gambler remove Fendy's revolver from the leather.

The gambler examined the blue Colt, then smiled, "Yup, .45 is our daisy, O'Brien."

Shawn tossed the box back into the bag. "Grab a couple of rifles from the rack and see if there's ammunition to go with them."

"I ain't much of a hand with a long gun," Sedley said.

"I'll teach you," Shawn said.

The gambler took down a couple of Winchesters, both in .44-40 caliber, and found a couple of boxes of shells to go with them.

Sammy, Fendy's blood crusted rust brown on his face, said, "You go now." He held up two fingers. "One, two horses outside."

"He's right, O'Brien, we'd better light a shuck," Sedley said.

"Hamp, there are three of us," Shawn said. "What about Sammy?"

The gambler looked quickly at the man. "You got a horse?"

Sammy shook his head. "I stay here."

"See, he wants to stay here, so let's go," Sedley said.

"What about the girl?" Shawn said.

"What about her?"

"They're going to burn her for a witch. I can't let that happen. She goes with us, Hamp, or we don't go at all."

Sedley looked stricken. "Are you out of your mind? She's at the hotel under guard. Ain't that right, Sammy?" Without waiting for an answer, he said, "There, Sammy says she's under guard."

Once again Sammy, looking more molelike than ever, his swept back hair starting just above his eyebrows, held up two fingers. "One . . . two . . . guards," he said. "Very bad men."

"You want to gunfight your way out of this burg, O'Brien?" Sedley said. "And with a woman in tow?"

"If that's what it takes," Shawn said. "I'm in not much of a mind to see another woman murdered." His eyes hardened. "I won't step away from this, Hamp. But you can. I won't hold it against you."

"Damn it all, O'Brien, and be double damned to ye for a crazy Irishman, but I won't run out on you now. Time is ticking—let's get it done."

Shawn smiled and put his hand on Sedley's shoulder.

"You're true blue, Hamp," he said.

"No, I'm true yellow," Sedley said.

CHAPTER NINE

The moon was up and its light lay on the dusty street like winter frost.

Holy Rood was so quiet the only sounds to be heard were the restless rush of the wind and distant yip of coyotes. But now and then the bell in the church tower dinged softly when the wind gusted, adding a small noise to the night.

"This way," Sammy whispered. He shuffled in his carpet slippers and still held the bloodstained club.

Shawn and Sedley followed, leading the two saddled horses. Who they belonged to and where they had come from, Shawn had no idea. But he was willing to bet the mounts were owned by a couple of Hank Cobb's boys.

He and Sedley slid their rifles into the empty scabbards attached to the saddles as they drew closer to the hotel.

Walking clear of the boardwalks where a man's

boots would sound like bass drums in the quiet, Sammy led the way toward the edge of town.

They passed a store with a disfigured hanging sign that creaked in the wind.

The sign had once read:

PETE WRIGHT & SON
GUNS, AMMUNITION
& FISHING SUPPLIES

The words GUNS and AMMUNITION had been whitewashed over, but were still fairly visible, the letters showing through like pale ghosts.

It seemed that Cobb didn't want the people of Holy Rood to have access to guns.

An alley opened up to Shawn's left and a bottle clinked somewhere in its rectangle of darkness. His Colt suddenly in his hand, Shawn stopped and so did the others.

Long, tense moments passed, and then a small calico cat stepped out of the gloom on silent feet. Startled by the appearance of the men, she turned tail and dashed back into the alley. Bottles chinked again.

Shawn realized that he'd been holding his breath and let it out in a relieved sigh.

"No need to panic, O'Brien," Sedley said. "It was only a cat."

Shawn glared at him. "Worked that out for yourself, huh?"

Sammy put a finger to his lips and said, "Hush."

"See, you talk too much, O'Brien," Sedley said.

"Hotel," Sammy said, pointing to a false-fronted building that marked the end of the street. "You go quiet now."

Shawn was not a whispering man, but he made the effort as he said to Sammy, "Where is the girl? I mean what room?"

The question stumped the man and Shawn could've sworn Sammy's nose twitched as he turned it over in his mind. Then his face lit up and he held up two fingers and said, "One . . . two . . . Miss Sally there. She a nice lady."

"Room 2, Sammy?" Sedley said, making sure.

The man nodded. "Uh-huh. One . . . two."

"He could mean twelve," Shawn said to the gambler. "Maybe she's in Room 12."

"Then let's go ask the night clerk," Sedley said. He took time to check the loads in his Colt, then punched a cartridge into the empty chamber that had been under the hammer. "If they got a night clerk, that is."

Sammy nodded vehemently. "Got night clerk," he said.

"Understands more than he lets on," Sedley said.

The Rest and Be Thankful hotel was a white-washed building, like all the other structures in town. A lamp burned in the office on the ground floor and spilled light onto the boardwalk that looked like pale orange paint.

Beyond the hotel, the wagon road was a ribbon of gray that abruptly disappeared into sooty blackness.

Shawn made a mental note of that. Once they had the girl, it was the route they'd take. They could lose themselves in the gloom—at least until the sun came up. He smelled sage in the wind and unsettled dust, but not a trace of the saloon odors of stale whiskey and beer, cheap perfume and crowded, unwashed bodies that were such staples of Western cow towns.

Holy Rood was a sterile, viciously cruel place, and it seemed the citizens preferred it that way.

But no matter. Shawn vowed that one day he'd come back and tear the town apart.

Tame it!

Wasn't that the expression the newspapers used?

But Shawn's growing hatred for Holy Rood was not in retaliation for all the humiliations he himself had suffered.

No, it was because of a cowboy Shawn didn't know, a freckle-faced youngster named Sandy Worth, whose decapitated head had rolled in front of him . . . and the boy's dying eyes that had begged for help that he could not give . . .

"Hell, O'Brien, let's get it done," Sedley said. "You look like you're standing there half asleep."

"Sorry," Shawn said. He pulled his Colt from the

holster and took the stairs that led to the surrounding porch with its extensive gingerbread trim, and stepped to the hotel's frosted glass door.

At that moment Shawn O'Brien was prepared to be a ruthless killer, no talk, no excuses, no mercy . . . just bang-bang.

He reckoned his brother Jacob would be proud of him.

The sleepy clerk at the front desk woke up in a hurry when Shawn stuck the muzzle of his revolver between the man's eyes.

"Where is the girl? And how many with her?" he said.

The clerk, a neat little man with his thin hair parted in the middle and pomaded shiny and flat, recovered enough to paste a now-see-here look on his face.

But it vanished quickly when Shawn thumbed back the hammer of the Colt, and said, "Mister, I swear, give me any sass and I'll blow your damned head off."

The clerk saw the writing, or his brains, on the wall, because he said quickly, "Twenty-one."

"How many?" Shawn said.

"Two. Maybe three. I don't rightly know." He attempted a smile. "You know how men are with a pretty girl."

Shawn was a man made strong by years of hard

work on the Dromore range and anger made him stronger.

He reached out, grabbed the clerk by his shirt-front and dragged him effortlessly across the desk and onto the floor.

Then, his eyes ablaze with blue fire, he said, "Get up there and show me how men are with a pretty girl."

Suddenly, the little man was afraid. "If I interrupt the reverend brothers at their pleasure, they'll shoot me."

"And I'll shoot you if you don't," Shawn said. "Choose a trail."

Hamp Sedley, uneasy at the delay, grabbed the clerk by the scruff of his neck and frog-marched him to the stairs.

"All right, my buck, let's get going," he said.

"The key," the little man wailed, balling and un-balling his hands.

"We won't need a key," Shawn said. "We'll knock, polite like."

The door of Room 21 was at the end of a wall-papered hallway, lit by a couple of oil lamps. There was no sound but the rush of the wind outside and far in the distance the clacking rattle of a south-bound freight.

The clerk's Adam's apple bobbed as Sedley forced him relentlessly along the shadowed hall toward the door.

Thick carpet covered the floor and absorbed the

sound of booted men and no one stirred behind the numbered doors that lined the corridor.

Then two things happened very quickly . . .

Suddenly the clerk wrenched himself free of Sedley, ran to the door and pounded his fists on the varnished pine.

"Help!" he yelled. "Help me."

Shawn taken by surprise, recovered, pushed the wailing clerk aside and kicked the door in.

In a shower of splintering timber, the door violently slammed inside and crashed against the wall.

Shawn stepped inside, his gun up and ready.

A bearded man had the tearstained, naked girl on his knee and she fell heavily to the floor as he jumped to his feet. He grabbed a Colt from the table beside him, swung on Shawn—and took a bullet between the eyes.

The big .45 shattered through the bearded man's skull and blew out the back of his head. A sudden fan of blood and brain splattered the wall behind him.

Beside Shawn, Hamp Sedley triggered a shot, then a second at a tall man, still wearing his monk's robes, who stood close to the fireplace.

Both missed.

Cursing Sedley, Shawn turned, his eyes targeting the surviving gunman who'd already skinned a gun from the holster at his side.

But at that instant Shawn was roughly pushed

aside and Sammy charged at the tall man, his bloody, knotted club raised for the kill.

For the space of a heartbeat the tall man's face was stricken, but he steadied himself and got his work in. Two bullets crashed into Sammy's chest, but the great, sleek mole absorbed the hits and kept coming.

The instant before he died, the tall man knew fear.

Even a third shot fired into Sammy's belly at point-blank range didn't halt the hurtling, lethal, downward arc of the club.

The gunman's skull collapsed under the impact with a distinct popping sound. Like a pumpkin hit by a sledgehammer, his head burst apart, scattering, not seeds, but blood and bone.

Sammy hit the floor a moment after the dead gunman and the weight of his massive body seemed to shake the hotel to its foundations.

"Oh, my God, we're all dead," Sedley yelled. "There's been too much shooting, so let's get the hell out of here."

"Damn it, Hamp, why didn't you tell me you couldn't shoot?" Shawn yelled, irritated and scowling.

"Sure I can shoot," Sedley protested. "But I can't shoot straight when I get nervous, and I was nervous. Now grab the girl and we'll go."

"What about Sammy?" Shawn said.

"Sammy's dead," Sedley said. He took a ragged breath. "And we're pretty close to being dead."

"Get dressed," Shawn said to the girl.

"She doesn't have time to get dressed," Sedley said. He removed his frockcoat and hung it over the girl's shoulders. "Pick up your duds and we'll get out of here."

"But I need to brush my hair," the girl said.

Shawn interrupted the string of curses from Sedley.

"Get her out into the hallway," he said. "I'll be right there."

"I told you he's dead."

"If he is, later I'll say a rosary for his poor soul," Shawn said. "But right now I want to make sure."

Sedley hustled the girl through the ruined doorway. She held her clothes bundled in her arms and a purple bruise stained her left cheekbone.

Shawn kneeled beside Sammy, but all the life that had been in the man was gone.

"May God rest you, Sammy," Shawn said, a strange, lost sadness in him.

Then he rose to his feet and followed Sedley and the girl out of the room.

A door opened to his left and a blowsy, middle-aged woman in a see-through nightgown stood framed in the doorway. She wore a black, lacy mask over her eyes and a seductive smile on her lips.

"What's all the shooting?" she said.

"Just high spirits is all," Shawn said.

"Then do you want to come in and join my masquerade, cowboy?" she said. She raised a white, blue-veined hand in an attempt to grab Shawn's shoulder. "I've got whiskey and cigars," she said. "And I'll give you a mask of your very own."

The woman put her forefingers against her temples like horns, made a grotesque face and her tongue darted in and out of her mouth.

"A devil mask," she said. "Sssssss . . ."

She sounded just like a snake.

CHAPTER TEN

Still shaken by his encounter with the woman, Shawn sprinted out of the hotel . . . and into a gunfight.

Hamp Sedley blasted shots into the moon-bladed street where a dozen shadowy figures scurried from cover to cover.

"Put the girl on your horse and get the hell out of here," Shawn yelled.

Sedley's head was bent to his Colt as he fed fresh rounds into the cylinder.

"I'll stick," he said.

A shot kicked up a startled exclamation point of dirt at Shawn's feet and a second chipped splinters from the wooden hotel sign above his head.

"The hell with that!" Shawn yelled. "Get up on your horse."

"What about you?" Sedley said.

"I'll follow you. Now go." He pointed into darkness. "That way."

As bullets split the air around them, Sedley read the urgency in Shawn's face. He grabbed the girl by the arm. "Come on, let's get the hell out of here," he said.

Shawn didn't wait to see the gambler and the girl leave.

He dived behind a zinc horse trough that stood just outside the hotel—and was rewarded by a volley of fire that sent up vees of water and started half a dozen leaks in the side of the trough.

Shawn swallowed hard, a tight knot in his belly.

Damn, even in the dark those gunmen of Hank Cobb's were good.

He rose up and thumbed off a shot at a crouched figure on the opposite boardwalk.

A clean miss.

The gunman faded into darkness and as shots buzzed around him like angry hornets, Shawn figured there were a dozen of Cobb's men out there, stalking him.

He knew then that he was going to lose this street fight. It was only a matter of time.

A cloud passed across the face of the moon and, for a few moments at least, Shawn had a chance to move. He jumped to his feet and sprinted for a parked freight wagon outside a feed store.

A few bullets chased him, but he reached the

wagon safely and crouched behind a wheel. Now he had a dark building behind him and wouldn't be outlined against the lit hotel.

So long as he crouched behind the wagon, Shawn's view of the street had narrowed to what was in front of him.

Now Cobb and his men would need to come at him in a rush instead of holding back to pick him off at a distance.

The big Studebaker protected his front and there was no boardwalk outside the feed store, so he had the door at his back.

The wind had grown turbulent and now it furiously gusted so much blown sand along the street and high above the buildings it obscured the face of the moon.

Shawn watched a wadded-up sheet of newspaper tumble past the wagon like a shotgunned jackrabbit and it seemed that every hanging sign in town creaked and banged on its chains.

It seemed like a dilly of a sandstorm was brewing and whether it would aid him or Cobb, Shawn as yet had no way of telling.

There was a lull in the firing as Cobb apparently considered his next move and Shawn took time to feed fresh shells into his Colt.

After that, all he could do was wait.

Hank Cobb held the cards in this game and right then he was standing pat.

But not for long . . .

* * *

They came at Shawn all at once, ten men wearing monks' robes, their heads bent against the wind and stinging sand.

Shawn fired once through the spokes of the wagon wheel and he saw a man grab his knee and go down.

No time for thinking!

He made an instinctive decision and stepped away from the wagon.

He'd die standing like a man on his own two feet, gun in hand, and give up his life in one, glorious, hellfire moment.

It was what his father would expect of him. What his tutor, grim old Luther Ironside, the colonel's *segundo*, would demand of him.

But it was not to be.

From Shawn's left, a racketing roar of rifle fire ripped through the night and he saw a man spin and fall, and then another went down, hit hard and screaming.

Cobb's gunmen scattered for cover as a man on a white horse drew rein beside Shawn, windblown sand driving into him. "Get the hell out of here!" he yelled above the savage roar of the storm.

No second invitation was needed.

Shawn sprinted to his horse, swung into the saddle and kneed his mount into a gallop, heading into the now sand-ripped darkness that had swallowed Sedley and the girl.

Behind him, he heard a man shout and guns fired.

Then there was a lull.

Shawn drew rein and looked behind him, his stinging eyes searching the gloom for a glimpse of the white horse.

He saw only the somber shroud of the night and the great, tumbling breakers of blown sand.

There was nothing in Shawn O'Brien's character and breeding that would make him flee the field of battle while a man who'd saved his life was in mortal danger.

He slid the Winchester from the boot and headed back toward Holy Rood at a trot. On both sides of the trail, yellow skulls watched him and grinned.

The sandstorm grew in intensity, but as Shawn rode closer to the town he heard a man's words carry above the venomous scream of the wind.

It was Hank Cobb's voice.

Angry, defiant, loud, roaring.

"Jasper Wolfden! You listen here to me!"

Shawn drew rein and all his senses reached into the cartwheeling night.

"Damn you, I'll kill you, Jasper Wolfden!"

There was no answer.

"I killed you once. I can kill you again. You hear me, Jasper Wolfden?"

But there was no answering shout, only the bellow of the wind and the serpent hiss of the swiftly shifting sand.

Shawn's mount, its head down, would go no farther. It rose up on its hind legs and turned, then stood stiff-kneed, refusing to face the bite of the sand.

For a moment, Shawn considered going ahead on foot, but then, from out of the darkness the white horse, riderless, its stirrups flying, passed him at a gallop.

From somewhere deep in the cavern of the night a wolf howled.

A moment later, Cobb called out again. This time his voice was edged with uncertainty and tinged with fear.

"Jasper Wolfden, I'll kill you again! Damn you, I'll bury you deep!"

The wolf's answering howl was as white as ivory.

To Shawn, the long, eerie wail sounded like an act of defiance.

But he knew full well that wolves were incapable of such an emotion. In the darkness a man's imagination can play tricks and lead him down shadowed pathways.

Brush rustled to Shawn's right. He racked a

round and slapped the forestock of the Winchester into his hand.

For a moment his eyes probed the gloom, wind and sand tearing at him, then he said, "Come out with your mitts in the air or I'll drill you dead center."

The darkness parted and took on the form of a man.

"Helluva way to greet a feller who just saved your life," the man said. For a moment, his eyes glittered, then faded.

"Are you Jasper Wolfden?" Shawn said, wondering about those eyes.

"Who the hell else would I be?" the man said. "If you can hear anything above this storm, you heard Hank Cobb calling out to me."

"Then I heard a wolf," Shawn said.

"Me too. Damned lobo spooked my horse," Wolfden said.

"I'm beholden to you for saving my life," Shawn said. "Sorry about the horse."

"He'll find me," Wolfden said.

People instinctively rebel against ordinariness, being thought average, but the man named Wolfden seemed to revel in it.

He was of average height, average build, his features ordinary in the extreme, his clothing ordinary as was his canvas gun belt and blue Colt.

Even his voice was ordinary, unaccented, unmemorable.

Only his eyes were unique, gathered points of

light glowing in their depths like fireflies trapped in amber.

"I will take you to your friends," Wolfden said.

"You met them?" Shawn said, surprised.

"I did not, but I know where they are."

"But how—"

"I said I know where they are," Wolfden repeated.

The man had made it clear that he wished to drop the matter, and Shawn didn't press him.

"Will Cobb come after us?" he said.

"No. He has four dead and another will die soon. He'll wait, lick his wounds for a spell."

"It seems that he wants to kill you real bad," Shawn said.

"And you too, my friend."

"He'll get his chance. I plan to take the town away from him."

"Why? The people of Holy Rood are nothing to you."

The wind tugging at him, Shawn said, "I'm doing it for a young cowboy."

Wolfden nodded. But he said nothing.

Shawn waited, expecting a you-got-to-be-crazy comment, but when none was forthcoming, he said, "We can ride double on my horse until you find your own."

"I'll bring him," Wolfden said.

He raised his head and made a strange huffing sound, barely audible above the shriek of the sandstorm. A few moments later, his horse appeared out of the murk like a gray ghost.

Shawn didn't say it outright, but he thought it. . . .

Whatever else he might be, Jasper Wolfden was a real strange fellow.

CHAPTER ELEVEN

The sandstorm had not yet blown itself out and the hour was late, but Hank Cobb rang the church bell to announce a meeting of the townspeople.

As the citizens appeared, most of them in night-clothes, Cobb and his gunmen steered them away from the church to the sheriff's office.

Cobb wanted to speak to only the most influential residents, the businessmen and their wives, and the others were left outside on the boardwalk, to take shelter from the still hard-driving sand as best they could.

After Cobb called the meeting to order, he told Shel Shannon to present the butcher's bill for the battle against what he called, "the terror riders."

Shannon read the warning in Hank Cobb's eyes and mentally reframed his statement to suit the mood of the curious crowd that had squeezed inside the sheriff's office.

"Brothers Amos, Gideon, Kent, Bernard and

Lemuel are all dead," he said. "Brother Matthias is gutshot and squallin' like a—"

"A grievous, mortal wound," Cobb said, his glare again flashing a warning to Shannon that he should watch his tongue. "And painful."

"Yeah, an' Brother Jeremiah's knee is bullet smashed and he ain't never again gonna walk again on two legs."

"Where is the witch?" a fat man with wet lips said. "We must burn the witch."

"Yes, we must, but did she escape?" a woman said.

"The terror riders took her," Cobb said. "Our brothers had no chance against such a host of gunmen and the witch, the devil's harlot, helped them prevail by casting her evil spells."

He pulled his cowl over his head and looked at the people around him from shadow.

"The good Lord is testing us," he said. "The brothers laid down their lives to protect this blessed town from outlawry, violence and witchcraft, but were laid low." His voice rose to a shout. "But we will prevail over evil. Those who cast envious eyes on our fair town and wish to destroy it will themselves be destroyed. This is the word of the Lord!"

This last drew a cheer, but a few of the women tugged their dressing gowns closer around their necks and exchanged fearful glances.

"Brother Matthias, we must have safety and security at any price," the fat man said. "Only then can Holy Rood regain its peace and tranquility."

"Where will you lead us, brother?" a man in a plaid robe and carpet slippers said.

"Perhaps we must flee and establish a new Holy Rood away from all danger," a woman said.

Cobb shook his head. "No. That is not the way."

"Then ease our minds and show us the way, Brother Matthias," a voice from the crowd said, to nods of approval.

"I say we execute outsiders with evil in their hearts right away and not keep them for trial before the Grand Council like we did the witch and the two men with her," the fat man said.

This brought another murmur of approval.

"Yes, mistakes were made, but they will not be made again," Cobb said. "We have lost holy and valiant brothers this night, but, as I prayed over their dead bodies in the street, God spoke to me."

A chorus of, "What did He say? Tell us, brother."

"He told me that I have brought three years of peace and prosperity to our town and He instructed me to bring many more," Cobb said. "He said it is His wish that more skulls of the evil interlopers who would do us harm line the road into Holy Rood."

There were a flurry of cheers and a few shouted questions, but Cobb held up his arms for quiet.

Ignoring the gesture, a thin, older woman, her mouth as tight and mean as a snapped-shut steel purse, raised her voice and yelled, "More rolling heads! It is the Lord's wish."

"Indeed it is, madam," Cobb said. "But first we must replace the holy warriors we lost with more heroes of the same stamp. The terror riders and the witch who now leads them must be hunted down and destroyed."

Recognizing his cue, Shannon called out, "Our town is in grave danger, Brother Matthias, but for pity's sake tell us where such brave men can be found?"

"Money will bring them, Brother Uzziah, and plenty of it," Cobb said.

His eyes glittered in the shadow of the cowl. "We will lure such paladins to Holy Rood with the promise of gold, saith the Lord to me, and then we convert them to our ways. Soon they will see the light and fight for peace and justice, just as the rest of our brethren does."

"Brother, I have but a few cents in my pocket," Shannon said. "But I give them to you freely for our holy cause."

"Blessed be the givers," a woman said. "And bless you, Brother Uzziah."

Cobb threw his cowl back and, his pitiless, criminal eyes blazing, he said, "Then ye'll pay for more crusaders, will ye?"

"Command us!" the woman with the mean mouth yelled.

"Just don't break the bank, brother."

This last came from white-haired Temple Carstairs,

the owner of the town's prosperous mercantile. As a major of Union infantry, Carstairs had fought well at Gettysburg and there was a hard edge to him.

But Cobb ignored the old soldier's outburst and said, "All of ye standing here tonight, do you want the best? Do you want to live your lives free from evil and men who would do violence to you and yours?"

"Aye, the best there is," another man said. "Keep us safe, brother."

"Then I'll find champions for you," Cobb said. "But know this, such men don't come cheap."

There was not the roar of approval that Cobb expected, but Shannon stepped into the breach again.

"We'll pay to restore Holy Rood to an island of peace in a sea of lawlessness," he said. "Name the price we must pay, Brother Matthias."

If anyone in the crowd thought that was big talk coming from a man with only a few cents in his pocket, he or she stayed quiet.

"Then thus spake the Lord to me," Cobb said. "From every man in town ye will collect watches, studs, rings . . . everything they have that's made of gold."

Talking into a shocked silence, he continued, "From every woman, jewelry of all kinds. Heed my warning, let no woman wear a ring, bracelet or necklace of gold after this tithe has been made or verily, it will turn molten and burn her like the very fires of hell."

The silence grew, deepened and stretched for long moments, and then Carstairs's voice shattered the quiet like a rock thrown through a plate-glass window.

"It's too much, Brother Matthias," he said. "You can't demand such a sacrifice from these people. I say we arm ourselves and form our own police force. Aye, even an army if need be."

Temple Carstairs didn't know it then, but Cobb did, that the large number of hear-hears from the crowd after his statement would prove to be his death warrant.

"I don't demand such a sacrifice from you," Cobb yelled. "God demands it!"

"A tithe like that would just about wipe me out," another man said. "I've worked hard for what I own."

"And surely you don't want our wedding rings?" a woman said.

"I don't want them, but God surely does," Cobb said. He saw mouths opening to speak and added, yelling, "Listen to yourselves, people! With God's help Holy Rood is a heaven on earth. We live free of crime, free of the violence that has so destroyed the Western lands. The only people allowed in our town are those honest souls who come to buy, sell or trade."

Shel Shannon once again decided to back up his boss.

"Look around you, citizens," he said. "There are no drunken cowboys or stinking miners staggering from saloon to saloon in search of demon drink, no painted women eager to satisfy their lusts, no pale-faced gamblers to fleece the unwary and no soulless outlaws to visit violence on our women and children. The law never comes to Holy Rood and why? Because they know it is a town of peace and good order."

His voice rising to a roar, Shannon poked holes in the air with his forefinger and said, "And the skulls of those who have tried to transgress against us are plain to see, a warning to others who might be tempted to do the same."

"Indeed, Brother Uzziah," Cobb said. "And we owe all this to you and others like you, the holy warriors who have kept the peace in Holy Rood with the gun, the noose and the falling blade. But now, to save this town from terror and witchcraft, we need more of your kind."

The reaction from the townspeople was luke-warm at best, and Carstairs made things worse when he said, "What you have told us is true, Brother Matthias. Holy Rood is a safe town, a place where women and children can walk without fear. But sometimes the price for such security can come too high."

"Brother Carstairs, you talk of forming a police

force, even a citizens' army, and that tells me you are a fool," Cobb said. "All you'd form is a rabble that would flee their first encounter with the terror riders."

Carstairs looked angry and opened his mouth to object, but Cobb shouted him down.

"Only the men I choose can be trusted with guns," he said. "We don't want an armed rabble here. Only the warriors I plan to hire can bring you the peace and security you desire."

"Peace and security at any price!" a woman yelled, and a few heads nodded in agreement.

"I suggest a meeting of the Grand Council to discuss the matter and that a vote be taken," Carstairs said. "I propose a citizens' police force, but others may think that a certain amount of money could be allotted for more armed men. No matter the decision, you'll have to work within a strict budget, Brother Matthias."

"I am your obedient servant, Brother Carstairs, and I will abide by the wishes of the Grand Council," Cobb said. "But know this, the witch who entered this town now leads a band of terror riders and Holy Rood faces a crisis the like of which it has never experienced before."

Cobb pulled up his hood again. "Bear that in mind when you speak in council, Brother Carstairs."

* * *

"Hell, Hank, that damned fool Carstairs is gonna upset all our plans," Shel Shannon said. "All that talk of his own police force."

"No he ain't," Cobb said, reaching for the whiskey bottle. "We'll still wring this hick town dry afore we light a shuck." He smiled. "An' I'll finally be glad to get rid of these holy-roller robes. Damn things are hot and itch like hell."

"But, Hank, I mean, how we gonna—"

"Part of your problem is that you ain't too bright, Shel," Cobb said. "An' that's why you don't think things through."

"But you do, huh, boss?"

"Damn right I do."

Cobb picked up his glass, stepped to the sheriff's office window and stared outside.

The storm still raged and ticked sand against the glass panes. Across the street a sign hung aslant on one chain and somewhere a screen door banged in the wind and a dog barked.

Without turning, Cobb said, "Temple Carstairs dies tonight."

He heard the grin in Shannon's voice as the man said, "You want me to gun him, boss?"

Now Cobb turned, took time to sip his whiskey, and said, "No, you idiot, you want to alarm the whole town again?"

Without waiting for an answer, Cobb said, "I

don't want a mark on him, understand? No bullet or knife wounds."

Shannon's mind was slow and he looked confused.

"But why fer that, boss?" he said.

Cobb walked to the desk and leaned over Shannon. His face, lit by the oil lamp, was hard, his mouth a thin, white gash.

"I'll tell you why fer that," he said.

CHAPTER TWELVE

Because of the shrieking wind and rasping sand Jasper Wolfden leaned from the saddle and yelled into Shawn's ear, "They're close!"

Wolfden saw the question on the younger man's face and said, "I can smell them."

"In this wind?"

"In any wind."

Shawn let that go. Raising his voice above the racket of the storm was too much of an effort. Besides, he'd already established in his mind that Wolfden was a mighty peculiar man.

To Shawn's east rose the massive escarpment of Sand Mountain and beyond that the rocky battlements of the Hurricane Cliffs. But both were lost in darkness. Ahead of him the visibility of the high timber country came and went as the wind gusted, but it was a likely place for a couple of fugitives to hole up for the night.

His hunch was proven correct when Wolfden

suddenly swung his horse to the west and pointed into the trees.

"There!" he yelled.

Wolfden, his head bent against the wind, led the way to a narrow creek, then followed its winding course north into the pines.

Here, sheltered by trees, the full force of the windblown sand was blunted and visibility increased to twenty or thirty yards.

Shawn heard growling on the opposite bank of the creek and saw half a dozen gray wolves tear at the belly of a downed whitetail buck. They raised their bloodstained muzzles as he and Wolfden rode past and the deer kicked and tried to rise.

But the wolves ravenously went back to their feast and the buck's agonized eyes, as soft as a woman's, fastened on Shawn in a hopeless plea for help.

He shuddered, like a man in an icy draft, and rode on.

"Stay right there and state your intentions. We ain't sitting on our gun hands here."

Hamp Sedley stepped out of the trees, a Winchester at the ready and a scowl on his face.

"It's me, Hamp, Shawn O'Brien. And another feller."

"Mister, you'd better be who you say you are," Sedley said, peering into the gloom. "We're twenty United States marshals here, all well-armed and determined men."

"Hell, Hamp, all you've got there is a woman,

and you can't shoot worth a damn," Shawn said. "Now put the rifle away before you hurt yourself. We're coming in."

Shawn took the lead and rode toward Sedley.

"Damn it all, O'Brien, it is you," the gambler said, lowering his gun.

"Of course it's me," Shawn said, stepping out of the saddle. "I hope the coffee's biling."

"I wish," Sedley said.

Shawn and Wolfden followed the gambler into the trees.

The girl sat with her back against a pine, her knees drawn up to her chin. Her yellow hair was undone and fell around her face in wind-teased waves.

"How are you holding up?" Shawn said. "Sally, isn't it?"

The girl nodded. "Sally Bailey."

She let it go at that and Shawn didn't push it.

"This here is Jasper Wolfden," he said. "He saved my life back at Holy Rood. Took on Hank Cobb and his men like they didn't matter."

"Here, I recognize you," Sedley said. "You were the ranny up on the ridge with a head on a pole, scared the hell out of everybody."

"Ah, yes. I've always had a flair for the dramatic," Wolfden said. "It comes naturally to a former actor, you see."

"I'd pegged you fer a preacher or something,"

Sedley said. "You mean you were on the stage with folks watching you?"

"Exactly what I mean," Wolfden said. "I've performed with Edwin Booth, playing Horatio to his moody Dane, and with Lillie Langtry, a truly beautiful woman. Let me see, ah yes, I did several turns with Oscar Wilde and on one memorable occasion, James Butler Hickok."

"You were on stage with Wild Bill in person?" Sedley said.

"Indeed, yes. But an actor he was not. He mouthed the words well enough, when he was sober that is, but never became the character he played."

"Good with a gun though, was Bill," Sedley said.

"I don't know about that," Wolfden said. "I never saw him shoot anything but blanks."

"Somehow a gun-fighting actor doesn't quite add up," Shawn said.

Wolfden tilted his head to one side and gave Shawn a wry look. "John Wilkes, Edwin's brother, did all right, didn't he?"

"Lincoln didn't have a gun," Shawn said.

"That is very true," Wolfden said. "As for me, I was always a keen target shooter. Then Hank Cobb and his rowdies and the good people of Holy Rood made me a gunfighter by necessity when they deemed actors were degenerates and not fit to live."

"Hank Cobb said he'd killed you," Sedley said. "We heard that plain. But you aren't dead, are you?"

The clearing in the trees offered protection from

blowing sand, but the wind tossed the tops of the pines, sending down showers of twigs and needles.

For reasons known only to themselves, the wolves howled over their recent kill and Wolfden turned his head and listened, his strange eyes glowing.

"Cobb said he'd killed you," Sedley prompted. "That's what he said, plain as ever was."

"Maybe the man doesn't want to remember that," Sally said. Her hair tossed in the wind as she raised her head and stared at Sedley. "Some memories are better left buried."

"It's all right, I don't mind," Wolfden said. "Right now we've got nothing else to do but tell stories, huh? Cobb thought he'd killed me. But his bullet had only grazed my head and I played dead." The man smiled. "It was one of my finer acting achievements, a consolation for flopping so badly in Silver Reef. I guess the miners didn't care much for a washed-up actor spouting bad Shakespeare."

"Nah, silver miners only want to see pretty women in pink tights," Sedley said. "Did Cobb shoot you in Silver Reef or in Holy Rood?"

"Neither. If it had been in Holy Rood I wouldn't have gotten away with it. No, it was southwest of here, at a place called Gooseberry Mesa. I was hiding out among thick stands of piñon and juniper, but Cobb drew a bead on me and shot me off of my horse."

"Why was Cobb so all-fired set on killing you, Wolfden?" Sedley asked.

"After the miners had more or less run me out of Silver Reef, I thought to settle in Holy Rood and write a play. It seemed such a peaceful town. Then I saw what was happening and took a set against Cobb and his men. We became bitter enemies and after a couple of attempts on my life, Cobb arrested me and sentenced me to death."

"So you were in his jail for a spell?" Sedley said.

"Only a couple of days," Wolfden said. "And that was bad enough."

"How the heck did you bust out of the jail in the first place?" Sedley said.

"A man helped me," Wolfden said. "Strange kind of fellow. I've always wondered what happened to him."

"Cobb's men killed him," Shawn said. He'd leave the details until Wolfden had finished his story.

"Too bad," Wolfden said. "Like I said, he was strange, but I kind of liked him."

"So you got burned across the head and then played dead until Cobb and his men rode away, huh?" Shawn said.

"Would it were that simple," Wolfden said. "No, they buried me."

"Alive?" Sedley said, his face shocked.

"Well, I was still breathing, so they could hardly bury me dead now, could they?" Wolfden said.

"Why did Cobb take time to bury you?" Shawn said. "That's not his style."

"As far as I can piece it together, there was a

United States marshal nosing around at the time and Cobb didn't want my body found."

"So, after Cobb left, you dug yourself out," Sedley said.

"I tried, but I was deep and no matter how I struggled, I couldn't dig myself free. Of course, by then I was suffocating, within a few minutes of death."

"But how—" Sedley began.

"A tame wolf and a tamer Indian saved me."

The wind had shifted and was blowing from the north. The girl shivered and rubbed her upper arms with her hands.

Shawn took off his coat and draped it around Sally's shoulders.

"I feel your warmth," the girl said. She smiled, shyly. "Thank you."

In that moment, Shawn remembered his dead wife's smile, shy like that sometimes, and it was like a knife to his heart.

Wolfden, seeing the eager expression on Sedley's face, spoke again. "The Indian was a Navajo, maybe he was a hundred years old, I don't know. But he and his wolf pulled me out of my grave. It had been a close-run thing, mighty close." He smiled. "Mr. Poe would've enjoyed that story."

"And what then?" Sedley said.

"There is no 'And what then?'" Wolfden said.

"All right, what about the Navajo and his wolf?" Sedley said.

Wolfden smiled. "Maybe they were both wolves.

Maybe they were both Navajo. I can't say. The old man didn't utter a word. He just left and a while later I heard the howls of hunting lobos in the woods. He did give me this." Wolfden opened his shirt and showed, on a rawhide thong, a snarling, fanged wolf's head, carved from bone.

"What does it mean?" Sedley said.

"I don't know what it means," Wolfden said.

"But you do, Mr. Wolfden," Sally said. "You know perfectly well what it means. What the old Navajo gave you means you became blood brother to him and the wolf."

Both Shawn and Sedley looked at the girl in surprise. But her eyes were hidden in shadow and she said nothing else.

CHAPTER THIRTEEN

Temple Carstairs was a widower who lived in a gingerbread house at the edge of town. Missing a woman's touch, the place was rundown and the front yard, where once flowers had bloomed, was overrun with cactus and bunch grass.

Carstairs's late wife had always polished the brass knocker that Shel Shannon used to a bright shine, but now it was dull with spots of green mildew.

It was almost midnight and the sandstorm had blown itself out, but the wind was now from the north and coldly slapped Shannon's unshaven cheek.

The hollow *rap-rap-rap* of the doorknocker echoed inside the house and it took a couple of moments before Carstairs appeared.

The old man wore a long nightgown, a sleeping cap with a tassel falling to his shoulder and a puzzled expression on his face.

"Brother Uzziah, why are you abroad at this time of night?" he said. "Keeping the town safe from harm, I presume."

"I've got an urgent message from the . . . from Brother Matthias," Shannon said. "He said to give it to you personal like."

"Then deliver it, brother, and leave me to my slumbers."

"I think I should come inside, Brother Carstairs," Shannon said. "It's a secret message and the night has ears."

"But there's no one to hear it but me," Carstairs said. The lit candle lamp in his hand guttered in the wind. "The whole town is asleep, as good Christian folk should be."

The old man looked irritated. "If it's about the tithe, can't it wait until morning?"

Shannon shook his head. "Sorry, Brother Carstairs, but I was ordered to deliver the message tonight."

Carstairs sighed. "Oh, very well then, come in, but make it quick."

"So quick you'll hardly notice," Shannon said.

He showed his teeth in a grin.

Candlelight rippled across the ceiling and glistened on flyspecked spiderwebs as the old man led the way into his study. The house smelled musty, old, like damp earth.

Carstairs laid the lamp on a table and turned.

His eyes widened, first in surprise, then in horror.

Shannon stretched a rope taut between his huge, hairy hands. He grinned like a hyena at a kill.

"What are you doing?" Carstairs said, his voice quivering in his throat.

"Killing you, you old coot, like the boss told me to. You've lived too long, old man."

Temple Carstairs was game, and he was spry.

He made a dash for an open rolltop desk and the Remington derringer stuck into a letter slot.

He never made it.

As fast as a striking cougar, Shannon growled and then looped the rope around the old man's neck.

Then he had fun.

Giggling like a teenage girl at her first cotillion, Shannon tightened the rope and Carstairs made gagging sounds as the rough hemp dug deep. His eyes popped and his lips peeled back in a grotesque grimace.

The garrote is a slow, painful way to kill a man. The victim convulses horribly before he eventually passes into death. Sometimes, as an act of mercy, an iron spike is incorporated into the garrote to break the spine and hasten the demise of the condemned.

But there was no such compassion for Temple Carstairs. He suffered his execution in full measure.

By the time it was over and the old man's body slumped to the floor, Shel Shannon, a big man and strong, sweated like a pig and his cackle was gone, replaced by heavy breathing, his chest rising and falling from his great effort.

But Shannon wasn't yet finished with Carstairs, not by a long shot.

He dragged the old man's body out of the study, then under the cobwebs where spiders devoured mummified flies, and out through the rear of the house into darkness.

Shannon paused for a few moments and listened into the night. He heard only the endless yips of coyotes in the hills and the harsh rasp of his own breath.

The sky was clear, the moon rising high, and bats flitted close to Shannon as he let go of his burden and found the can of coal oil he'd already hidden in the brush.

Working quickly, he doused the corpse in oil and then thumbed a match into flame and set it alight.

Carstairs's body burned well and Shannon was delighted.

Who would have thought that the old man had so much fat in him?

When the body was charred, Carstairs's left arm had bent at the elbow in the flames and his open hand looked like a bird claw.

Shannon was pleased with the effect. It looked

like the old man, in his final agony, had reached out for help from the deity, and that would suit the boss's plan admirably.

Now to hide the empty oil can and proceed with the rest of Hank Cobb's scheme.

As he ran toward the church, Shannon smiled to himself.

Damn it, the boss was brilliant. Only Cobb could cook up a plan like this and only he, Shel Shannon, could make it work perfectly.

Shannon pulled on the church door and it creaked open. It was dark inside, but for the beams of moonlight that bladed through the stained-glass windows and splashed pale rainbows of color on the polished wood floor.

The door to the bell tower lay to the gunman's left.

Hitching up his monk's robes, he ran for the door, yanked it open and sprinted up the wooden staircase, his boots thumping on pine, spurs chiming with every step.

Ahead of him the bell rope dangled and Shannon grabbed it and pulled.

The rewarding clash and clang of the bell urged him to greater effort and the clamoring carillon shrilled ringing echoes throughout the waking and thoroughly alarmed town.

Panicked voices were raised outside the church, but Shannon, laughing like a demented Quasimodo, yanked faster and faster on the bell rope.

Feet pounded on the stairs and Hank Cobb burst onto the platform, a couple of concerned citizens in his wake.

"Brother Uzziah, what in the world are you doing?" Cobb said, feigning surprise as he played his role to the hilt. He held a Bible in his right hand, pressed close to his chest, his forefinger jammed between the pages as though marking his place.

A nice touch, Shannon thought, as he let go of the rope and the bell chimed slowly into silence.

"Brother Carstairs is dead," Shannon said.

"But how . . . what . . ." Cobb said.

"I found him behind his house," Shannon said. "All burned up, as though he'd been struck by lightning."

"There has been no lightning," one of the citizens said. "The sky is clear and full of stars."

"Yes, clear by God's grace, but there's enough evil abroad this night to darken any sky," Cobb said. He stared at Shannon, his face empty. "Quick now, Brother Uzziah, lead us to the good brother's body and keep your revolver handy."

A large crowd, all of them in sleep attire, shuffled after Shannon to Carstairs's house.

"The poor man is out back where he was struck down," Shannon said. He waved the people forward. "Follow me, brothers and sisters and prepare yourselves for a terrible sight."

"Aye, that we will," Cobb said. "The air is thick and hard to breathe and smells of sulfur. It means that there's witchery and wickedness afoot."

If the crowd didn't think that the air was hard to breathe and smelled of sulfur before, they did now, and a few of the women were audibly gasping.

Cobb turned to a man at his side and said, "Brother, fetch yonder storm lantern from Brother Carstairs's porch. We'll need it in this hellish gloom."

The man nodded. "The night does smell strong of witchery, brother."

"Indeed, it does," Cobb said. "But never fear, we'll hunt the vile creature down and burn her in the fire."

Shannon stepped to the charred form sprawled on the ground, the left hand raised in macabre supplication.

The man with the lantern held it high. The fire had burned Carstairs's face to a blackened skull, white bone showing here and there through the skin.

Before anyone could talk, or speculate, Cobb said with all the authority he could muster, "Struck down by a bolt of hellfire. That's plain to see."

The man with the lamp raised his nose and tested the air.

"The poor brother's body smells of kerosene," he said. "Like the lamp I hold in my hand."

Cobb gritted his teeth. Damn the man for a meddling pest.

But aloud he said, "And think ye that kerosene doesn't fuel the eternal fires of hell?"

"Yes, it is the devil's way," another man said. "Kerosene burns hot."

A gray, slat-sided dog nosed its way through the crowd and sniffed the corpse's crotch, its teeth bared.

Cobb kicked the dog away and glared at the woman. The damned stupid sow threatened to ruin the atmosphere he'd created.

He ratcheted up his rhetoric several notches.

"Many have been killed by the witch's evil spell," he said. "It was she who cursed the stage that brought her here and caused it to overturn. It was she who destroyed the brothers who so gallantly fought her to save this town, and it was she who hurled the bolt from hell that killed the good and honorable man who lies at our feet."

Cobb raised his arms and his voice rose to a shout.

"Aye, and it was she who then fled into the night with Jasper Wolfden, the dead man who still walks the earth."

"It's the truth, by God," Shannon said. "And she'll try to kill us all."

A woman screamed in terror and pointed at the sky.

"I saw her! I saw the witch."

Even Cobb was unnerved by the woman's shriek, a hysterical screech that slashed through the fabric of the night like a knife blade.

He stared at the sky and yelled, "Where?"

"The witch just flew across the face of the moon on a gigantic bat," the woman said. She gagged in her throat and her face seemed to melt into a mask of fear. "God . . . help . . . us . . . all. . . ." she said.

"I see her!" Cobb said. "There!" He jabbed a finger upward. "And there! And there! And she has other demons with her!"

Shel Shannon, slow of wits but impulsive, drew his Colt and slammed shots at the cobalt-blue, star-strewn sky.

The firing added to the mob hysteria and people began to drift hurriedly away, seeking the safety of their homes.

Cobb noted the exodus and yelled, "Now do any of ye say we don't need more fighting brothers?"

"Anything, Brother Matthias," a man called out, his voice ragged with fear. "Just keep us safe from the fiends of hell."

"Then ye heard it," Cobb said. He raised his Bible

for dramatic effect. "My brothers and me will begin to collect the tithe tomorrow, and woe betide those of you who hold back, for ye shall surely be struck down by the witch and her familiars."

Again Shannon thought that an excellent speech on his boss's part. He had no idea what "familiars" meant, and he suspected Cobb didn't either.

Caught up in the enthusiasm of the moment, Shannon gestured at the sky and screamed, "She's coming back!" He raised his gun again, but the hammer clicked on spent cartridges and ruined the effect.

But it was enough.

The crowd scampered, all but one tall, potbellied man who had a sour, slack look on his fleshy face, as though his before-sleep sex had been interrupted.

"Surely you will not tithe the bank, brother?" he said.

"Especially the bank," Cobb said. "But you needn't pay the tithe unless we really need it and there is no other course."

It seemed like a magnanimous gesture on Cobb's part. But it wasn't. He wanted all the bank's money in one place where he could get at it easily.

Banker Reuben Waters apparently didn't see it that way. He took Cobb at face value.

"I trust the tithe will generate enough money for

the men you need, Brother Matthias," he said. "And without my bank's involvement."

"I'm sure it will, Brother Waters," Cobb said, figuring he could afford to humor the man.

"Well, good night then," Waters said. "Brother Matthias, you are indeed a fair and honorable man."

CHAPTER FOURTEEN

The crowd had dispersed and Shel Shannon, grinning, raised a hand to the sky, made a gun of forefinger and thumb, and said, "Pow! Pow! Pow! I got the witch."

Hank Cobb chose not to be amused.

He toed Carstairs's body and said, "One of you get the undertaker and get this buried. Then Shel, you and the boys start collecting the tithes at first light. I want every damned ring . . . I mean every piece of jewelry in this town."

Cobb lifted his right hand and made a tight fist. "Squeeze them, Shel, squeeze 'em hard until their tongues hang out and their eyes pop. After we've wrung them dry, we'll empty the bank and then quit this hick town forever."

"Maybe we can head for Old Mexico, huh, boss?" Shannon said. "Money goes further there. I hear the whiskey and the señoritas come cheap."

"I'll study on it some," Cobb said. "But I'm partial

to the big towns. That's where the easy money's to be made." He grinned. "Plenty of saloons and dark alleys, if you catch my drift."

Then Cobb, a small-time crook with a politician's smarts, had a moment of diabolical inspiration.

"Hold up just one damned minute," he said. "I have an idea."

"Hell, boss, you're full of ideas," Shannon said, grinning, proud to be associated with such a genius for business.

"Listen up, Shel, before you start on the collection, you and the boys arrest . . . what's her name? The old bird that thinks her dead husband and son are still to home."

"Annie Gaunt, you mean? Her old man and son went marching off to the war and never came back."

"Yeah, her. Folks think she's crazy anyhow, talking and cooking dinner for two men who ain't there. At first light in the morning arrest her fer a witch. I think a burning before breakfast will show the good citizens of Holy Rood that there is"—he smiled—"evil in their midst and we're taking care of it. I reckon it will make 'em more inclined to be generous, like."

Cobb slammed a fist into his open palm and swore. "I've got another idea, but it's too late for that now."

Cobb's gunmen had gathered around him and one of them said, "What was your idea, boss?"

"To put a bullet into the old gal, somewhere that

wouldn't kill her right away, and . . . wait a minute, we don't need to hold on until sunup. We can do it right here and now. Everybody's so scared in this town they won't be asleep anyhow."

Answering the question on Shannon's face, Cobb said, "Shel, forget the undertaker for now. I want you and one of the boys to bring the old woman to me, while Carstairs's body is still lying here. Beat her up some so the bruises show, but don't kill her, understand?"

He saw no light of understanding in Shannon's eyes and said, "After the good folks of Holy Rood retired for the night, we shot her out of the sky and she fell to earth with a thud. Now do you get it?"

Shannon's chin dropped and he gave an open-mouthed smile. "Hell, yeah, boss, now I catch your drift."

"Good, then go fetch her. Hurt her, but not real bad."

"Got it, boss. Hell, do you want me to shoot her? I never liked the crazy old biddy anyhow."

"No, I'll do that," Cobb said. "When you come back with her you can shoot at the sky."

Annie Gaunt was old, frail, with lost, empty eyes that had faded to the color of bleach. She wore a black, hooped dress of the Civil War era, made from bombazine, that dull, lusterless fabric, a widow's cap, and her cuffs and collar were also black.

The townspeople thought Annie wore the mourning gown because her husband and son had been killed in the war. But since the old lady thought they were still alive, that was not the case.

No, she dressed in black out of sympathy for old Queen Vic who'd lost her husband to typhoid in 1862. After an initial exchange of letters, Annie and the queen had been corresponding regularly for twenty-five years and Victoria called her, "my dearest friend, confidante, and willing shoulder on which to shed my many bitter tears."

Later, a two-bit gunman by the name of Frank Steele, acting on Cobb's orders, would throw the queen's letters into the flames of Annie's execution pyre.

But that was then and this was now. . . .

When Shannon roughly dragged the old woman to Hank Cobb, he ran a critical eye over the deep bruises on Annie Gaunt's face and arms and smiled his approval.

"Bring her here, Shel," he said.

Shannon pushed the old woman forward and she said, "I'm old and sick and I want to go home. Why are you doing this to me?"

"Because you're a witch," Cobb said.

"I'm just a poor old woman who never harmed

anyone," Annie said, pulling her torn nightgown around her. "I could be your own mother."

Cobb said nothing. He believed that some people, the poor, the sick, the old and the powerless weren't worth talking to.

"All right, boys, start shooting at the sky," he said. "Let's hear the fire of the festive revolver."

As pistols racketed around him, Cobb swung his boot and scythed Annie's legs out from under her. He ignored her screams and cries for mercy as matters of no importance, drew his Colt, placed the barrel parallel to the woman's forehead and pulled the trigger.

The effect was exactly what he wanted.

The .45 bullet grazed the old woman's head, inflicting a shallow wound. But the powder burn and bleeding looked dramatic enough and Annie was stunned, so that would keep her yap shut.

"Shel, go ring the bell again," Cobb said after the firing had died away. "Get them out here. By God, there'll be no sleep in Holy Rood for anyone tonight."

Summoned by the clanging clamor of the bell, the citizens of Holy Rood stumbled, heavy eyed, out of their houses.

Cobb's men ran among them waving excited arms that rose above the crowd like tentacles.

"We got us a witch! Shot her out of the sky!"

Still half asleep, the townspeople blinked and staggered toward Cobb, who dragged Annie Gaunt's frail unconscious form into the street.

He let go of the old woman and she fell onto her back.

"Why, that's Annie Gaunt," someone said in a shocked voice.

"Aye, that's her all right," Cobb shouted. "But a few minutes ago she was riding across the sky on a scarlet bat."

The people crowded closer. A few of the more timid stopped at a distance and craned their heads forward to see.

One of them said, "She's dead."

"No, she lives," Cobb said. "Only fire can kill a witch." He pointed at the sky. "See yonder bright star, she fell from there, and look you, only a few bruises."

"Her head is bleeding," a woman said.

"That's where my bullet hit her," Cobb said. "But mortal bullets can't destroy a witch."

He knocked off Annie's nightcap, then grabbed her by the hair and hauled her into a sitting position.

The old woman looked around at the increasingly hostile crowd and screamed loud in apprehension and fear.

"Listen to her curse you," Cobb said. "The witch is alive and still a danger to us all."

"Is she such a danger?" said a voice in the crowd.

"Yes, she's a danger," a woman yelled. "She is

visited by her dead husband and son and she talks with them. I've heard her."

"Lay to that," Cobb said. "That she does, and worse. With his own ears Brother Uzziah heard her talk to . . . I can't bring myself to say it." He waved at Shannon. "Tell them, brother. The witch has closed my throat and I can't go on."

Despite his slow wits, Shannon rose to the occasion.

"It was a cold evening last winter as I passed the witch's house that I heard her speak with a demon. Aye, and not any demon mind ye, it was the Earl of Hell himself. Old Harry come to earth to plot mischief and evil."

A gray-haired woman with yellowed store-bought teeth reacted as though she was in a revival tent.

"Tell us, brother!" she shrieked. "Was it really the devil?"

"It was him all right," Shannon said. "Beelzebub, Lucifer, the Prince of Darkness, call him what ye will, but I heard him plain, talking in a growl like a wolf. An' I heard him and Annie Gaunt touch glasses and drink to the evil they planned to befall this town."

"Then the witch must burn at sunup, before the tithing begins," Cobb yelled. He looked around him. "Can somebody give me an amen?"

A few people muttered the required word and then Cobb dragged the old woman to her feet.

"This will be the first of the damned evil brood to

burn. But there will be more and we must fight them," he said.

A child squealed at the edge of the crowd where she and a couple of older boys were using sticks to beat a rat. The rat, out of fear or because a blow had ruptured its bladder, urinated into the dust and the girl shrieked again.

One of the boys had a diseased eye and when he looked at Cobb and grinned in the moonlight, it gleamed like an opal.

The only sane person in Holy Rood that night was Annie Gaunt.

And now her fellow citizens bayed for her blood.

CHAPTER FIFTEEN

Shawn O'Brien woke with a start from shallow sleep, Judith again lost to him as his dream of her alive, laughing, beautiful, faded into transparency, then vanished into mist.

My God, had it only been six months?

Judith had been dead for a hundred and eighty days.

It seemed like a lifetime. A hundred lifetimes. Yet the pain he felt over her death was still raw and scarlet red, a wound that would never heal.

Shawn tilted back his head and stared through the lacy pine canopy at the star-scattered sky, a sky much different from the one that had cast a dark pall over the English countryside the night . . . the night . . .

The night his life ended.

He looked down at Sally Bailey lying asleep with her head on his lap. She was covered by Shawn's frockcoat and Jasper Wolfden had made her a bed of pine boughs.

Wolfden and Hamp Sedley were sleeping by the fire. Normally, a campfire to warm the night was a comforting presence, but without a coffeepot simmering on the coals, it was so much less than that.

Wishful for a cigar, but having none, Shawn faced yet more sleepless hours, as he had since Judith was murdered.

Unbidden, a man will often let his memory return to a place he no longer wishes to visit, and Dartmoor, with all the horrors it held for Shawn, was such a place.

Maybe the trouble was the night it all ended for him was so vivid, so just yesterday in his memory, that he couldn't let it go . . . would never let it go.

He looked down at Sally's face, so peaceful and pretty in sleep.

How had Judith's face looked that night, the night she'd died in pain and terror?

A steel blade twisting into his gut, Shawn reluctantly let himself live that night again.

It was a time and place he'd no wish to remember . . . but the siren song of the moor once again drew him close and would not let him forget.

A moon as thin as a slice of cucumber hung high above Dartmoor and its wan light glittered on the hoarfrost that enameled every tree, bush and blade of grass.

Shawn O'Brien's breath smoked in the air as he turned to Sir James Lovell and said, "Did you bring your revolver?"

The man nodded. "I have my Enfield."

"Then keep it close. You may need it."

Shawn rose in the stirrups and studied the bridle path though the marsh that showed in the moonlight as a twisting white ribbon.

"The tracks of Judith's horse look as though she headed straight for the tor," Shawn said. "We'll search there."

"Drago Castle is a couple of miles west of the tor," Sir James said. "She may have been overtaken by darkness and headed there to spend the night. Judith and Lady Harcourt have been friends since childhood."

"The tor first," Shawn said. His face was grim, lines of concern cutting deep like wires. "If I was an escaped convict that's where I'd hole up. From the top of the hill, a man could hide among the rocks and scout the moor for miles around."

"There are other tors on the moor, Shawn," Sir James said.

"I know. And I'll search each and every one of them."

Sir James reached inside his coat and produced his watch.

"It's almost midnight," he said. "There are storm

clouds coming in from the north. Soon it will be too dark to see."

"Then let's press on," Shawn said.

He saw the exhaustion on his father-in-law's face, the deep shadows under his eyes and in the hollows of his cheeks. Sir James was no longer young and the search for his daughter was taking a toll on him.

But he was a proud man and it didn't enter into Shawn's thinking to suggest he turn tail and head for home.

Sir James Lovell would be wounded deeply by such urging, a terrible slight to his honor that he would neither forget nor forgive.

What Shawn did say was, "I reckon we should leave the horses here and cover the rest of the way to the tor on foot. The police inspector said the convicts had raided the prison armory before they broke out, and they may have rifles."

Sir James nodded. "A sound plan, Shawn. We're sitting ducks on horseback."

Then, as gently as he could, Shawn said, "How are you holding up?"

"Oh, I can't complain, old boy. Elderly English gentlemen with weak hearts love to take midnight strolls on dangerous moors in the middle of winter, don't ye know?"

Shawn managed a slight smile. "To say nothing of hunting down escaped convicts."

"Oh, yes, I'd quite forgotten about those," Sir James said.

But he hadn't, of course . . . and neither had Shawn O'Brien.

They both had a feeling, for better or worse, the dreary, dreadful night would end with men dead on the ground.

The tor was a rugged outcropping of bare granite rock that rose fifteen hundred feet above the surrounding mire. Treeless, scoured by the winds, snows and rains of centuries, the hill looked like the skeletal backbone of an enormous hound.

Gray mist hung above the marshes like smoke and ice fringed the mud puddles. The night air was sawtoothed with frost and painful to breathe.

"Here," Shawn O'Brien said. "It happened right here."

Even Sir James, never schooled in the tracker's art, could read the sign plain.

"It looks like Judith was dragged from her horse at this spot," he said. He looked like a man who'd just read his own death notice in *The Times* of London.

Shawn nodded. "Three men. Judging by the depths of their boot prints and the lengths of their strides, all of them are tall and heavy."

"Just the kind who could kill their guards and escape from a prison," Sir James said.

Shawn nodded but said nothing. He took a knee and studied the tracks, most of them already obscured by snow and ice.

"They dragged Judith toward the tor," Shawn said. "And one of them led her horse."

Sir James suddenly looked old and tired.

"Shawn, there are two hundred tors on Dartmoor," he said. "This may not be the one."

"It's the one," Shawn said. Even in the gloom his eyes gleamed with blue fire. "There is no other."

The Anglo-Saxons have never understood, or quite believed, the Celtic gift of second sight, and Sir James had a right to look confused.

However the ability, called in Gaelic the *an dara sealladh*, is not considered a gift by those who possess it, but rather a curse, for it imposes a terrible burden—the faculty to sense death, be it near or far.

Now Shawn felt death reach out to him, its thin fingers as cold as the night, and he knew in that single, awful moment that his wife was no longer alive.

Sir James Lovell watched the change in Shawn's face, the skin draw tight to the bone, the mouth become a hard line. He had a fearful, haunted look, as though a wild, ancient war song heard in a nightmare had intruded into his waking consciousness.

And then the older man knew what Shawn knew.

"We're too late, aren't we, Shawn?" Sir James said. "My daughter is dead, isn't she?"

Shawn had no answer, or at least none he wished to make.

He opened his coat and drew his Colt from the leather. With numb fingers he fed a round into the empty chamber that had been under the hammer and holstered the revolver again.

"Let's get it done," he said.

Sir James remembered words like these from his time in the West, said by hard men committed to following the code of an eye for an eye, a tooth for a tooth, no matter the cost or the consequences.

When uttered by a man like Shawn O'Brien, there would be no turning back. Not now. Not ever.

It was Sir James who first saw the man walking along the path through the mire, appearing through the mist like a gray ghost.

Shawn, the instincts of the gunfighter honed sharp in him, saw the older man's eyes narrow and he swung around to face the danger, the Colt coming up fast.

"No shooting!" the stranger yelled. His voice croaking from cold and frost, he said, "It's only harmless old Ben Lestrange as ever was. I mean harm to no one."

"What the hell are you doing here?" Shawn said. "I could've plugged you square."

He knew the ragged, bent old man was not one of the convicts, but right then he wanted to kill him real bad. It was as though an unwelcome stranger had walked into a private funeral.

"What am I doing here, ye say. And I answer that old Ben has walked this moor, man and boy, for nigh on fifty year," Lestrange said. He laid the pack he carried on his back at his feet and winked. "I know the secret places and where the ancient bodies lie buried."

"Did you see men on the tor?" Sir James asked.

Lestrange's wrinkled face, weathered to the color of mahogany, took on a sly look. "Old Ben seen a dead 'un, squire."

"Where?" Shawn said. "Speak up, man."

"At the foot of the tor. Only she wasn't a man." Lestrange shook his head. "Oh, dear no, she were a lady."

He reached inside his filthy greatcoat and brought out a silver chain with a heart-shaped locket. "Took this from her, and if it's what you're wanting, well it's old Ben's, not yours. Finders keepers, I always say."

"Let me see that," Sir James said.

Lestrange turned away, the locket pressed against his upper chest.

"It's old Ben's," he said. "Why would a fine gentleman like yourself want to steal what's mine?"

"I warn you, my man, let me examine the locket or I'll have you in the dock at the next assizes, charged with vagrancy and theft from the dead,"

Sir James said. "You'll end your days at a penal colony in the West Indies."

Lestrange angrily shoved the locket at Sir James.

"Here, take it and damn you for a thieving toff," he said.

Sir James ignored that and examined the locket, turning it over in his gloved hands.

"Is it Judith's?" Shawn said. "It's not something I've seen her wear."

"No, it's not Judith's. The chain is silver but the locket is cheap, made of tin."

Sir James opened the locket, turned it to the pale moonlight, and stared at it for a long while.

"What do you see?" Shawn said, stepping closer.

"Two people and I recognize their likenesses." He held out the open locket to Shawn. "It's George Simpson the blacksmith and his wife, Martha. Their daughter Mavis was one of the girls abducted from the village."

Shawn swung on Ben Lestrange. "Take us to the girl," he said.

"I told you, she's a dead 'un. You need have no truck with her, young gentleman."

"Take us to her," Shawn said. "Show us where she lies."

Lestrange looked sly. "Do I get my chain back?"

"Here," Sir James said. He dropped the locket into Lestrange's hand. "I rather fancy that Mavis has no further use for it."

The old man grinned, knuckled his forehead and picked up his pack.

"Follow me, gents," he said. "Mind you don't step into the mire"—he cackled— "or you'll end up dead 'uns like poor Mavis Simpson, God rest her."

The girl's plump, naked body lay tangled in a gorse bush at the base of the tor. That she'd been badly abused and raped was obvious.

"Found her lying there," Lestrange said. "There's frost all over her and that's why at first I thought she was a silver woman. There are some who will pay plenty for a woman made out of silver."

Shawn's bleak eyes searched the top of the hill, and then he lowered them to the tramp. "Go away," he said. "Get the hell out of here."

"Can you spare me a shilling, squire?" Lestrange said. "Then you'll never see old Ben again."

"No, Shawn!" Sir James placed his hand on the younger man's gun arm. "Killing this poor, demented creature won't bring Judith back to you."

For a moment Shawn teetered on the edge, breathing hard. Finally, he brought himself under control.

To Lestrange he said again, "Just . . . go away."

Sir James fished in his pants pocket and came up with a coin.

"Here, Lestrange, take this and go," he said. "You've done us a service."

The tramp stared, big-eyed at the gold sovereign in his palm and knuckled his forehead. "Thank'ee," he said. "You're a real gent as old Ben knowed when he first set eyes on you."

Then, after a quick, frightened glance at Shawn, the old man shuffled quickly down the path and the moonlight cast his rippling shadow on the frozen earth.

"I'd say the girl was murdered and then her body was thrown from the crest of the tor," Sir James said.

Shawn nodded. "Seems like."

The older man was quiet for a few moments, as though he was taking time to choose his words carefully.

Finally, he said, "Shawn, let me go alone. I can use a revolver quite well."

"Why do you say that?"

"Because . . ." Sir James searched for the words. "Because I don't want you to see Judith like"—his eyes moved to the girl's stark body—"like her."

"You're her father. Do you think that you can stand it?"

"No. No, I can't. But I'm an old man. You are young, Shawn. If you don't keep seeing a terrible picture in your mind, you can recover from this."

"Recover if I don't see what happened to my wife? Is that it?"

Sir James floundered, his face strained. "Something like that." He shook his head. "Be damned to it all, Shawn, I just don't have the words."

Shawn looked at the sky. "It will rain soon and we'll lose the moon to clouds."

"Then we both must face what's before us in full measure," Sir James said. "There can be no sparing you."

"No, I can't be spared. As my father says, I'll soon sup sorrow with the spoon of grief. But there's no stepping away from it."

"Then let us climb the hill together," Sir James said.

The way up the tor was difficult, especially in darkness and a cold, ticking rain.

Shawn and Sir James scrambled through gorse bushes and grabbed the twisted limbs of stunted birch trees to navigate the icy slope.

Every now and then the moon entered a break in the black cloud and afforded a view of the granite rocks at the crest of the tor.

Up there nothing moved and no sound carried in the rising wind.

After fifteen minutes of climbing, the top of the hill still seemed a long way off and Sir James stopped on a flat ledge of rock to take a breather.

Now the rain had turned to a slashing sleet, carried on the knifing north wind, and the night grew colder and darker.

After scanning the tor, Sir James pulled the collar of his coat closer around his face, like a turtle retreating into its shell, and said, "There's a wild sheep on the tor. Would it remain there with men around?"

"I don't know," Shawn said. "Show me."

"There," Sir James said, pointing.

Shawn saw what the older man had seen, but with younger, farseeing eyes.

How does a man look when everything inside him suddenly dies?

He looks as Shawn O'Brien looked that night.

Broken.

The only possible word to describe it.

There was no sheep on the tor.

It was the slender white body of Lady Judith, spread-eagled on a flat slab, a naked sacrifice to the lusts of men who were not fit to breathe the same air as the rest of humanity.

"Oh, my God," Sir James whispered, reading Shawn's face. He buried his face in gloved hands. "Oh, my God . . ."

Shawn did not cry out in his pain and rage; instead, he was silent, filled with an icy calm, his hands steady, as is the way of the gunfighter when there's man killing to be done.

Without waiting to see if Sir James followed, he climbed the hill.

* * *

When Shawn kissed his dead wife's lips, they were as cold and lifeless as marble. Pain that was beyond pain knifed through him and he wanted to turn his face to the torn sky and scream his grief.

But that must come later. . . .

Biting sleet cartwheeling around him, Shawn stood in darkness, gun in hand, and watched the dull orange glow of a fire among the rocks ahead of him.

He was aware of Sir James stepping beside him. The man no longer wore his coat.

Shawn accepted that without comment.

Then, in a whisper, he said, "They're camped out among the rocks, sheltered from the wind."

Sir James nodded.

"This will be real close. When you get your work in, aim low, for the belly. A bullet in the gut will stop a man."

Again, Sir James nodded and said nothing. His eyes were lost in shadow.

His face a stiff, joyless mask, Shawn said, "Then let's get it done."

Their steps were silent on the slushy, uneven ground. Half-hidden behind the shifting shroud of the sleet, the two men advanced on the rocks.

Shawn smelled wood smoke and the heavy odor of wet earth and the sword blade tang of the sleet itself, cold and raw and honed sharp.

The three convicts sat between a pair of massive

boulders, and had pulled over their heads a makeshift roof of thin sheets of black shale.

Later, Shawn would not be able to recall their faces.

When he brought the scene to mind, he saw again the small campfire and the three convicts dressed in blue canvas jackets, pants of the same color and heavy, steel-studded boots.

The men were vicious predators who'd stalked a peaceful, pastured land with impunity. But the man now towering above them was no pale, puny, prattling prelate who'd just watched them rape his wife and loot his village church's poor box.

Shawn O'Brien was a gunfighter, schooled by gunfighters, and that night he was death.

Startled, the convicts dived for the Martini-Henry rifles propped against the boulders . . . but they never made it.

At a distance of less than six feet, Shawn O'Brien didn't miss.

He thumbed three fast shots and all three men went down, hit hard. The face of one convict crashed into the fire, erupting flame, sparks and a scream of sudden agony.

Shawn scored two headshots, killing the convicts instantly. The third man, his booted feet gouging the ground as he cringed away from a visitation from hell, had taken Shawn's bullet in the throat. The side of his neck between earlobe and shoulder was a mass of red, mangled meat that pumped blood.

Sir James, gun in hand, stepped beside Shawn and looked into the smoke-streaked hideout.

In a wet, gurgling voice the wounded convict screamed to the older man, "Help me! I'm hurt bad and I need a doctor!"

Sir James, in shock, turned to Shawn and said, "He needs a doctor."

Shawn nodded. He thumbed back the hammer of his Colt and shot the man between the eyes.

"He just got one," he said.

The time for vengeance was over. Now came the grief.

Shawn spent the rest of the long night with his dead wife in his arms, holding her close to his chest as the slanting sleet bladed around him.

Come the dawn, Sir James, his face gray as ash, gently tried to take his daughter from Shawn's arms and said, "I'll bring the horses."

"No," Shawn said. "I don't want the horses."

He lifted Judith's body, her face as beautiful in death as it had been in life, and said, "I'll carry her. I'll carry my wife home."

The memories of that different time and place flowed out of Shawn's mind like water as the dawn chased darkness from between the pines and the new aborning day came in fresh and clean and full of promise.

Sally's head stirred in his lap and she opened her eyes and smiled that sleepy, sweet smile a woman often gives a man when she first wakes in the early morning.

Without moving, she said, "I hope I didn't keep you awake. I do wiggle sometimes."

"No," Shawn said, deciding on a small lie, "I slept just fine."

Over by the dull glow of the campfire, Hamp Sedley got to his feet and stretched the kinks out of his back.

"Had a damned rock under me the whole night," he said. He glanced down at Jasper Wolfden and said, his face sour, "How the hell can a man sleep like that, all curled up like a dog?"

Sedley never got an answer to his question because a man's voice cut through the morning quiet.

"Hello, the camp!"

CHAPTER SIXTEEN

Shawn O'Brien gently raised Sally Bailey to a sitting position, and then rose to his feet, his right hand dropping to his holstered Colt.

"Come on in, all smiling and friendly, like you were visiting kissin' kin," he called out.

A few moments later a small, plump man on a bay horse rode out of the pines. He had a booted Winchester under his left knee.

"Howdy," he said. "I'm sorry to intrude."

Wolfden was on his feet and he didn't look like a man about to unroll the welcoming mat.

"You from Holy Rood?" he said, his words hard edged.

"Of course, I got food," the small man said. "I got a ways to ride and a man needs to eat."

"He said, are you from Holy Rood?" Sedley said.

"Eh?" the small man said, cupping a hand to his ear.

This time Sedley shouted, "You from Holy Rood?"

"Yes, I'm from Holy Rood," the small man said. "And be damned to ye for a mumbler. Pronounce your words properly, young man."

"State your intentions," Sedley said.

"Eh?"

Sedley tried again. "Why are you here? Speak up now. Be quick."

"Eh?"

The man on the horse held up a hand. "Wait one all-fired minute. Lord, I can't abide a whispering man."

He reached into the pocket of his coat, an action that merited the sound of triple clicks as three Colts cocked.

"Hold on, now," the small man said. He looked like a jolly German toymaker. "I was just getting me ear trumpet so I can damned well hear mumbling men."

The man produced a contraption that looked like a brass horn, stuck the thing to his ear and said, "Eh?"

Sedley, with the irritated tone of a man fast running out of patience, said, "State your intentions."

"My intentions?"

"You heard me."

"No I didn't. I read your lips."

"Well, state them anyway," Sedley said.

"Hell," Wolfden said, "we'll be here all day,"

"No need to keep me at bay," the small man said. "I'm your friend. As to my intentions, I plan to ride clear to Albuquerque and leave behind this hellish country forever."

"Then light and set," Shawn said.

"Eh?"

This time Shawn yelled the invitation so loud, it set the jays in the pines fluttering in panic.

"No need to shout," the little man said. He had red apple cheeks, bushy gray side whiskers and looked to be about seventy years old. "You should learn some respect for your elders, young feller."

Before he swung out of the saddle, the man said, "Name's Nathan Scruggs. Scruggs by name, Scruggs by nature, I always say."

The little man tethered his horse to a pine branch, and then stepped to the fire that Sedley had fed with wood.

"No coffee?" Scruggs said.

"We don't have any," Sedley said.

"Eh?"

Irritated, Sedley yelled directly into the ear trumpet, "We ain't got no coffee!"

Scruggs nodded and said to Shawn, "There's coffee and a pot in the poke tied to the saddle, sonny. Go get it and then look for water."

He shook his head. "Then I have a sad story to tell you." His eyes lighted on Sally. "It will chill the young blood in your veins."

Shawn was going to say, "About Holy Rood?" But he held his tongue. Yelling into Scruggs's trumpet was too much of an effort.

A mossy stream ran through the trees at a distance from camp and soon coffee bubbled on the fire.

Sedley, who had appointed himself the camp spokesman, said, "Tell us your story."

"Nah, let it bile a little longer," Scruggs said.

Sedley was spared having to shout again, when the little man said, "They're burning a witch this morning in Holy Rood." His eyes wounded, Scruggs's voice was hollow, distant. "Only she's not a witch—she's my dearest friend."

"Who is she, Mr. Scruggs?" Sally said.

A woman's voice is pitched higher than a man's and Scruggs seemed to hear the girl better because he answered her question without hesitation.

"Her name is Annie Gaunt. People say she's crazy because she thinks her dead son and husband are still alive, and maybe she is, but then, Queen Victoria doesn't reckon so and that's good enough for me."

Scruggs looked around at blank faces and said, "Annie and old Queen Vic have been exchanging letters since Prince Albert died, nigh on twenty-five years ago. I know because I'm a calligrapher by profession and when Annie got older, I copied her letters for her and fine letters they were too."

Shawn leaned forward slightly, and said, "Why are they—"

"Eh?"

He turned to Sally. "Ask him why they're burning the old woman."

The girl repeated the question, and Scruggs said, "Burning her for a witch. I already told you that." He pointed to Sally. "Young lady, Brother Matthias says he shot Annie out of the sky while she was flying a bat across the moon with you."

"With me?" Sally said.

"Eh?"

"But that's ridiculous," the girl yelled.

"I know it is, but they'll burn poor Annie just the same," Scruggs said.

Shawn looked at Jasper Wolfden, but the man shook his head and said, "Nothing we can do, Shawn. She's already dead."

Shawn opened his mouth to speak, but Scruggs, with a deaf man's disregard for ordered conversation, said, "I fled town in the dark. I'm a friend of Annie's, her only friend, and I reckoned I'd be next for the stake or the chopping block."

Scruggs lifted his tin cup and motioned to Shawn.

"Here, sonny, fill this up," he said. "I don't want to burn my hands, me being in the profession I'm in."

After Shawn poured the coffee, Scruggs said, "We only have but one cup, so we'll pass it around. Just don't get your damned mustaches into it." He smiled at Sally. "Of course, that doesn't apply to you, dear lady."

"Did you ever think Annie was a witch?" she asked him.

The little man heard and he answered.

"Of course not. Annie was the only sane woman in a town gone mad." His eyes moved to Wolfden. "You lived in Holy Rood for a while. Is it possible? Can a whole town go mad?"

"It's happened before in history," Wolfden said. "Salem comes to mind."

Now Shawn asked Wolfden another question.

"Why would Hank Cobb murder a harmless old woman?" He shook his head. "I can't come up with any reason for it."

"I don't know," Wolfden said. "To scare folks, maybe."

Scruggs had been watching the two men intently, reading lips.

"It's all about the tithe," he said.

Shawn said to Sally, "Tell him we're not catching his drift."

"Eh?" Scruggs said, looking around him.

"We don't understand," Sally said.

"Huh? What wonderland?" Scruggs said.

"We didn't catch your drift," Sally yelled.

"What's to catch?" Scruggs said. He accepted the coffee cup from Sedley. "Didn't put your mustache in it, did you?"

"Yeah, I sure did," Sedley said.

"Just as well you didn't," Scruggs said. "It isn't hygienic."

He sipped the coffee, passed the cup to Shawn and said, "I believe Annie was condemned to burn because the tithe has been increased and Brother Matthias—"

"Hank Cobb," Shawn said.

"Eh?"

Now Shawn roared at the top of his voice.

"He isn't Brother Matthias. He's a two-bit crook by the name of Hank Cobb!"

Scruggs winced and quickly unplugged the trumpet from his ear.

"No need to shout, sonny. I reckon your pa should've taken a switch to your backside when you were a younker and taught you some manners."

"Sorry," Shawn said.

"He says he's sorry," Sally yelled, doing her best to suppress a grin.

"And so he should be," Scruggs said. "Raising your voice like that, young man. I declare, the very idea!"

But somewhat mollified by Shawn's apology, the little man told how the tithe had been increased to buy gunfighters to protect the town against witches and their familiars.

"Of course, you four are included in that distinguished group," he said.

Scruggs glanced at the brightening sky like a man gauging if it was time to leave.

But he shoved a half-burned stick back into the fire and then said, "By tonight there won't be a piece of jewelry, a wedding ring, watch or gold coin that won't be in Brother . . . I mean Hank Cobb's hands."

"What about the bank?" Shawn said.

"Eh?"

"Ask him, Sally," Shawn said.

"What about the bank?" Sally yelled.

"The money in the bank stays where it is for now," Scruggs said. "I reckon maybe fifty thousand in deposits. Brother . . . uh . . . Hank Cobb says he'll tithe the deposits if and when he needs them."

"He'll need it," Wolfden said. "He's planning to blow town, I reckon. Get all he can get and then light a shuck, and that includes the money in the town bank."

"Seems like," Shawn said. "Unless we stop him."

"Are the people in Holy Rood worth it?" Sedley said.

"It's not for them," Shawn said. "It's for all the victims of Hank Cobb, including a young cowboy who died for nothing and now a crazy old woman who was the friend of a queen."

"Shawn, there's three of us," Wolfden said. "Now I don't know how many gun hands Cobb has left, but I figure he's got enough. We'd be bucking a stacked deck."

"And you can count me out," Sedley said. "I'm not drawing iron against professional gunfighters. Man can get himself killed playing that game."

"If we can stop Cobb collecting the tithe as he calls it, we can keep him in town for a while and deal with him there," Shawn said.

"I repeat, there's three of us," Wolfden said. "How do you figure we can pin Cobb in Holy Rood."

"Two. I've opted out, remember," Sedley said.

"Three," Shawn said. "Hamp, here's today's lesson. You draw your gun, get your work in and take your hits until the smoke clears. Gun fighting isn't real complicated."

"Thanks, O'Brien, now I feel a lot better," Sedley said.

"What are you three whispering about?" Scruggs said.

"It's none of your business," Wolfden said.

"You're talking about my baldness?" Scruggs said.

"Yes, we are," Wolfden yelled.

"Then I won't stay here any longer to be in-sulted," Scruggs said.

He opened the lid of the coffeepot, poured the dregs into the fire and picked up the empty cup. When he'd shoved them both back into the sack on his saddle, he turned and said, "Nine."

He noted the puzzled faces and said, "Cobb has eight gunmen and he makes nine."

Scruggs swung into the saddle, gathered the reins and said, "Read your lips." He smiled. "Maybe I'll see you folks in Albuquerque. That is, if you ain't all dead by then."

"The little man might be a prophet, you know," Wolfden said.

"Not too hard to predict that if we don't get out of this country we'll all be dead soon," Sedley said.

"Not me. I've got a score to settle with Cobb and the whole damned town," Shawn said. "I won't step away from it."

"You're fixing to set yourself up as a town tamer, huh, O'Brien?" Sedley said.

"Yeah. Something like that."

"Then what do we do?" Sedley asked. "Walk down Main Street with guns blazing?"

"We could, but I don't think we'd last too long," Shawn said.

Smiling no longer came easily to Shawn O'Brien, but he managed one now as his thoughts amused him.

"I have an idea if we can make it work," he said. "Maybe we can beat Hank Cobb at his own game."

After a few moments silence, Wolfden said, "Well, let's hear it."

"Not yet," Shawn said. "I have to find a volunteer."

He saw the alarm in Sedley's face and said, "Not you, Hamp. I need a volunteer that Cobb won't recognize."

"And where are you going to find one of them?" Wolfden said.

"I've already found him," Shawn said. "You're sitting right there, Jasper."

CHAPTER SEVENTEEN

The burning had gone really well.

The old woman had screamed enough to impress the crowd, but not too much that it might have made some sympathetic to her suffering.

Cobb's only disappointment was that the search for Annie Gaunt's friend, a man called Scruggs, had turned up nothing. He would have burned with the old woman, but it seemed that the man had scampered.

Still, Cobb grinned as he drank his morning coffee and studied the pile on the table in front of him.

"Good work, Brother Uzziah," he said.

"Hell, boss, that's only the beginning," Shel Shannon said, huge in his monk's robe. "I ain't near through squeezing them yet."

Cobb idly picked up a gold ring with a ringlet of hair enclosed in its locket-like setting and turned it in his fingers.

"It's what they call a mourning ring," Shannon said. "The woman who owned it said it was a lock of hair from the head of her daughter who died when she was six or seven. I don't rightly recollect." The gunman grinned. "Damned slut didn't want to part with it until I convinced her that a ring wasn't worth a broken finger."

"How much?" Cobb said.

"Hard to say, but I reckon it will bring a hundred easily in Texas."

Cobb tossed the ring onto the heap of jewelry and gold watches on the table.

"How much is all this in front of me worth?" he said.

"Five, six thousand," Shannon said.

He saw the disappointment on Cobb's face and said, "The boys are still gathering stuff, boss. By tonight we'll have twice that and maybe more."

"I know, but it isn't gonna be near enough," Cobb said. "But we'll make it up with the bank money."

Shannon nodded. "I asked some questions about that, discreetly, like you said. Ain't that the word you used?"

Cobb nodded and Shannon said, "There's gold miners' money in there and a few cattlemen's accounts. Seems like they figured a law-abiding town like Holy Rood was a safe place to leave it."

Cobb smiled. "Their mistake. How much?"

"Near as I can figure, twenty, maybe thirty

thousand. But there could be twice that, I reckon. Only Reuben Waters knows for sure."

Cobb considered that, then said, "All right, we'll pay off the hired guns with the jewelry and stuff, and split the bank money between us."

"Seems fair to me, boss," Shannon said, pleased.

Cobb picked up the mourning ring and after a while found a tiny clasp at the side of the setting. He opened the locket and let the lock of hair inside fall to the floor.

"I'm keeping this," he said. "When I kill Jasper Wolfden, I'll put a chunk of his beard in it." He grinned at Shannon. "I'll wear it on my finger to mourn him, like."

"Will we have time for that, boss?" Shannon said. He looked concerned.

"We'll make time," Cobb said. "I want Wolfden and them other two that he helped escape. And most of all, I want that girl."

"You gonna gun her too, boss?"

Cobb shook his head, his eyes gleaming. "No, I got other plans for her."

The coin was heavy, but most of the bank's assets were in paper money and Reuben Waters easily handled the burlap sacks he threw into the back of the surrey. The horse in the traces was a Morgan and it would do its job.

Waters had been pilfering the accounts for the

past year, but not so much that it would be noticed by his clerk without a careful audit.

The big banker nodded to himself and smiled his satisfaction.

He estimated there was close to sixty thousand in the surrey, enough to last him the rest of his life if he stayed to cheap whiskey and cheaper whores.

As for his dear wife, Prudence, fat and snoring in the marital bed, she could fend for herself. Hey, maybe Brother Matthias would name her for a witch and burn her.

Waters's smile broadened. Serve her right. She really was a damned witch after all.

The virgin dawn blushed pink in the sky as the banker checked the loads in his Smith & Wesson .38 and returned it to the pocket of his frockcoat.

A big-bellied man, and heavy, the surrey lurched and creaked when Waters climbed into the seat and clucked the Morgan into motion.

Holy Rood was still asleep as the banker swung the surrey into the street and headed south through long morning shadows.

Waters was mightily pleased with himself.

If he kept to the main wagon and stage route, by tonight he'd be in Silver Reef where he and his money would be safe.

Then a few drinks, a good dinner and a woman to share his bed, and he'd hit the road again and head for the Arizona Territory where nobody knew him.

And after that . . . well, the world was his oyster.

Waters slapped the horse into a trot, anxious to be gone from the damned town forever. The surrey trailed a plume of dust as it cleared the business area, then the livery stable and finally the sheriff's office.

He didn't see a soul.

But a dog trotted out of an alley, a burned chunk of bone in its mouth, and watched Waters go. The dog dropped the bone, then squatted and scratched and scratched and scratched. . . .

"There he goes, boss, just like you said he would," Shel Shannon said. "Runnin' like a scalded cat."

Cobb stepped to the window in time to see the surrey's dust settle back to the street.

He smiled. "I don't know how many mistakes Waters has made in his life, but this is his biggest."

Cobb moved away from the window and said to Shannon, "Who's to the south."

"McCord and Hooper. I told them to bring him back dead. Figure it's easier that way."

"See the money is returned to the bank and I want a two-man guard on it until we ride out of here," Cobb said.

He smiled as a thought struck him.

"Hell, we'll burn the place on the way out. Wipe this burg off the map."

"Easier that way," Shannon said, repeating himself.

"Ain't it, though?" Cobb said, his tight-skinned face alight.

Bargain with the coin and save the notes, Reuben Waters told himself as the two riders, dressed in monkish robes, rode out of the trees and blocked the road.

"Howdy, Rueben," one of the men said. "What brings you out so early in the morning?"

Jason McCord was a Texas gunfighter who'd been a close friend of John Wesley Hardin and had gone drinking and whoring with him on numerous occasions. He was so sudden on the draw and shoot that Hardin called him Fast Draw McCord, and meant it.

Waters searched for mercy or understanding in the man's pale blue eyes but found neither.

Beside McCord, a rifle across his saddle horn, Tom Hooper had an amused smile on his lean, narrow face, his mouth showing teeth under a great dragoon mustache.

Waters believed that the lives of such rough men revolved around women and whiskey, and he decided to play to both vices.

"I'm headed for Silver Reef, boys," he said. "I keep a woman there an' figured it was high time I got some of my money's worth." He winked. "She also supplies the whiskey."

"Well, good for you, Reuben," McCord said. "What does your old lady say about that?"

Waters tried a grin that ended up a grimace. "Well, the wife don't know nothing about my spare woman. Like, I told her I was headed to Silver Reef on banking business."

"So what you got in your poke behind the seat?" McCord said.

"Oh, that?" Waters said.

"Yeah, that," McCord said.

"It's money I plan to invest in certain business ventures in Silver Reef." Waters tried the smile again. "As you brothers know, I believe in giving the good folks of Holy Rood an interest second to none, more than they'd get in them big banks in New York or Boston. And the secret to supplying that interest rate is sound investment after sound investment. And always keeping a sound head, of course."

The two gunmen said nothing.

Waters sweated in his broadcloth and wiped his round, glossy face with a large, blue bandana. Suddenly, he found it hard to breathe and he heard a wheeze in his chest.

"You don't look so good, Reuben," McCord said. "A might peaked, like a man with a misery."

"I am a sick man, brother. That's another reason I'm headed for Silver Reef, for some well-earned rest and relaxation."

"I never could relax with a whore," McCord said. "Could you, Tom?"

Hooper shook his head. "Nah, I was always too busy to relax."

"Ella Campbell is not a whore," Waters said, pretending to be outraged about his pretend woman to make his reason for travel more believable.

"She's a kept woman, you said." Hooper grinned.

"Well, yes, she is."

"Then she's a whore," McCord said. He turned in the saddle and said, "Tom, check out them sacks."

"Wait!" Waters said. He shook his head, the wattle under his chin wagging, panic in his eyes.

"I told you a lie, brothers," he said quickly. "I'm stealing the bank's money."

"We know you are, Reuben," McCord said. "Now just sit back and enjoy the morning while Tom takes a look."

"Seems like it's all there to the last penny," Hooper said.

"Now much you reckon?" McCord said.

"Hell, I don't know, and it would take me all day to count it," Hooper said. "But it's a lot. I can tell you that."

"Fifty thousand," Waters said. "We can split it three ways and head for Arizona." His hands outstretched, pleading, he said, "What do you say, boys? Is it a deal? Let's have no unpleasantness here."

McCord said, "You lied to us, Reuben, and you know what happens to bad boys who tell lies, don't you?"

"They get shot," Hooper said.

Waters's eyes unmasked and now they glittered with anger.

"Scum!" he yelled. "You damned scum."

He went for the revolver in his pocket.

It was another big mistake, and the last one he'd ever make.

The Smith & Wesson was still in the broadcloth when Hooper hit him with a heavy-bladed machete he'd drawn from a scabbard on his saddle.

Waters screamed as the honed edge bit deep into the roll of fat at the back of his neck and blood spurted.

His face ugly with fear and horror, the banker rolled off the seat and hit the ground hard. He tried for the gun in his pocket once more, but Hooper had dismounted and he swung the machete again.

The sharp steel blade split open Waters's skull like a ripe watermelon and he was mercifully dead when more of Hooper's blows rained down on his head and shoulders, and blood and brain fanned into the morning air. . . .

Finally sated, the gunman straightened up and let the gory machete dangle at his side. His face was covered in streaks of scarlet and gray and it looked as though he wore a red silk glove on his right hand.

McCord leaned from the saddle, his forearm on the horn.

"Never seen a man killed like that before," he

said. "Never figgered a blade could cause that much damage."

Hooper grinned. "Got a taste for the steel when I was just a younker and done fer my pa with a wood axe. Besides, a blade saves a bullet, considering what a box of decent .45s cost these days."

"Hitch your hoss to the wagon, Tom," McCord said. "We'll take the money back to town."

"What about him?" Hooper said.

"Just leave him where he lays. I don't reckon he cares much one way or t'other."

Hooper gave McCord a sly look. "We could just grab the money an' run, Jason. Just like ol' Reuben said."

McCord nodded. "We could. But do you want to spend the rest of your life looking over your shoulder for Hank Cobb? Years might pass, but one day, when you least expect it, you'll turn and he'll be there."

Hooper considered that, and then said, "I was only joshing."

"I wasn't," McCord said.

CHAPTER EIGHTEEN

"I don't like it, Shawn," Jasper Wolfden said. "It's too thin. I could end up dead real easily."

"You're an actor," Shawn O'Brien said. "All I'm asking you to do is act."

"I'm willing to part with my hair, if that's what it takes," Sally Bailey said. "I'll cry a little, but that's what women do, isn't it?"

Wolfden said nothing, but his concerned face spoke volumes.

Hamp Sedley turned the two jackrabbits roasting on a stick, and then said, "Wolfden, you're a shape-shifter. All O'Brien's asking you to do is shift shapes."

"Who says that?" Wolfden said.

"Says what?" Sedley said.

"That I'm a shape-shifter."

"Folks. And one of Hank Cobb's boys said it."

"Folks say a lot of things that aren't true. Folks say what they'd like to be true, that's all."

"You were on the stage, Jasper," Shawn said. "Actors shift shapes all the time, become somebody else. You ever play Richard the Third?"

"Of course I did. Not as well as Booth and some others, but in Boston town I played the evil Yorkist prince to considerable acclaim."

"You had to shift shape for that, I imagine," Shawn said. "Wasn't Richard a hunchback with a bad leg?"

Wolfden sighed. "Run your wild scheme by me again."

"Jasper, it's not so wild," Shawn said, smiling reassurance.

"Easy for you to say," Wolfden said. "You're not the one sticking his head in the noose, or on the chopping block, more to the point."

"I'm not an actor," Shawn said. "I'd never pass muster in Holy Rood."

Wolfden sighed again. "Let me hear it."

"We must keep Cobb and his boys in town for a couple of days," Shawn said. "If he bolts to open ground, we'll never get him."

"So far, so fairly reasonable," Wolfden said. "'Lay on, MacDuff.'"

"To do that, we need somebody in the inside who can maintain a disguise," Shawn said. "And who but an actor can play that role?"

"As a federally appointed witch-finder general," Wolfden said. "Hank Cobb won't swallow a big windy like that."

"You're right, he won't. But the people of Holy Rood will, hook, line and sinker," Shawn said. "They accepted Cobb's story that he could make their town a paradise on earth by the use of the guillotine and the stake to execute undesirables, didn't they? Cobb aimed high, Jasper, and so will you."

Wolfden shook his head. "O'Brien, you've got my brain bound with so much baling wire I can't think."

"It's easy," Shawn said. "The first thing you do is get the people on your side. According to Scruggs, Cobb's tithe has already caused ill feeling. When you tell them their valuables will be returned once you smell out all the witches in town, they'll listen."

"And what does Cobb do in the meantime, apart from shooting me?" Wolfden said.

"He can't go against the will of the people," Shawn said. "I'm betting that he'll be stuck in town until you leave. I think the good citizens of Holy Rood won't stand by and watch him skedaddle with their valuables and money while the federal witch-finder is in town to sort things out."

Wolfden slapped the Colt at his side.

"I can't wear iron," he said.

"We'll hide it on you somewhere," Shawn said.

"If Cobb figures the witch-finder is me, he won't come at me straight up and true blue; he'll shoot me in the back," Wolfden said.

"He won't figure it's you, not if you're a halfway decent actor," Shawn said.

"I was, but I'm not any longer," Wolfden said.

Sedley grinned. "Cheer up, Wolfden. Sally's donating her hair. So you glue it under your hat with a mix of pine sap and charcoal and let it fall over your face in ringlets. Ol' Hank Cobb an' them will be fooled. Trust me."

"Gambler, I wouldn't even trust you to play honest poker with my own marked deck," Wolfden said.

Sedley nodded and smiled. "Wise man."

"Well, Jasper?" Shawn said.

"All right, I'll do it," Wolfden said. "It's a challenging role with a difficult audience, but it could be my greatest triumph."

"Sally, we're asking you to make a big sacrifice," Shawn said. "You've got such beautiful hair. Reminds me of . . ." He smiled. "Well, it just reminds me."

"No need for that," Wolfden said.

He removed his hat and a mane of black locks tumbled over his shoulders.

"I let it grow sometimes," Wolfden said. "It's a little eccentricity of mine. All actors, even washed-up ones, have them."

"Well, it ain't near as pretty as Sally's," Sedley said. "But I guess it will do."

"I'll be back," Wolfden said.

He rose to his feet, picked up his saddlebags and walked into the pines.

After the man had gone, Sedley said, "What was all that about?"

"I don't know," Shawn said. "But you don't question a man who excuses himself from camp and steps into the trees."

Sally's eyes locked on Shawn's and her mouth compressed into a small, pink flower.

"What's on your mind?" Shawn said.

"I just looked up at the sky and had a vision of death. Many deaths," the girl said.

Shawn didn't question the girl's gift.

"Who will die?" he said.

"I don't know," Sally said. "Just . . . many deaths."

Sedley shivered. "Well that kind of talk spooks the hell out of me. Makes me think of ha'ants an' such."

"Shawn, I think we should go away from here," the girl said. "Leave this place behind."

Shawn shook his head. "Holy Rood is an evil place, Sally. I'll cleanse that town or destroy it."

"Hell, O'Brien, why do you care?" Sedley said.

"You know why I care."

"The cowboy, you mean?"

"Yes. Him and all the others. And I plan to kill Hank Cobb. His shadow has fallen on the ground for way too long."

Sedley looked at the girl. "There's your answer, Sally. Ol' Shawn ain't leaving."

"And you, Hamp?" Sally said.

"I'll stick. I'm as big a fool as O'Brien is."

"Sally, you don't have to stay," Shawn said. "You can take my horse and put a heap of git between you and Holy Rood. Hell, a pretty girl like you can find work anywhere."

Sally smiled. "I'll see how it ends. I guess that makes all three of us fools, doesn't it?"

"Sure does," Sedley said. "But, girl, you got more sand than most men I've run acrost, including my ownself."

Shawn rose to his feet as the rising sun filtered through the tree canopy and the songbirds greeted the new day. The air smelled sweet of pine and wood smoke and the tang of the cooking rabbits.

"Hamp, do you have a knife?" he said.

The gambler nodded. "Still got my Barlow."

Shawn extended his hand. "Let me have it."

He read the question on Sedley's face and said, "Every witch-finder needs a badge of office. I'm going to make one."

CHAPTER NINETEEN

Shawn O'Brien returned to camp carrying a long, straight tree branch that was wide at its base but slimmer at the top so it would bend like a fishing rod under any kind of weight.

Hamp Sedley was unimpressed.

"That's it?" he said. "It ain't much of a badge of office."

"It's not quite done yet," Shawn said.

He held up a roll of trimmed creeper vine that was stronger than twine.

"For the finishing touch," he said.

"And what's that?" Sedley said.

"All in due time, Hamp. All in due time."

But Sedley paid no attention. He looked beyond and behind Shawn, then jumped to his feet, his gun coming up.

"Hold up right there, mister," he yelled. "Or I'll drop you right where you stand."

"Hell, Sedley, on your best day you couldn't hit me at this distance."

It was Wolfden's voice, but it came from a small, hunchbacked man with the pinched, intolerant face of a Spanish Inquisition torturer.

The man had sunken cheeks and great black shadows under eyes that glowed with a fanatical fire. His pallor was ashen and lank, dirty hair hung about his face. The mouth was thin, pinched, cruel, merciless.

"Well, what do you boys think?" Wolfden said. "I always carry my stage makeup. Never know when I might need it."

"Well, you scared the hell out of me," Sedley said. "Another minute and I'd have plugged you for sure."

"Perfect," Shawn said, grinning. "The very model of a model witch-finder general if ever I saw one."

Wolfden stepped to the fire and Sedley decided to play critic.

"The clothes let you down, and can you keep yourself hunched over like that all day?"

"I'm an actor," Wolfden said. "I don't know about all day, but I've played the hunchbacked prince for hours at a time."

He looked down at his black frockcoat, pants of the same color and the scuffed toes of his boots. "But I agree with you about the duds."

"Cobb won't remember what you wore," Shawn said. "You'll need to lose the gun belt, of course."

"Wait, I have an idea," Sally said.

She stepped to the carpetbag that she'd insisted on taking from the hotel and rummaged inside. "Let me have your hat, Mr. Wolfden," she said.

"The name's Jasper, remember?" Wolfden said, smiling as he said it.

"No. You are Mr. Wolfden," the girl said. "Now let me have the hat."

Sally folded up the brim until it lay flat against the crown, and then she pinned it in place with a brooch she'd taken from the bag.

"It was my mother's, a cameo of nymphs dancing in a glade," she said. "But it looks like something a witch-finder might wear in his hat. At least, I think it does."

"Naked nymphs, Sally," Sedley said. "Or hadn't you noticed?"

"No, they're witches," Sally said. "That's what the witch-finder will tell anyone who asks."

"It makes me look kind of weird," Wolfden said, settling the hat on his head.

"That's the general idea, general," Shawn said. "Now do something about the iron."

Wolfden's coat was cut baggy in the fashion of the time and his revolver disappeared into an inside pocket.

"Fine," Shawn said, standing back to admire him. "You look just fine. You could fool your own mother."

"I don't know about that," Wolfden said. "Hell,

this isn't going to end well. I can feel it in my water."

"Oh, ye of little faith," Shawn said. "I'll raise such hell in the damned town that half the time no one will notice you."

"What kind of hell?" Wolfden said.

"Once I've figured that out, you'll be the first to know, Jasper." He shoved the pole at the man. "Here, take this. It's your official badge of office."

"It's a pine branch," Wolfden said.

"Well, it isn't quite finished yet," Shawn said. "Now, let's be on our way. You'll ride double with me."

"What's wrong with my own horse?" Wolfden said.

Shawn shook his head. "Jasper, Jasper, Jasper. Cobb may not remember your duds, but he'll sure as hell recollect a white stud that goes seventeen hands high and has a mean disposition."

"Then I'll take—"

"No, you walk into Holy Rood," Shawn said. "Witch-finders don't ride horses."

"Who says?"

"I do. Now let's hit the trail. Time's a-wasting."

"What about the rabbits?" Wolfden said.

"They're nowhere near done yet," Shawn said. "We'll save you some."

Riding double, Shawn and Wolfden dropped out of the trees and onto the wagon road, and then swung south toward Holy Rood.

The high mountain land around him lay still and silent, drowsy from the growing heat of the day. Only the distant Harmony Mountains to the north looked cool, purple peaks against a cloudless sky that shaded from blue to the color of mint.

For fifteen minutes, Shawn and Wolfden rode in silence, the only sounds the soft plod of the horse and the creak of saddle leather.

Then Shawn said, "The first of them coming up, Jasper."

"Maybe this isn't such a good idea," Wolfden said.

Shawn turned his head in the saddle and grinned.

"You'll look great," he said. "Like a witch-finder should look."

"Yeah, if the people in Holy Rood are stupid enough to believe it."

"They're stupid enough."

Shawn drew rein and studied the skull on the post nearest him.

"Well?" Wolfden said.

"Not quite right," Shawn said. "It's a bit too weathered." He nodded to the other side of the road. "Same with that one. Real brown instead of yellow."

Wolfden looked over Shawn's shoulder. "Lord, these damned skulls go on forever," he said.

Shawn's far-seeing eyes scanned the road, a dusty vee that disappeared into shimmering distance.

Somewhere beyond the heat shimmer was Holy Rood.

"I'd say close to fifty, twenty-five a side," he said. "It looks like Cobb was busy for a spell when he and his boys first rode into town. Who were these people?"

Wolfden stared at the brown skull and said, "Whores, gamblers, goldbrick artists, dancehall loungers, drunks and vagrants. Alas, the poor Yoricks, I knew them all."

Wolfden leaned over in the saddle and pointed into a patch of scrub at the side of the trail. "See that rotten wood in there?" he said.

Shawn allowed that he did.

"It had a name on it once—Dawson's Draw, the name of the settlement when it was a town like any other. Hank Cobb changed the name when the killing started."

Shawn kneed his horse forward. "And you tried to stop him."

"Yeah, I did. Then he killed me."

"Or so he thought."

"Yeah, Shawn, something like that."

Holy Rood had emerged through the shifting landscape when Shawn found a skull that suited him. It was a white, fine-boned example that looked female, and it still had all its teeth.

Trying hard not to speculate too much about the

skull's previous owner, Shawn took it from the post and said, "Right, Jasper, from now on you walk."

Wolfden jumped off the horse and then Shawn swung out of the saddle.

"What the hell are you going to do with that head?" Wolfden said.

"Let me have your staff of office," Shawn said.

"You mean this dry stick?"

"Yes, and remember to bear it with pride, my man," Shawn said.

Using the creeper vine, as tough as rawhide, Shawn lashed the skull to the pine branch.

The weight of the skull bent the pole over at the top, an effect Shawn declared was, "Crackerjack!"

"Jasper, carry the staff over your shoulder and walk into Holy Rood like you owned the place," he said. "Remember, you're the official witch-finder general and everybody's afraid of you."

"We'll soon see if that's the case," Wolfden said. "Cobb is a piece of dirt, but he's hard to fool."

"I know," Shawn said. All the good humor drained from his face, and was replaced by concern. "Jasper, you're putting your life on the line and what you're about to do is dangerous. Just . . . just be careful."

"I'll pin Cobb in town for as long as I can," Wolfden said. "The rest is up to you."

"You see the skulls around you," Shawn said. "A town that sanctions that isn't fit to exist. I've declared war on Holy Rood, Jasper, and I'll finish what I start."

Wolfden smiled. "I pegged you for a rich man's son, but never a town tamer."

"Me neither," Shawn said, "but I guess that's what I've become."

The road lay ahead of Wolfden and Holy Rood shimmered white in the noon sun.

"I best be on my way," he said. He grinned. "Maybe I'll get something to eat, on account of how I'm missing my last six meals."

"Wait," Shawn said.

He reached into his pocket. "This is a rosary. My father gave it to me when I left home for England. It will help protect you."

Wolfden smiled. "Sounds like popery to me."

"It sounds like it because it is," Shawn said.

He removed Wolfden's hat and hung the coral rosary beads around his neck. Then he replaced the hat again.

"My gun-fighting brother, Jacob, carries one, and he's about as good a Catholic as a Cheyenne dog soldier. Same goes for Luther Ironside, only he's even worse."

"I guess if a fast gun like Jacob O'Brien doesn't mind the beads, then neither do I." Wolfden smiled. "Shawn, thanks. I won't let you down."

"And I won't let you down either," Shawn said.

* * *

Shawn watched Wolfden leave, the white, grinning skull over his shoulder bobbing behind him.

The day was as bright as a newly minted coin, the land around Shawn rippling with heat, yet he felt a chill, as though the cold winds of Dartmoor were once again blowing on him.

CHAPTER TWENTY

Jason McCord talked loud above the clamor of the church bell.

"He died screaming like a pig," he said. "Hooper took a machete to him."

"Save a bullet that way," Hank Cobb said.

"Hey, that's what Hooper said."

"Waters have a gun on him?" Cobb said.

McCord pulled the Smith & Wesson from his belt and laid it on the desk.

"I reckon if a man carries a belly gun, he's got to be good with it," he said.

"Did he get off a shot?" Cobb said.

"Nah. He didn't even get his piece drawed afore Hooper done for him."

Cobb picked up the revolver and stepped to the sheriff's office window.

The surrey was parked outside in the street

under guard and a curious crowd had already gathered.

"Well, I'll go talk to them," Cobb said. "Put their minds at rest."

"When are we pulling out of here, boss?" McCord said.

"Soon. Maybe tonight," Cobb said. "Before we quit this burg I plan to burn it around their stupid ears."

He motioned to the people outside. "Listen to them babble to each other about their precious bank money. A bunch of sheep waiting to be fleeced."

"Know the old feller who owns the livery?" McCord said.

"Yeah. What's his name . . . Rhodes, isn't it? Matt Rhodes. He's as mean as a caged rattler, that one. But he's good with horses so I let him be."

"He was with Sherman in Georgia, damn his eyes," McCord said.

Cobb smiled. "And you want to put a bullet into him before we leave?"

"That's my intention."

"Then be my guest," Cobb said. "I don't give a damn what happens to these people. I may gun a few of them myself before this day is over."

Cobb adjusted his monk's robe, hating the feel of the rough wool against his throat, and opened the office door.

When he appeared, Waters's .38 in hand, the crowd fell silent.

"And then, as though the theft of the town's money was not a heinous enough crime, Reuben Waters drew this . . . *murderous revolver* . . . and attempted to shoot the apprehending brothers," Cobb said.

He paused and his eyes swept the crowd, gauging their mood.

Reuben Waters was not liked, but he was a pillar of the town and most faces showed a mix of surprise and apprehension.

"My friends, only a buzzard preys on his own kind, but Waters's end was swift and richly deserved," Cobb said. "With admirable speed and dexterity, our very own brothers McCord and Hooper returned fire."

Cobb paused again. This time for effect.

"The robber, Reuben Waters, died *weltering in his blood!*"

That last drew a ragged cheer and a relieved Cobb struck while the iron was hot.

"The money will be returned to the bank and placed under guard," he said. "When the tithing is complete, you may then reclaim your deposits and hold on to them until a new banker is appointed."

"When will we be able to get our money?" a voice from the crowd asked.

"First thing tomorrow morning," Cobb said, lying smoothly.

"Hell, the money's right there in the wagon," the man said. "Why not divvy it up right now?"

This drew murmurs of agreement that Cobb quickly squelched.

"Do you have your bankbook, brother? Your proof of deposit?" he said.

"No, but I can get it right quick," the man said.

"No. We'll do this legally," Cobb said.

The irony was not lost on Shel Shannon, who watched from the office window and grinned.

"Yes, I said legally," Cobb said. "The bank will open for business at seven tomorrow morning. Those with money to collect, come with bankbook in hand."

There may have been further discussion, but the crowd's attention was caught and held by the strange apparition walking down Main Street.

Wolfden played his role to the hilt.

"Make way for the federally appointed witch-finder general," he yelled in a strange, hollow voice. "I have come to rid this benighted town of witches, sorceresses, enchantresses, magicians, spell-casters, warlocks, crones, hags, she-devils, ogresses . . ."— Wolfden ran out of names—"and all such hellish creatures and entities."

Hank Cobb stood on the boardwalk and looked stunned.

The crowd was shocked into silence, and Wolfden

was well aware that his fate—and life—hung in the balance.

As an actor he'd learned how to please an audience—and he tried desperately to please one now.

Wolfden raised his arms, the skull dangling above his head, and roared in a powerful voice that had once carried all the way to "the gods," a theater's upper balcony where the poorest of the poor were seated.

"Soon ye'll find who among ye consorts with the powers of evil and ye'll chase them from your midst," he said.

Hank Cobb recovered his wits and his anger flared.

He stepped down from the boardwalk, pushed people aside and stood in front of Wolfden. "I don't know what your game is, mister," he said. "But you git right now or I'll take your damned head off."

"No, let him speak," a man said. "He looks like a witch-finder, sure enough."

Using what he called his Richard the Third voice, a rusty, grating rasp, Wolfden shook his staff so the skull danced and spat at Cobb, "Back I say, back! Ye wear a holy robe but you might be a warlock yourself. Aye, or even a demon in disguise."

At that moment, Cobb badly wanted to gun the man who claimed to be a witch-finder. He had not yet seen through Wolfden's disguise, but something about the man troubled Cobb, as though he'd met him before.

He did know that the moment for shooting had passed. The crowd had slipped away from him and was now intently staring at the stranger. Worse, the women had moved to the front for a better view . . . always a bad sign.

"How did you find us, Mr. Witch-finder?" one of them asked.

"Your plight is well known, even in the halls of Washington," Wolfden said. "It has long been rumored that Holy Rood is beset with witches and I was ordered by President Grover Cleveland* himself to put an end to it."

"We don't need your help," Cobb said. His face was iron hard and slick with sweat. "We'll rid ourselves of our own witches."

Wolfden shook his staff again and roared, "Ye will, will ye? Look at the people gathered here, a hundred strong, I'll be bound, and among them I already can sniff out a baker's dozen of the devil's brood."

The crowd gasped and instinctively shrank from one another and somewhere among them a child shrieked in fear.

"My name is Stanley Starlight of Salem town. Will ye put your faith in me or those who have already led you to the very brink of hell?" Wolfden yelled.

---

*By a strange quirk of fate, Cleveland is believed to have passed through Holy Rood, by then a ghost town, in the winter of 1897, two months before the end of his second term.

He knew he had the crowd and it didn't disappoint.

"You speak the truth, witch-finder. Tell us what to do," a pretty brunette woman cried out, hugging her crying child close to her skirts.

Wolfden stole a glance at Cobb's face.

The gunman was beyond anger. He was in an impotent, killing rage, exactly where Wolfden wanted him.

"What burdens this surrey?" Wolfden said, guessing that the burlap sacks were full of money.

"It is the deposits from the bank," the brunette said. "The banker tried to steal it, but Brother Matthias's men stopped him."

"He's dead, missing his damned head," Hank Cobb said, his voice flat. It sounded like a threat and it was.

An errant wind lifted dust from the street and the tin rooster weathervane atop the livery stable screeched as it moved this way and that and frantically tried to pin down the direction of the breeze.

"Well, now I am very concerned," Wolfden said.

Getting into his role, he made his eyes both shifty and shrewd.

"I smell treachery here," he said. "Treachery spawned in the deepest pits of Hades."

"What the hell are you talking about?" Cobb said.

The gunman's mind was working overtime.

Was this ugly hunchback really who he claimed to be? And what was it about the man that made him seem familiar?

Cobb had no time to ponder those questions, because Wolfden spoke again.

"This is the town's money, is it not?" he said.

"Every last penny of it, except for some bank bonds held in trust for others," a man said.

"Then it must be made safe ere it be used to fund the devil's work," Wolfden said.

"It will be returned to the bank and kept there under guard," Cobb said. "I already told these people that."

Wolfden shook his head and then his staff. The skull bobbed and grinned.

"No," he said. "That will not do. I will take the money in charge, using the emergency powers granted me by the government of the United States."

Cobb grinned in triumph.

"There, brothers and sisters, you heard it from his own lips," he yelled. "This is no witch-finder, but a common thief who aims to steal your money."

That last brought a hostile murmur from the crowd, and Wolfden knew he had to talk fast or he'd lose them.

"Did ye not hear me talk of treachery?" he yelled. "I trust no one in this town until my investigation is over and that is why your money must be guarded."

Then he played his hole card.

"D'ye see yonder ridge?" Wolfden said.

He pointed to the ridge where he'd earlier held up the decapitated head for Cobb to see.

"The surrey must be taken there and remain in full view of the town until I smell out every witch and warlock among ye. Only then can the money be returned to the bank in safety."

Wolfden allowed to himself that there was some convoluted logic in what he said. But now would the good citizens of Holy Rood buy it?

To his surprise, Cobb readily agreed. Too readily.

"That's as good a plan as any," he said. "But a couple of my brothers will stay on guard."

"As will I," Wolfden said. "I plan to stay on the ridge tonight, where I can pray in peace and have a full view of the town. I will keep good watch for the creatures of darkness who flit through the gloom like phantoms."

It seemed to Wolfden that most of the townsfolk were really worried about the safety of their money, because they enthusiastically agreed to his plan.

But their bloodlust was still in evidence.

"When will the burnings be, Mr. Starlight?" the pretty woman said. Her eyes were of different colors; one brown, the other green, and she had a mole on her left cheekbone that looked like a speck of mud.

"When the smelling out is done and the evil ones are found," Wolfden said. "Aye, pile the faggots high, because ye will need them. There will be much burning to be done."

To Wolfden's disgust this drew scattered cheers from the crowd and the pretty woman smiled, white teeth gleaming.

The good citizens of the Salem* of the West were again baying for blood.

*More than 160 people were accused of witchcraft in Salem. At least 25 were executed or died in jail and the rest lost their property and legal rights.

CHAPTER TWENTY-ONE

The rabbits, a less than satisfying meal, were eaten and the hot afternoon had begun its slow shade into evening when the Missouri mule walked into camp, a saddle hanging under its belly.

Hamp Sedley grabbed the animal's trailing reins and patted its neck. "Where did you come from, huh?" he said.

"I'd say the road," Shawn said. "She smelled our fire, I guess."

"Must've thrown its rider," Sedley said.

Shawn nodded. "I'll go take a look."

Sedley had stripped the mule of its saddle. "Want me to saddle your horse, O'Brien?" he said.

"No. I'll take the mule."

"Your funeral," Sedley said. "She's got a mean eye."

"So do I," Shawn said.

He climbed onto the back of the mule that stood

placidly enough, just as Sally Bailey returned from bathing at the creek.

The top buttons of her dress were undone, revealing an expanse of creamy skin and the swell of the top of her breasts. Her hair was damp and hung over her shoulders in tendrils of yellow curl.

The girl looked at the mule, then Shawn. "What did I miss?" she said.

"Jenny just wandered into camp," Shawn said. "I'm going to look for her rider."

"Be careful, Shawn," Sally said. "It would be just like that Hank Cobb person to set a trap."

Shawn nodded. "I'll remember that."

He rode out of the trees and down the incline to the wagon road.

After scouting around he found the mule's tracks in the hard-packed earth, coming from the south. Around Shawn rawboned ridges thrust themselves from the scrub flat, their furrows and crevasses filled with dark blue shadow.

Shawn pushed the mule south. In front of him a dust devil danced, and in the distance, the land, not yet cooling, still shimmered.

Thus it was that the man who walked the trail ahead of Shawn at first appeared tall and elongated, like a Gothic saint. But then, as he stepped closer out of the dancing heat waves, he settled down to his normal size, and that was small indeed.

Shawn drew rein and watched the man come.

He was a little fellow, wearing a brown-checked,

high-button suit and a bowler hat of the same color. A celluloid collar with a dark red tie completed his unlikely appearance. He carried a carpetbag and used a cane to assist his left leg that had a definite limp.

When the man was within speaking distance, Shawn said, "Howdy."

The small man stopped, wiped off his sweaty face with a handkerchief, and then said, "Found my mule, I see."

"She found me. Walked into my camp."

The man jerked a thumb over his shoulder.

"The confounded animal got spooked by something in the brush about two miles back and took off." He looked down at his feet. "Elastic-sided boots were never made for walking."

Shawn smiled. "No boots are made for walking. Name's Shawn O'Brien."

"Fordham J. Platt at your service. Most folks just call me Ford, when they call me anything." Then, as though he felt it necessary, he added, "I came up from Silver Reef."

"Pleased to make your acquaintance," Shawn said.

Platt was silent for a few moments, then said, "The cast of your features reminds me of a friend of mine. Would you be related to Jacob O'Brien from down in the Glorieta Mesa country of the New Mexico Territory?"

"I would. He's my brother." Then the shock set in and Shawn said, "You're a friend of Jake's?"

"Does that surprise you?" Platt said. "I mean, apart from meeting your brother's friend in the middle of a wilderness."

"Big country, few people, I guess," Shawn said. He smiled, taking the sting out of what he was about to say next. "You just don't seem the type to be a friend of Jake's. He's a mighty rough-natured man who lives by his gun."

"Don't judge a book by its cover, Mr. O'Brien," Platt said. "I mean, who could tell by looking at Jacob that he's an accomplished pianist? I consider his interpretation of Chopin's Nocturne in E-flat Major to border on sublime, like a meteorite through the soul."

"You ever see him shoot?" Shawn said.

"Again sublime, Mr. O'Brien?" Platt smiled.

"That's the word for it, all right," Shawn said. He swung off the mule and extended his hand. "Any friend of Jake's is a friend of mine."

"And me likewise. Any brother of Jacob's . . . et cetera . . . et cetera."

"Where are you headed, Ford?" Shawn said.

"A town called Holy Rood, to the north of here," Platt said.

Shawn was taken aback and before he could stop himself, he said, "Don't go there!"

"I must, I'm afraid."

"Why?"

"I was hired by Wells Fargo to investigate the disappearance of a stage, its driver and four passengers."

Platt spread his hands apologetically, including the one holding the cane.

"Wells Fargo contacted the authorities, of course. But they were told that the loss of a stage was sheer carelessness and hardly a matter for the army, the only authority in these parts."

"The army is stretched thin," Shawn said. "It isn't going to spare men to look for a stage."

"Ah, yes, so Wells Fargo was informed. And that's why they hired me."

"Are you a detective, Ford?" Shawn asked.

"Of sorts. I dabble in many things. I got my start in life in the train-robbing profession. Then one time up in Kansas it all went bad. Held up a train and all I had to show for my efforts was a bunch of bananas, a round of Double Gloucester cheese and eleven dollars and six cents."

"Too bad," Shawn said.

"It was even worse than that. The train was passing through buffalo country and it seemed that every ranny on board had a sporting rifle with him. I ended up with about a hundred fellers taking pots at me as I lit a shuck out of there. Lost a two-hundred-dollar horse and chunk out of my leg."

Platt raised his cane. "As you can see."

"Train robbing can be a rewarding but dangerous profession," Shawn said. "Or so I was told."

"Indeed, it can. But after that disaster I mentioned, I chose a safer line of work as a clerk in an assay office in Silver City. That didn't work out, so I became a lawman down Texas way, then a range detective and now . . . well, you see me."

"I have news for you, Ford," Shawn said. "I'm one of your missing passengers."

Now it was Platt's turn to be surprised. "You don't say?"

"I do say. I think you should come back to camp. You'll meet two more of my fellow travelers there, and we've got a tale to tell."

"I imagine you do," Platt said. He glanced at the sky. "Be dark soon. I might as well open my investigation here." Then, remembering his aching feet, "Not far I hope."

"Our camp is close, such as it is," Shawn said. "You can ride the mule if you like."

"The thought of sitting on the bony back of that vile animal fills me with dread," Platt said. "I'll walk."

Shawn smiled. "You should get yourself another horse."

"One's quite as bad as the other," Platt said.

CHAPTER TWENTY-TWO

After Ford Platt drew himself up to his full five-foot-four, bowed and kissed Sally's hand, she smiled and declared him, "A most gallant gentleman."

And, indeed, the others considered the little man an affable companion, especially when he produced a bottle of Old Crow from his bag and shared it around.

As darkness fell, Platt listened intently as Shawn told the story of their dramatic arrival in Holy Rood and what had transpired since.

When Shawn was done talking, Platt said, "And you hope Jasper Wolfden, the actor, will convince Hank Cobb and the townspeople that he's a witch-finder? How deliciously droll."

"I want to keep Cobb in town for a couple of days until I can figure a way to deal with him," Shawn said. He hesitated, then said, "And take back the town."

"From what you've told me, is Holy Rood worth saving?" Platt said.

"Sedley asked me that, and the answer is I don't know," Shawn said. "There must be some decent people living there, but I'm not doing it for them. I'm doing it for the cowboy I told you about, him and others."

Platt said, "You may have to destroy Holy Rood to save it."

"If that proves to be the case, then that's what I'll do," Shawn said.

The little man sat thinking for a while, and then said, "I believe Hank Cobb suddenly realizes that he's in over his head. He'll want to pull stakes and leave with all he can. Is there a bank in town?"

"Yes, there is," Shawn said.

Platt nodded. "If he cleans it out, Holy Rood will never recover."

The little man brooded in silence for a while, and then said, "I'm here because I'm being paid. Miss Sally, Sedley, what's your stake in this?" He looked at Shawn. "And what about you? You said that your pa is the richest man in the New Mexico Territory. Why don't you go home and court the beautiful Santa Fe señoritas, or whatever it is sons of wealthy ranchers do?"

"Not until I see this business through," Shawn said.

"Mr. O'Brien, you puzzle me. Why are you even here, in this . . . desert?" Platt said.

"Since my wife died, I've been drifting, walking a mental gangplank afraid to fall off," Shawn said. "I guess a rogue wave washed me this way."

Hamp Sedley stepped into the silence that followed. "For me it's payback," he said. "I was badly handled by Cobb and I take that from no man."

"And you, Miss Sally?" Platt said.

"I want Holy Rood wiped off the map, as though it never existed," the girl said. "I'll stay to see it done."

Sally's long hair swung on her shoulders and there was a strange glow in her eyes that could not be explained by the firelight or the whiskey.

Shawn noted that glow and wondered at it.

"And I can't get any of you to change your mind, huh?" Platt said.

"That's how it stacks up," Shawn said.

"Then let me say this," Platt said. "If all what you've told me is true, and I've no reason to believe that it's not, there could be gunplay involved. If that becomes the case, I want you to step aside and leave the shooting to me."

Platt had mild brown eyes and the kind of delicate features that wouldn't be out of place on a particularly devout nun.

"Gunfighting is not for the faint of heart," he said. "It is dangerous, violent, bloody and an almighty sudden affair. I will tell this same thing to your actor friend when I see him. I'm afraid that in real life, dead men don't get up and go for cake and ice cream when the curtain falls."

Shawn had it in mind to say, "Mister, you couldn't shade me on your best day," but was searching for a less belligerent way to express it when something happened that forever changed his opinion of Ford Platt.

It began innocently enough.

Hamp Sedley had stepped into the trees and returned with an armful of firewood. He apparently considered one of the branches too long for his purpose and snapped it across his knee.

This happened behind Platt's back.

The breaking wood cracked loud.

And Platt moved.

In one smooth motion, as controlled as an athlete, he drew a .36 caliber Remington police revolver from under his coat, turned, threw himself on his belly and laid the sights on Sedley.

"No!" Shawn yelled.

Sedley threw up his arms, his face frozen.

"Don't shoot!" he said.

Several slow seconds ticked past. Then Platt rose to his feet, the Remington dangling at his side.

"Don't . . . ever . . . do . . . that . . . again," he said to Sedley.

"It sure ain't likely," Sedley said. "I thought I was done for."

"Mighty touchy, aren't you, Ford?" Shawn said.

"Live longer that way," Platt said.

He slid the revolver into its shoulder holster, then looked around him.

"Sorry," he said. Something akin to regret flickered in his face, then died. "I didn't mean to alarm you all."

"Well, mister, you sure as hell alarmed me," Sedley said. He picked up his wood. "Where the hell is the bottle?"

As though to make up for the trouble he'd caused, Platt passed the whiskey to Sedley and smiled. "Well, it could've been worse, I suppose."

"That crossed my mind," Sedley said.

Then he took a swig, his hand holding the bottle trembling slightly.

Platt sat down again, his back against a tree. He saw Shawn watching him, his eyes speculative, and said, "I've killed seven men in my life, all in honest fights."

The little man shrugged, an oddly expressive gesture. "It's not something I'm particularly proud of, but now you know."

Shawn made no comment. It was not the time for idle boast.

"Where do we go from here?" he said.

Platt stared at the rising moon that had impaled itself on top of a pine. Far off in the darkness a hunting wolf pack howled and an alarmed owl asked its question of the night.

Finally, he said, "Tomorrow morning I'll ride into Holy Rood and take a room at the hotel. If things are as you told me they are, I'll start to take down Cobb and his boys one by one."

"There's a lot of them," Shawn said.

"Then I'll be sneaky."

"Find a way to get in touch with Jasper Wolfden," Shawn said. "He's smart and he's good with a gun."

Platt nodded. "Just as you say."

He reached into his coat and Shawn stiffened, his hand dropping to his holstered Colt.

Platt smiled. "Cigars. I feel like a smoke." But his hand stayed where it was.

Now it was Shawn's turn to smile. "You have fast hands, Ford. Slow down the one inside your coat considerable."

The little man's eyebrows crawled up his forehead.

"Could it be that I've underestimated you, Mr. O'Brien?"

"A little. I'm faster than Jake."

"Ah, yes, but no matter the odds, Jacob will stand," Platt said.

"And so will I."

"All right then, watch closely, Mr. O'Brien. I'll be like molasses leaking from a barrel."

Platt's right hand moved out from under his coat with exaggerated slowness. It was holding a silver cigar case.

Sally laughed and clapped her hands. "Huzzah for the man from New Mexico!"

"He took my measure, didn't he, Miss Sally?" Platt said. His grin was wide and good-humored as he extended the case. "Seems like you just won a cigar, Mr. O'Brien."

But as Shawn reached out to take the cigar

case, Platt let it drop and extended his fingers. A Remington derringer suddenly appeared in his fist.

"This is what I meant by being sneaky," he said.

Shawn was caught flat-footed. The twin muzzles of the belly gun looked like an hourglass, telling him his time was running out.

But Platt shoved the derringer back into his sleeve, then rolled it up to reveal a spring-loaded contraption strapped to his forearm.

"A gunsmith in Dallas made this up for me," he said. "It's called a sleeve holster and he said it might come in handy one day."

"Hell, you ever get the drop on somebody with that rig?" Sedley said.

"Nope. Only Mr. O'Brien here," Platt said.

Shawn grinned. "There's one born every minute, huh?"

"It was only a conjurer's parlor trick," Platt said. "And you fell for it."

"And that's why I'm glad you're on our side," Shawn said.

Platt stretched his arms and yawned.

"Well, I think I'll turn in," he said. "Busy day tomorrow."

Shawn rose to his feet.

"Not me," he said. "It's time to start shaking up Hank Cobb."

"I'm not catching your drift," Platt said.

"Me neither," Sedley said.

"I promised Jasper Wolfden I'd start to stir things

up in Holy Rood and keep Cobb on edge. If I can scare him badly enough, he'll make mistakes."

"What kind of mistakes?" Sedley said.

Platt answered the question. "The kind that gets a man killed."

"It might be you that gets killed, Shawn," Sally said. "Let Mr. Platt do his work first. He's obviously capable."

Platt smiled. "No, Shawn has a point. I think it's better he goes alone. One man can hide in the dark better than two."

He spoke to Sally but looked at Shawn.

"If Cobb gets irritated enough, he'll go at the problem like a charging bull," he said. "That's when men of patience and reason like myself and Mr. O'Brien can join forces and use clever strategy to take advantage of him."

"Stay out of my head, Ford," Shawn said. "I'll do this my own way."

"Then you have a plan?"

"Not really."

"I advise you to come up with one fast," Platt said.

Shawn nodded. "I'm studying on it." Then, for Sally's sake, "I'll be back before first light."

Without a moment's hesitation, Platt said, "Know this, Shawn, should you fall, I'll see to it that Miss Sally is taken care of. And I'll personally shoot Cobb for you, then burn down Holy Rood."

"Thanks," Shawn said. "That makes me feel much better."

"I'm glad. Go in peace, Mr. O'Brien," Platt said.

CHAPTER TWENTY-THREE

The moon hung high in the sky and, staring at it, Jasper Wolfden felt an ancient stirring, as old as mankind itself, to strip off his clothes and go hunting with the wolves.

He smiled to himself.

How wonderful that would be, to run through a pine forest misty with moonlight and howl with the pack, the musky scent of deer strong, like incense in his nostrils.

But there was no need for that . . . plenty of wolves right here in Holy Rood.

Two watched him now, predators more cold and deadly than the most ravenous lobo.

Despite their monk robes, Wolfden recognized them both. Tom Hooper, a mental case who enjoyed killing for killing's sake, and Jason McCord, a Texas hard-ass of reputation.

Wolfden pegged the gunmen in his mind as the Deadly Duo, and the alliteration pleased him.

Both of them had been present when Hank Cobb buried him alive.

The men sat about twenty feet apart from Wolfden, close enough that a skilled revolver fighter like McCord could get his work in, but far enough away to discourage any gun or knife play the witch-finder might make.

Wolfden commented on it.

"You boys don't trust me, huh?" he said. "Sceered I'll bring the lightning down on you."

Hooper, who'd been honing the edge of his machete with a whetstone, sneered and said, "You don't scare us, mister."

"And why not?" Wolfden said. "Though I have no intention of scaring either of you."

"Because there ain't no such things as witches. And if there ain't no witches, there ain't no witch-finders."

"Hank Cobb doesn't think so," Wolfden said. "That's why you and McCord are here."

"We're here because of the money," Hooper said. "Hank hasn't figured out your angle yet, hunchback. But he will."

"And then?"

"And then he'll kill you. Or we will." He turned to McCord. "Pass the damned whiskey, will you? You been hoggin' it all night."

McCord surrendered the bottle, and then said, "Your name is Starlight, ain't it?"

"As ever was, man and boy," Wolfden lied smoothly.

"Then why don't you make it easy on yourself, Mr. Starlight?" McCord said. "Admit to Cobb in the presence of the townspeople that you came here to steal the bank's money and he'll go easy on you."

"Hell, he might cut you in for a share," Hooper said. "The boss is a generous man."

"Shut your trap, Tom," McCord said. Then to Wolfden, "You know you're not leaving this burg alive unless Cobb says so."

"I have a job to do," Wolfden said.

"There ain't witches in Holy Rood, mister," McCord said. "I already told you that."

Wolfden smiled. "I know. But there's a bunch of killers and outlaws here. And they're just as evil as witches."

"Listen, hunchback, are you some kind of law?" Hooper said.

Wolfden shook his head. "No. I'm a witch-finder."

Hooper hissed his frustration and held up the machete so the moonlight gleamed on its edge.

"You know why I'm sharpening this knife?" he said. "Because I blunted it on a feller's skull this morning. I damn near cut his fool head off. Now I'm thinking about doing the same to you. Maybe cut that hump off'n your back."

"He isn't joking, Mr. Starlight." McCord grinned. "Good ol' Tom's a demon with that there machete."

Wolfden had been sitting on a rock. Now he rose to his feet and his back straightened.

Surprise showed on the faces of the two gunmen

as they all at once beheld a tall, straight man, not a hunchback.

"Good ol' Tom, try to hit me with the big knife and I'll kill you before you cover three paces," Wolfden said. "You really feel like wading through a half dozen bullets to get to me?"

Hooper was not a smart man, and he might have gone for it.

But the sudden clangor of the church bell froze him in place, as it did McCord.

The Texan recovered first. "What the hell?" he said.

He ran to the rim of the ridge and stared at the moonlit church, then ducked as shots rang out.

"Is it Cobb?" Hooper yelled above the din.

"Hell, I don't know," McCord said. "I can't see a thing."

"We'd better get down there," Hooper said.

"No. You boys stay right where you're at."

The heads of both men swiveled in Wolfden's direction. He stood tall and terrible in the darkness, Colt in hand.

"Damn it," McCord said. "I should've pegged you for a gun."

Wolfden shook his head. "No, you should've pegged me for who I am, Jason."

McCord peered hard at Wolfden and the scales fell from his eyes.

"Jasper Wolfden, by God," he said. "I helped bury you."

"Not deep enough," Wolfden said.

"Damn you, then this time I'll make it stick."

McCord drew.

And died.

The Texan was fast, but drawing from the leather against a man who already had his own gun out and knew how to shoot it was a doomed play.

McCord went down with two bullets in his chest that clipped half-moons from the tag of the tobacco sack that dangled from his shirt pocket under the monk's robe.

Hooper watched McCord fall. He screamed in rage and charged Wolfden, the machete raised for a killing downward stroke.

Wolfden had earlier prophesized what would happen.

Three bullets tracked upward, following the recoil of the Colt.

Hooper stumbled a few steps with a .45 in his belly, chest and throat.

He died with his eyes wide open, horrified at the time and manner of his death.

The demanding bell dinged into silence, its sound replaced by random shots, pounding feet and the hoarse yells of angry men.

Wolfden smiled.

Shawn O'Brien was sure playing hob.

Now it was his turn.

The idea had come to him out of the blue. To be sure, it was a grandstand play, but he considered it crackerjack. Best of all, it would take the pressure off Shawn, who might even now be fighting for his life.

Wolfden pried the machete out of Hooper's dead hand and stepped to the ridge. The unblinking moon rode high, surrounded by a halo of pale blue and red.

People were flooding into the bone-white street and he thought he heard Hank Cobb yelling orders.

Wolfden turned his head into the wind. There was a good breeze, sufficient for his purpose.

Grinning, he set to work.

He opened the sacks of paper money and shook them into the wind. The bills fluttered off the ridge and scattered like a flock of released pigeons.

Now for the coin.

The keen-edged machete easily slashed the burlap sacks open and Wolfden emptied them into the bottom and the seat of the surrey.

When every sack was empty, he stepped to the edge of the ridge.

"Hey, you down there!" he yelled, throwing his actor's voice.

Blurred white faces turned in Wolfden's direction and one of Cobb's men took a pot at him.

The bullet went wild and Wolfden laughed and yelled, "Watch this, pilgrims!"

A strong man, he put his brawny arms to the surrey.

The carriage tipped and then teetered perilously on two wheels.

Wolfden put his back into it and the surrey toppled over the edge.

He stood and listened to the tinny tinkle of coins chime over the rocks, and then a ragged crash as the surrey hit the flat and shattered apart.

Stepping to the edge of the rim again, Wolfden yelled, "Hey, Hank! You just lost your money!"

He was answered by loud curses and shots slapped across the night.

A few of them were close. Too close.

Standing on the rim, Wolfden realized he was like a duck in a shooting gallery.

He faded back into the darkness, looking for a way out.

As far as he could tell, there was none.

CHAPTER TWENTY-FOUR

Shawn O'Brien waited until the midnight hour before yanking on the bell rope.

It was gratifying to see how the racket woke up the town, people running this way and that, as though he'd just stepped on an ant nest.

But when men appeared wearing nothing but long johns and gun belts and bullets rattled into the tower and pinged off the bell, he decided it was high time to scamper.

His boots pounding on the bell tower's pine steps, Shawn ran directly into the church and then headed for a door that stood ajar to the right of pulpit.

He'd come in that way, and it seemed the best bet for an exit.

But as Shawn stepped through the door, a bullet chipped wood from the jamb and another kicked up dirt at his feet.

He stared into the darkness, his mouth suddenly dry.

A man wearing a long red nightshirt stood on the porch of a gingerbread house, a rifle at his shoulder.

He was not one of Cobb's gunmen, but one of the good citizens of Holy Rood who'd somehow managed to hold on to his firearm.

The man fired again, his rifle flaring orange in the moonlight, and Shawn's anger surged.

The idiot was shooting at a target he hadn't even identified as the phantom bell ringer. He was just some rooster who wanted to take pots at somebody . . . anybody.

Shawn drew and fired, aiming to scare, not kill.

He thumbed off three fast shots that split the air close to the rifleman's nightcapped head.

It was enough. The man squealed, dropped his rifle and ran into his house, the bottom of his nightshirt flapping around his skinny, hairy legs.

Shawn was pleased that he'd put the crawl on the rifleman, but the sound of firing had alerted Cobb's men.

He heard shouts mingled with curses and the sound of feet running across the wooden floor of the church.

His horse was picketed just north of town, but Shawn decided against making a run for it. Cobb's men were too close, and those boys knew how to shoot.

Sweat beading his forehead, he scrambled past the side of the gingerbread house and into an open patch of sandy ground where islands of brush and bunch grass surrounded isolated piñon and juniper trees.

Shawn ran for the nearest cover, took a knee behind a piñon and studied the situation.

His heart thumping in his chest, he fed shells into his Colt as his eyes scanned the darkness.

He'd made only a half-baked plan to begin with. By ringing the bell he'd hoped to put the town on edge and force Cobb into doing something rash. That was the plan, its entire focus and beginning and end.

Now he'd run out of options and was trapped like a rat.

Cobb's men had reacted quicker than Shawn had expected and they were between him and his horse. Not only that, it seemed like every rooster in town was willing to take a pot at him if he could.

He cursed under his breath and told himself that it was high time to come up with a daring, clever plan.

But he didn't have one of them.

He didn't even have a timid, stupid plan.

Three men carrying rifles walked between the church and the gingerbread house. The man in the nightshirt yelled at them to hold up and he stepped off his porch.

His voice loud and edged with hysteria, he pointed to the waste ground and said, "He went that way. Just a minute ago."

"Just one?" a gunman asked.

"Yeah, and he was a handful," nightshirt said. "Damn near killed me."

The three men stared into the darkness where the moonlight cast long shadows.

"Let's go get him," a man said.

Shawn wiped his sweaty palm on his pants, and then grasped his Colt again.

He'd let them get a little closer, then jump to his feet and cut loose.

Trained in the way of the Colt by grim old Luther Ironside, his pa's *segundo* back at Dromore, Shawn suffered the same disadvantage as most revolver fighters.

The fast draw and shoot was an effective weapon, but only up close at spitting distance. These were Hank Cobb's handpicked men and they'd be no bargain in a fight . . . at any distance.

He'd need to wait until they halved the open space between him and them, and even at that range one against three was a mighty uncertain thing.

Shawn swallowed hard. He had no other option. He had to do it.

Only one of the gunmen wore boots. The other two had rushed into the street at the sound of gunfire and walked on bare, hesitant feet, wary of rocks and cactus.

They came on slowly, carefully. Shawn touched his tongue to his dry top lip and waited.

Ten yards . . .

Seven . . .

Five . . .

One more yard and it would be time to open the ball. . . .

Gunfire erupted, somewhere in the darkness behind him.

"Frank, he must've made it to the ridge above town," a man said, his tone urgent.

The three gunmen stopped in their tracks, and listened into the night.

"Hell, the money's up there and so is that damned witch-finder," the man called Frank said. "He must be in cahoots with the feller we're chasing. You two stay here and keep a sharp eye out. I'll go find Cobb and take a looksee on the ridge."

"The ranny we're after ain't here, Frank," one of the barefooted men said. He wore a black-and-white cowhide vest over his undershirt. "He must be on the ridge."

"We don't know that," Frank said. "Maybe McCord and Hooper shot the witch-finder."

"We'll go with you," the man said.

"Do like I told you and bide right where you are," Frank said. "If you see the man we're after, go get him. I'll be back."

Shawn heard the man's booted feet make tracks into the street toward the sheriff's office.

The barefooted men stood in moonlight, their eyes scanning the waste ground.

"Damn it, I know he ain't here," the man with the cowhide vest said again.

"Yeah, well, Frank said to bide, so we'll bide," the other gunman said.

"You see anything?"

"Not a damned thing."

"Me neither. I reckon he's long gone."

The odds were reduced by one and Shawn worried that Wolfden was in trouble, maybe badly wounded.

It was time to jump the broom.

He sprang to his feet, his Colt coming up fast.

"Damn—" cowhide vest yelled. It was the last word he'd ever say in his life.

As the man swung his rifle, Shawn shot him twice, the black-and-white vest a splendid target in the moonlight.

Shawn didn't watch the man go down. He turned on the second gunman and snapped off a fast shot.

Too fast. A clean miss.

But it was enough. It seemed that the second gunman had no belly for a fight, at least that night.

Shawn's bullet had furrowed the air so close to the man's head that he threw down his rifle and scampered for the gingerbread house, yelling for nightshirt to open the damned door.

A quick glance told Shawn that the big .45

rounds had torn great holes in the chest of the downed man and he was as dead as he was ever going to be.

He took time to reload his Colt, then swung around and ran in the direction of the ridge.

Shawn pulled to a halt when he heard a splintering crash ahead of him, and then more gunshots.

What the hell was happening? Was Wolfden playing hob, or had Cobb and his gunmen cornered him?

Even in moonlight, the darkness held no answers.

Shawn's inclination was to clear out of Holy Rood and make a run for his horse. But as soon as the thought entered his head, he dismissed it.

He couldn't leave Wolfden alone. For all he knew, the man might be badly wounded or already dead, but he had to find out for sure.

Besides, the plan was to put Hank Cobb on edge and force him into making a bad move. And that seemed to be succeeding.

But Shawn was forced to admit that only the first part of his scheme had been successful.

Judging by the racket of the gunfire ringing from the ridge, it seemed Cobb had the situation well in hand and had cornered Wolfden.

Since it was located behind the main street,

Shawn had never seen this part of Holy Rood before.

Around him, as though they'd wandered into the wilderness and lost their way, gaunt, tarpaper shacks with tin roofs and crooked iron chimneys were scattered here and there with no sense of planning or order.

No lights showed in any of the cabins and the ground around them was unmarked by footprints or horse tracks. The air smelled musky of stagnation and slow decay.

Shawn guessed that these were the hovels where the whores, gamblers and other undesirables lived before Cobb sacrificed them for his own gain.

Beyond the shacks rose the dark bulk of the ridge. The shooting had stopped, but Shawn was close enough to hear angry yells and curses as men stumbled around in the gloom as though searching for something.

Jasper Wolfden maybe? Or his body?

Like a moth attracted to a flame, Shawn again walked toward the looming bulk of the rise.

"I would stop right there, if I was you."

The voice came from his right. A woman's voice.

Shawn swung in her direction, his Colt coming up fast.

"If you shoot, you're dead," the woman said. "Hank's boys are on the prod and they'll come after you."

His eyes probed the darkness and Shawn saw the

upper part of the woman's body silhouetted in the window of the nearest shack.

He stepped closer, wary of an ambush, and then stopped when he was a few feet away.

As far as he could tell in the gloom, the woman was young, with long dark hair cascading over her shoulders. The top buttons of her filmy robe were undone, revealing the white mounds of large, firm breasts.

"Are you going to stand out there until you get shot, or are you coming in?" the woman said. "Don't be afraid. I won't bite."

The gunshots had roused people from bed and a babble of talk filled the street.

Above the din, Shawn heard Cobb yell, "Damn you, find him!"

And then a woman screamed loudly and in a hysterical voice yelled that she'd just seen witches and warlocks dancing with the devil on the ridge.

Somebody fired, shooting at shadows, and Cobb called out, "Did you get him? Is it O'Brien or Wolfden?"

Shawn's narrow smile was grim. Jasper was still alive and in hiding, and he felt a surge of relief.

But Cobb's voice and the gunshots were too close for comfort and he made up his mind and quickly stepped through the open door into the shadowed, candlelit shack.

The woman walked in front of Shawn and told him to close the door behind him. From the rear, she looked firm and round in all the right places, as though her body had been turned on a lathe.

Shawn closed the door and then turned to talk to her . . . and found himself staring into the black, unwavering muzzles of a very fine L.C. Smith scattergun.

CHAPTER TWENTY-FIVE

It didn't surprise Jasper Wolfden that after he tipped the surrey over the rise, all kinds of hell broke loose.

And he knew he was in big trouble.

To the north was an ancient talus slope and Cobb and his boys were already slipping and sliding on gravel as they climbed toward him.

The slope was the only way down, and Wolfden was trapped.

The rise, really a weatherworn mesa, dropped off in sheer cliffs on its other three sides. In daylight, a careful man with good feet and hands could probably make it to the flat.

But in darkness it was impossible.

Damn!

Wolfden swore as he realized that he'd emptied his Colt and hadn't taken the guns of McCord and Hooper.

He ran to remedy that mistake, but skidded to a

stop when Shel Shannon stepped through the darkness like the specter of death.

The gunman had a Colt in his hand and a grin on his cruel, thick-lipped mouth.

Shannon raised the revolver.

"Say good night, Jasper," he said.

Like a drowning man clutching at a straw, Wolfden made a desperate play for time.

"Before you pull the trigger, how did you know, Shel?" he said.

The muzzle of the Colt dropped an inch.

"A man can change his appearance, pretend to have a hump on his back, but he can't change his eyes," Shannon said. "You got wolf eyes, Jasper. There ain't no hiding those."

Another straw, another frantic grab.

"I should've known I couldn't fool you, Shel," Wolfden said, his mind racing.

Charge him. Try to get the gun.

Better that than just inviting the bullet and dying like a dog.

Wolfden tensed. Got ready.

"It was Hank who pegged it, not me," Shannon said. "Now, my bucko, you get it . . . right between the eyes. . . ."

"Shel, no!"

Hank Cobb stepped out of the gloom.

"I want him alive," he said.

Shannon reluctantly lowered his revolver. "Whatever you say, boss."

Two other gunmen stepped beside Cobb and one of them said, "Hell, what happened to his hump?"

Cobb grinned. "He isn't a witch-finder, his name ain't Starlight and he doesn't have a hump. This here is Jasper Wolfden, a failed actor whose big mouth once caused me no end of trouble."

"Boss, didn't you kill him already?" the gunman said.

"Sure I did, but it didn't take," Cobb said. His eyes met Wolfden's in the darkness. "I'm going to bury you alive all over again, Jasper."

"Gun me, Cobb," Wolfden said. "Shannon wants to put a bullet between my eyes, so get it over."

"You just don't listen, do you, Jasper?" Cobb said. "Let me say it again: I'm gonna bury you alive. Then I'm gonna piss on your grave and I won't move from there until the piss dries. This time I'll make sure you're dead, dead, dead."

Cobb stepped closer to Wolfden. Without warning he raked the barrel of his heavy revolver across the other man's face, opening a cut on Wolfden's cheekbone that instantly spurted blood.

"Who's down there?" Cobb said. "Is it O'Brien? Is it the pretty boy?"

"I don't know what the hell you're talking about," Wolfden said. His swollen right eye cried scarlet tears.

"You have an accomplice, Jasper. Who is he?"

"You go to hell."

A man stepped beside Cobb. "Lewis is dead."

"Who the hell killed him?" Cobb said.

"I don't know boss." The man hesitated. "Some ranny that knows how to shoot. Lewis took two rounds in the chest and he was dead when he—"

"Damn it, don't draw me a picture," Cobb said.

He was irritated beyond measure.

He'd lost three good men, his money was scattered to hell and gone and it would take days to recover it all, if ever.

Now he was down to five men and, apart from Shannon, they were the least of them.

A curse died on Cobb's lips, replaced by an order.

He pointed at Wolfden. "Shel, take that man to the damned jail and lock him up. Then join me at the spot where Lewis was shot."

He answered the question on Shannon's face.

"We're going to search for O'Brien. And when we find him, we'll kill him."

"Maybe he'll find you first, Hank," Wolfden said. He smiled and blood ran over his lips and into his mouth. "He can shade you on your best day."

Cobb's only reaction was a smile of his own.

"Damn you, Jasper, I'm gonna bury you so deep, you'll shake hands with the devil. And maybe I'll have O'Brien join you. You two can rot in the grave together."

CHAPTER TWENTY-SIX

"So it was a trap," Shawn O'Brien said. "I should've known as much."

"I've never seen you before," the woman said.

"I've been around."

"Are you one of Hank's men?"

"Hell, no."

"Then who are you?" She corrected herself. "What are you?"

"Do you really care who or what I am? Call Cobb and get it over with."

"I'm not your enemy," the woman said.

She was beautiful in a dark, flashing, Mexican way. Her eyes were as black as midnight, her glossy hair even darker, if that were possible. But her skin was creamy white and her voluptuous figure was the kind that keeps a man awake o' nights, remembering.

"If you're not my enemy, are you my friend?" Shawn asked.

"Maybe."

The shotgun still pointed at Shawn's belly and he knew he was only a finger twitch from getting cut in half.

"My name is Shawn O'Brien, out of the Glorieta Mesa country in the New Mexico Territory," he said. "How's that for starters?"

"You killed a man tonight, didn't you?"

"Yes. One of Cobb's men."

"Why?"

"Because he wanted to kill me. Hank Cobb is my enemy and I aim to see that he pays for his crimes." Then, almost as an afterthought, "And I'll make this town pay as well."

"And he's also my enemy," the woman said. "And this town is my enemy."

"So maybe we can be allies," Shawn said. Then, smiling, "You know my name but you didn't give out yours."

"My mother's name was Rodriguez. My father was Irish but my mother never said his name aloud. He left us when I was three, went to the goldfields and never came back."

"So what do you call yourself? Rodriquez?" Shawn said.

"Ruby La Monde. At least that's what I called myself when I met Hank. I was working the line in Dodge before he brought me to Holy Rood."

The woman propped up the shotgun in a corner.

The cabin was tiny, barely large enough to accommodate a brass bed, an armchair by the potbellied stove, a small dresser and a clothes closet.

"I wouldn't have shot you," she said.

"That's good to know."

"Would you like a drink?"

"I could sure use one."

Shawn glanced out the open window, but saw only a rectangle of blackness.

"Will Cobb look for me here?" he said.

"Maybe. But I doubt it," Ruby said.

She poured whiskey into glasses and handed one to Shawn. Then she picked up the makings from the table and held them up where he could see.

"Smoke?"

"Yes, thank you."

Ruby tossed Shawn the makings and said, "Back in the day, I learned the habit from the Texas cowboys who came up the trail."

"And they learned it from the vaqueros who are much addicted to tobacco," Shawn said. He smiled. "As I am."

He built a cigarette and Ruby thumbed a match into flame and lit it for him.

"Those punchers taught you a lot, huh?" he said. "I've only seen a man light a match like that."

Ruby nodded. "They taught me stuff, all right. Both good and bad. I was a prize package back then."

"You still are, Ruby," Shawn said, meaning it.

The shouts of men echoed loud in the darkness

and the glow of lanterns danced in the street like fireflies.

The woman closed the window and pulled its ragged curtain closed.

"I only have one chair, but you're welcome to sit in it," she said.

"I reckon I'll stand," Shawn said.

Ruby understood the implications of that statement and said, "Once the search dies down, you can get away from here."

"Cobb still visit you?" Shawn said.

"Now and again. He says a man has his needs."

"I understand there were other girls in Holy Rood," Shawn said.

"Whores like me, you mean?"

She saw Shawn fumble for the right words and let him off the hook. "Yes, there were. The miners used to come in and a few cowboys. But then Hank got his brilliant idea to drain this town dry and he killed all the girls or forced them out of town. Killed a fair number of their clients too. Now nobody visits Holy Rood and I don't know how the town survives."

"Buy and sell among themselves, I guess," Shawn said. "Cobb didn't kill you? Why not?"

"Only because I was his property, bought and paid for. A man like Hank doesn't destroy something he owns."

Ruby took the makings from Shawn and expertly rolled a cigarette. After she lit it, she said, "When I saw what was happening, I tried to escape. But Hank came after me and brought me back."

Her cigarette trailed blue smoke as Ruby pulled back her hair and revealed a white, twisted scar where her left ear had been.

"He took my ear as a punishment and told me that if I tried to run again, he'd cut off the other one."

She let the hair fall back in place. "I'm Hank's prisoner and he'll kill me soon, I think."

"You better come with me," Shawn said. "I have a camp near here and there's another woman with us."

"Your wife?"

"No. Sally Bailey is just another of Cobb's victims."

"I haven't been out of this cabin in months," Ruby said. "The sky might fall on me."

"The sky will fall on you for sure if you don't get out of this town," Shawn said. "Cobb is fixing to leave."

"And he won't take me with him?"

"What do you think?"

"As I said, I think he'll kill me. Tie up all his loose ends before he rides out."

Shawn said nothing. Now it was up to the woman.

It didn't take long for Ruby to make up her mind.

"I'll come with you," she said. "I can't stay locked up in this town any longer."

Ruby blew out the candle and plunged the shack into darkness.

"You ever watch a woman get dressed from the skin out before?" she said.

"I was married once," Shawn said.

"Well, you weren't married to me, so turn around anyway."

"I'll stand at the door," Shawn said, grinning.

Then, as though she felt he was due an explanation, Ruby said, "I was a modest whore."

"I never met one of them," Shawn said.

After Ruby rummaged in her closet, she dressed hurriedly and the result, even in the gloom of the cabin, was pleasing.

She wore a tan canvas skirt, split for riding, a white shirt and over that a vest the same color as her skirt. She wore boots and a flat-brimmed, low-crowned black hat tied under her chin.

"So how do I look?" she said.

Shawn smiled. Even facing mortal danger, it was a question only a woman would ask.

"Real purty," Shawn said. "Like an English lady."

"I've never seen an English lady. Or any other kind of a lady, come to that."

"If you ever did, she'd look you up and down and then eat her heart out with envy."

It wasn't the most elegant of compliments, Shawn decided, but he meant every word of it.

Ruby smiled and opened her mouth to speak, but as footsteps shuffled outside Shawn put a forefinger to his lips and drew his gun.

The steps stopped at the door. Then after a few

moments a man whispered, "Ruby, darlin', you awake?"

Shawn recognized the voice. It was Shel Shannon.

The woman stepped closer to him, her eyes wide with apprehension.

Shawn put his finger on Ruby's mouth, and then pointed to the bed.

She caught on quickly and said, "Shel, I'm in bed, half asleep. All the shooting kept wakening me."

"In bed is where I was hoping I'd find you, darlin'," Shannon said. "I'm coming in and we'll talk, maybe have us a drink or two, huh?"

Shawn moved behind the door and at his nod, Ruby opened it wide.

Shannon grinned his words, "Want it as bad as me, huh, little gal?"

"Come in, Shel," Ruby said. "Quickly."

Laughing, Shannon stepped into the dark cabin . . . and then his voice became a growl. "What the hell, Ruby? Why are you dressed like that? You maybe planning to—"

Shawn swung his Colt. He hit the gunman on the right side of his head, just under his hat, and Shannon fell to his knees. But a buffaloed man with a thick skull can drop from the blow yet still hold on to consciousness.

Shannon cursed and groggily reached out for Ruby and Shawn hit him with the heavy Colt again.

This time Shannon fell on his face and lay still,

but the O'Brien brothers had not been raised in the ways of trusting men.

Shawn's booted toe kicked Shannon's head hard and when the man groaned, he kicked him again, harder.

When he was satisfied that Shannon wasn't going to get up again, he jerked the gun from the unconscious man's holster and tucked it into his waistband. He grabbed Shannon's ankles, dragged him into the cabin and told Ruby to shut the door.

Shawn let Shannon's ankles drop, then stepped to the window.

He pulled back the curtain an inch and stared outside. He saw only darkness and a bobbing lantern in the distance as the crowds of townspeople thinned.

"I don't think anybody saw Shannon come to your door," he said.

"What are you going to do with him?" Ruby said.

"I want to kill him, but I won't. At least, not yet. If Jasper Wolfden's been captured by Cobb, maybe I can trade Shannon for him."

"We can't stay here much longer," the woman said. "There's only a couple of hours left until sunup."

"I know. We're getting out of here and good ol' Shel is going with us. Any of those Texas cowboys you entertained leave you a rope?"

"No, only money," Ruby said. There was strange hurt in her eyes.

"Sorry," Shawn said. "I shouldn't have said that."

Then, because he felt his apology was inadequate, "I'm on edge, I guess."

"And me too," Ruby said. "I guess." She motioned to the bed. "Tear up my sheets for a rope. I won't have any use for them again."

It was only the work of minutes for Shawn to rip the sheets into strips and knot them together to fashion a rope, except for two pieces he used to gag Shannon and tie his hands behind his back.

The gunman stirred, cursed, and made a grab for Shawn. He again got thumped on the head for his trouble and flopped like a rag doll into unconsciousness.

Shawn held up his revolver for Ruby to see. "Full factory-engraved Colt, the barrel cut back to four inches and the action tuned by Hermann Ulrich, the El Paso gunsmith, and I'm bending it over the head of this idiot. It would make a grown man cry."

The woman seemed unimpressed by the Colt's pedigree or Shawn's grief over its abuse.

"We'd better get to your horse," she said. "Shannon's a tough man and he could give us trouble when he recovers."

Shawn nodded. "Now's as good a time as any, I reckon."

He coiled the sheet rope and looped it over his left shoulder. Then, a strong, well-muscled man, he effortlessly hauled Shannon to his feet and grabbed the gunman by the back of his shirt.

Shannon's eyes rolled in his head, still out of it.

"Let's go," Shawn said.

He held Shannon's collar in his left fist, his Colt in the right.

Ruby opened the door and together they walked outside into the star-bright night.

CHAPTER TWENTY-SEVEN

The night was cool and the wind was in the trees as Shawn and Ruby left the cabin and made their way toward the northern edge of town.

The smell of the tall pines to the west was in the air and a drift of wood smoke and the tang of coffee and frying bacon as some of the citizens of Holy Rood had apparently decided that after being awake all night there was no point in going back to bed.

Keeping away from the ridge where there were still sounds of activity and moving lanterns, Shawn let Ruby lead the way since she was more familiar with the town than he was.

They kept to the east of the now dark street and Shawn noticed that light gleamed around the window blinds of the sheriff's office.

What that boded for the fate of Jasper Wolfden he did not know.

Shawn pushed the stumbling Shannon in front of him, but the terrain made for easy going, as flat as a dance floor, tufted with sparse grass and a few scattered junipers.

Ahead of him, a bottle clanked into another as Ruby took a misstep, and she froze as the sound rang loud and sharp in the silence.

Shawn stopped and glanced around him. The entire area was littered with empty bottles and he guessed they were walking behind what had once been a saloon.

Shannon groaned and sank to his knees and Shawn let him stay there.

It seemed that the sound had gone unnoticed because the darkness lay silent and unbroken around them.

Jumpy, and irritated with himself for being so, Shawn whispered, "Damn it, Ruby, can't you be more careful?"

The woman turned, angled at him one of those angry female looks that can freeze a man's blood, and walked on.

Feeling foolish, Shawn took it out on Shannon.

He roughly yanked the man to his feet and pushed him forward.

Shannon shook his body, trying to free himself from Shawn's iron grasp, and then made an attempt to talk around his gag. He failed, but his furious eyes said it all . . . black with anger and filled with murder.

* * *

To Shawn's relief, he and Ruby left Holy Rood behind them without further incident.

His horse was still tied to the bush in a grassy patch where Shawn had left it and displayed no ill will at being left for so long.

Shannon was fully conscious but was quiet. Something cold and ugly had settled inside of him and he was content to bide his time.

But Shawn had other plans for him.

He untied the gunman's gag and said, "All right, what happened to Jasper Wolfden?"

Shannon stretched his mouth open and shut for a few moments, then smiled and said, "You go to hell, O'Brien."

Shawn's sainted mother Saraid had been a sweet, gentle person, but his father and the sons he'd raised were the very opposite, neither sweet, gentle or forgiving.

Shawn's fist crashed into Shannon's mouth and the man dropped as though he'd been pole-axed.

After he dragged the gunman to his feet, Shawn said, "I asked you politely, Shel, but you gave me a most impolite answer. I'm really surprised at you."

He smiled and patted Shannon's hairy cheek.

"Now here's how it's going to work, just so you know," he said. "I'll ask the question again, and if you still give me an impolite answer I'll shoot off your left thumb. Then I'll ask the question a second time, and if the result is the same, I'll shoot off your right thumb. And then will come the third time, and you know what I'll shoot off then, don't you, amigo? The ladies will hate me for it, but what else can I do?"

Shannon saw determination and a distinct lack of sympathy in Shawn's eyes. The man was prepared to do exactly what he'd promised.

"Wolfden is alive, damn you," he said. "But he'll be dead soon, and so will you."

Shawn smiled. "You're such a pleasure to be around, Shel."

He made a noose at the end of sheet, looped it around Shannon's neck, then stepped into the saddle. He leaned over and offered Ruby a hand and a stirrup.

When the woman was settled behind him, he said, "Shel, I reckon you had those Texas boots of yours made on a narrow last. You've got some walking to do, so I hope they don't punish you too much."

Shannon's face was black with rage. "I'm gonna kill you, O'Brien," he said. "I swear to God I'll tear you apart. . . . I'll skin you alive."

"A wise precaution, Shel. Never trust a wolf until it's skun, they say."

Shawn jerked on the rope and kneed his horse into a walk.

Behind him, Shannon stumbled forward and turned the moon-dappled air blue with his curses.

* * *

"My witch-finder idea didn't work worth a damn," Shawn said. "Hank Cobb has Jasper Wolfden"—he nodded in Shannon's direction—"and I've got his idiot."

"There's still coffee in the pot," Ford Platt said.

"Is that all you have to say?" Shawn said. "There's coffee in the pot?"

"What else is there to say?" Platt said. "You tried something that didn't work and now we're back to square one. What else can I add?"

Shawn frustration showed. "I don't know . . . say something . . . anything." Then, after a few moments of reflection, he said, "Hell, I owe Jasper Wolfden my life."

"And now you have the idea of trading Shannon for him?" Platt said. "That's a wild guess."

"Well, you're right. It's my plan exactly."

Platt moodily poked at the fire with a stick. "Might work. But it might not. Kinda like the last plan you had." Platt smiled. "No offense."

"Hank doesn't care about Shannon. He doesn't care about anybody but himself," Ruby said. "If he wants to kill Wolfden bad enough, he won't trade."

"He wants to kill him bad, all right," Shawn said.

"Then all you'll do is take cards in a rigged game," Ruby said. "A game you can only lose."

Hamp Sedley poured coffee into the only cup and handed it to Ruby.

"Share that with O'Brien," he said. "He looks like he could use it."

Then, to Platt he said, "You'd better tell him."

"Tell me what?" Shawn said.

Platt sighed, as though telling the story would be an unpleasant chore.

Finally, he said, "I'm a restless man, and I don't sleep much. After you left, Shawn, I saddled the mule and rode down to the wagon road."

"Why?" Shawn said.

Platt shook his head. "Hell, if I know. Well, studying on it, I do know. I half-expected to see you riding hell for leather away from Holy Rood with Cobb and his boys right behind you."

"Not too wild a stretch," Shawn said, accepting the coffee from Ruby.

"No, I guess not," Platt said. "But who do I meet on the road but a traveling preacher, a Reverend Micah something or other." The little man waited until Shawn drank some coffee, then said, "He had a story to tell."

"Then tell it, Platt," Sedley said. "Damn, but you're a slow-talking man."

Sally chided the gambler. "In his own time, Hamp, please."

"It's not too long in the telling," Platt said. "But I'll make it even shorter."

He glanced into the pines where arrowheads of green pierced the pale pink of the dawn sky, then said, "The little reverend told me that Mink Morrow is headed for Holy Rood."

Shawn smiled. "Even a little reverend can tell a

big windy. Mink never leaves the Mogollon Rim country. Everybody knows that."

"Everybody but Mink, I guess," Platt said.

"Where did the preacher get his information?" Shawn said.

"He says he was in a saloon in Silver Reef, lecturing the drunks on the evils of demon drink, when he struck up a conversation with a feller you mentioned, Shawn, by the name of Nathan Scruggs."

"You can't have a conversation with Scruggs," Sedley said. "He's as deaf as a cow skull."

Platt said, "He may be deaf, but he's a talking man and he told Mink Morrow about Hank Cobb and the good thing he's got going in Holy Rood. Well, Mink listens and then says, and this according to the reverend, 'Hell, I'm gonna cut me off a piece of that action.' As I said, that's what the reverend told me he said, and I don't figure he'd any reason to lie."

Shawn thought about the implications of that for a while, then said, "Mink Morrow is a gun for hire. Plenty of work for a man with his talents in a boomtown like Silver Reef. Why leave a sure thing and buck Hank Cobb, who isn't any man's bargain?"

"There's a tough sheriff in Silver Reef who's mighty sudden with the iron his ownself," Platt said. "Maybe ol' Mink decided to up stakes and head for pastures anew."

"Or he isn't as fast as people say," Sedley said.

"Mink Morrow is a friend of my brother Jake's,"

Shawn said. "That ought to tell you something about how good he is with a gun."

He turned and stared at Shannon.

"Hey, Shel," he said, "Mink Morrow is headed for Holy Rood. What's your opinion on that?"

"You're a damned liar, O'Brien," Shannon said. "Mink never leaves the Rim."

"He's left it," Shawn said. "He wants ol' Hank to cut him in on the Holy Rood action."

"There is no Holy Rood action. The bank money is scattered to hell and gone and what's left wouldn't keep Mink in whiskey and whores for a month."

"Better tell Mink that," Shawn said.

"Hank will. Hell, he can shade Morrow."

"No, he can't, not on any day of the week."

"Why tell me this, O'Brien?" Shannon said. "I can't do anything about it sitting here."

"No, you can't, Shel," Shawn said. "But you're my bargaining chip. That's why you're still breathing. Even though you're an idiot, I'm just bringing you up to date on the current situation."

"I'm not gonna help you, O'Brien. You can kiss my ass."

Shawn rose to his feet. He drew his gun, stepped to Shannon, shoved the muzzle between his eyes and thumbed back the hammer.

"I had this here iron set up with a two-pound trigger pull, and I want to kill you real bad, Shel," he said. "If a fly lands on my finger, this thing will go bang. You catching my drift?"

"Damn you, O'Brien, you'd do it, wouldn't you?" Shannon said.

He looked like a man who'd just been taken with the seasickness on an ocean steamer bucking a force ten gale.

"Tell me to kiss your ass again, Shel. See what happens," Shawn said. "Let me hear if you're as stupid as I think you are."

It didn't take Shannon long to think that through.

"All right, O'Brien, I'll play ball for now," he said. "What do you want me to do?"

"Nothing much, Shel. Just be a good boy and behave yourself until we get to Holy Rood."

"Sure, sure, but after that, all bets are off," Shannon said. "I still plan to kill you, O'Brien, lay to that."

"You're true blue, Shel," Shawn said. He eased down the hammer of the Colt. "You said exactly the right words at the right time. I'll play ball was music to my ears. Just as well, otherwise you'd be dead right now."

The muscles of Shannon's jaw bunched, but he said nothing.

Shawn sat by the fire again and Platt said, "How do you want to play this, Shawn? I mean with Shannon."

"Nothing complicated like the last time," Shawn said. "Good ol' Shel and I will ride into . . ."

He stopped abruptly as a realization hit him like a blow.

He hadn't thought about Judith in . . . my God, how long?

Days? A week?

He closed his eyes and again recalled her face in his mind, but hazy, as though he saw her reflection in a steamed-up mirror.

It hurt. And that helped.

He needed to hurt. Judith deserved that much.

Then the pain was replaced by anxiety.

"Dear God in heaven, don't let me forget her this easily."

Shawn didn't realize he'd spoken aloud.

He opened his eyes and Ford Platt was staring at him in puzzlement. So was Sedley and the women and even Shannon looked bemused.

"You all right, O'Brien?" Sedley said.

Shawn pulled his mind into the present.

"Yeah," he said, "I'm fine, just fine. I . . . I just remembered something."

Sally Bailey's eyes met his, searched deep and saw inside him.

The woman had the Celtic gift, Shawn knew. And what he saw in his mind, she saw.

His eyes broke from Sally's steady gaze and he said to Platt, "Where was I? Oh, yeah, we ride into Holy Rood and dicker with Cobb for Wolfden."

The little man's gaze was just as intense as Sally's had been.

"You having second thoughts? You were acting kind of strange there for a minute."

"No second thoughts. This is how I want to play it," Shawn said.

Shannon sneered. "Listen to the dead man talk."

"If O'Brien dies, you will too, Shannon," Platt said. His eyes glittered cold, like a flicker of light along a steel blade. "Depend on it."

For the second time that morning, Shannon bit his tongue.

Platt looked like a bank teller, but there was something dangerous about the little man that Shannon couldn't pin down.

Then it dawned on him.

It was Ford Platt's eyes, brown, soft as a woman's. . . .

Yet now they stared at Shannon as though they were tangled in barbed wire . . . the eyes of an avenging angel . . . or a killer.

CHAPTER TWENTY-EIGHT

The morning was brightening into afternoon as Shawn O'Brien and Platt took the trail to Holy Rood. Behind them, tied up like a bale of cotton, Shel Shannon sat astride Wolfden's white horse, a permanent scowl on his face.

"I could've handled this by myself, Ford," Shawn O'Brien said. "In fact, it's high time I did."

"Could be. But Wells Fargo isn't paying me to sit on my butt," Platt said. "I want to find out what I'm facing in Holy Rood and then get the job done. I was deputized by a U.S. marshal to make arrests, and to dig a grave for them that don't cotton to being arrested."

"It's not difficult to sum it up for you," Shawn said. "What you're facing is Hank Cobb and his hired guns."

"And Mink Morrow, do you think?"

"Maybe. If he throws in with Cobb."

Platt's skin tightened on his face. "He could be

riding a reputation he doesn't deserve, you know. A lot of gunmen like Morrow aren't near as good as folks say they are. You ever see him shoot?"

Shawn thought on that, but only for a moment.

"No, I never saw him shoot, but my brother Jake did. Do you recollect a feller by the name of Scrap Page out of Gonzalez County, Texas?" Shawn said.

"Can't say as I do," Platt said.

"Scrap was a gun hand, ran with John Wesley Hardin and the Taylors and that hard crowd, and the word going around was that he'd killed eight white men."

Platt's mule decided to act up and when he finally convinced the animal who was boss, Shawn resumed his story.

"Well, one time down in the Colorado River country, Mink and my brother Jake were in a saloon, and Scrap stood with his back to the bar, bragging to all and sundry that he was the fastest man with the iron south of the Red."

"Was he?" Platt said.

"I'm coming to that," Shawn said.

"Figured you would."

"Now Jake was playing a Chopin nocturne on the piano and didn't pay Scrap any mind, but Mink was losing at poker and the man's boasting began to irritate him. Finally, he got to his feet, called Scrap for a braggart and a Texas jackass, and then the two of them had it out."

"And what happened?" Platt said.

"Well, just before he died that night, Scrap Page found out that he was the second fastest man south of the Red."

"So Mink really is good with a gun like folks say, huh?" Platt said, frowning, as though that realization troubled him.

"Damn it, let me finish my story," Shawn said. "I'm getting to the best part."

"Oh, sure, sorry," Platt said. "Finish away."

"Well, my brother Jake got real mad, told Mink that his damned shooting had ruined the nocturne's last movement for everybody."

"Is that a natural fact?" Platt said.

"Yeah, it's a natural fact. Mink was so sorry about kicking Chopin up the ass, he set up the bar and he bought Jake a shirt."

"A shirt?"

"Shawn nodded. "Jake is always kind of raggedy, so Mink bought him a new shirt."

"All things considered, that was playing the white man," Platt said.

"I guess so. But it all happened a good few years ago and a man changes," Shawn said.

"Let's hope it's for the better," Platt said. "But I doubt it."

Behind them, astride Wolfden's white horse, a scowling Shel Shannon said, "Hell, that ain't a good story. There ain't no whores in it and what kind of man who plays a pianny needs a shirt?"

"I could tell you what kind of man, Shel," Shawn said, "But I don't think you'd understand."

He turned to Platt. "What do you—"

But Shawn didn't finish his sentence.

Platt stared straight ahead of him, his sharp little features chalky.

"This is an obscenity, and outrage," he said, drawing rein on his mule.

They'd ridden up on the skulls lining the wagon road. The skulls grinned at them amid a vast silence.

"Who are they?" he said to Shawn.

"Folks Hank Cobb and the good people of Holy Rood deemed undesirables," Shawn said.

His hands were bound behind his back, but Shannon kneed his mount forward and the blackness of his soul blazed in his eyes.

"Whores, pimps, gamblers, goldbrick artists, drunks, dancehall loungers, wasters . . . we got rid of them all," he said, grinning. "They weren't fit to live."

Platt, small, slender and insignificant, nonetheless surprised Shawn by his sudden burst of violence.

He jumped from his mule, stepped to Shannon's horse, and like David toppling Goliath, he dragged the big man from the saddle.

Shannon's back hit the ground and Platt immediately put the boot in.

Thud-thud-thud . . . kicks pounded into the gunman's ribs and Shannon cried out in pain and rage.

"Is the Wells Fargo driver among the skulls?" Platt's lips snarled back from his teeth. "And is the dead passenger there?"

Shannon was finding it hard to breathe. But he glared at his tormentor and managed, "Damn you, I'll kill you."

"Are their skulls on posts?" Platt yelled. "Tell me!"

"You go to hell," Shannon said.

The little man didn't say anything, but he screamed like a wounded cougar.

His Remington flashed from under his coat and he two-handed the revolver and aimed at Shannon's head.

"No!" Shawn hollered in sudden panic. "Ford, we need him!"

Platt's gun didn't waver. Shannon's eyes were as big and fear-shiny as silver dollars and he didn't move a muscle.

A tense moment passed . . . then another. . . .

Platt's stiff shoulders relaxed and he slid the gun into his shoulder holster. He was breathing hard and said to Shawn, who stood by his side, "I . . . I don't get angry often because when I do, bad things happen."

"I can see that for my ownself," Shawn said.

"You, get the hell up," Platt said to Shannon.

His face wary, the big man struggled to his feet, his boot heels gouging the sandy gravel of the road in his haste.

"Turn your back," Platt said.

His face like stone, he quickly untied the gunman's hands, then said, "Now, get to work."

"Damn you, runt, doin' what?" Shannon said.

"You'll walk ahead of us all the way to Holy Rood and remove the skulls from the posts. You'll lay each one by the side of the road so they can be collected and later given a decent burial."

Platt read insolence and hesitation in Shannon's eyes and said, "Please, give me any excuse to kill you. You've already run out of room on the dance floor."

Shannon stood for a moment, read signs he didn't like, and then stepped to the nearest post.

He removed the skull and threw it into the brush.

"I said lay it by the side of the road," Platt said. "Now pick that up carefully and do what I told you."

Shawn stared into the distance, where the Holy Rood buildings rode the heat waves like a white fleet bobbing at anchor.

"Ford, this is going to take a lot of time," he said.

"We can spare it," Platt said. "Cobb will be in no hurry to kill Jasper Wolfden. I've got the feeling he'll want to draw it out and enjoy it."

Unfortunately, in that he was right.

CHAPTER TWENTY-NINE

Mink Morrow's arrival in Holy Rood would have normally caused a stir among the citizens, but since Hank Cobb had every man, woman and child on the ridge scavenging for his money, the coming of the gunfighter went unnoticed.

Morrow rode into a changed town.

Gone were the monkish robes, the brotherly names, the pretense of religious fervor.

The raw truth about Cobb's plans for Holy Rood was now on display for all to see.

The hard-faced gunmen who stood guard over the foragers on the ridge slope were no longer paladins of monkish virtue. Now they looked like what they were . . . hired guns who wouldn't think twice about killing any man, woman or child so long as the money was right.

Morrow dismounted outside the hotel and studied the empty street and the laboring throng on the hill.

His eyes lingered on the guillotine, its triangular

blade stained scarlet with fresh blood, then at a man's sprawled, headless body thrown carelessly into the dirt.

A far-hearing man, he made out the angry shouts of the gunmen on the ridge, barking dogs and the alarmed shrieks of women.

And Morrow, a man who feared nothing and no one, felt a twinge of unease as he wondered what he'd gotten himself into.

He glanced at the late morning sky. To the north, white, cumulus clouds piled high above the lonely land like gigantic boulders, but there was no hint of rain. The air was dry, musty, like mummy dust on the tongue.

His eyes on fire from the sun glare, Morrow stepped into the cool shade of the hotel, palmed the clerk's bell with a black-gloved hand and waited.

The casual observer would be struck by the fact that everything about Mink Morrow was angular, as though the template for his shape had been cut from cardboard with a straight razor.

His pockmarked face was lean to the point of gauntness, the cheeks sunken under, with prominent, square cheekbones. When seen from the front, his shoulders were perfectly horizontal, with no suggestion of a stoop, like the Jack of Spades on a playing card.

His black frockcoat, worn with a boiled white shirt and string tie, had been tailored with sharp scissors and thin needles, cut straight and severe with no embellishment.

The gunfighter's eyes were hidden behind round, dark glasses. Bright light tormented him ever more brutally as he grew older and it was getting worse with every passing day.

Morrow wore a plain, black cartridge belt and holster, the ivory-handled Colt on his right hip his only apparent vanity.

That morning he looked what he was . . . a dangerous man and one to step around.

Irritably, he slapped the bell a second time.

The sharp *ting!* echoed into silence.

"Is there anybody to home?" he called out.

Even to his own ears his voice sounded hollow, like a man shouting in a sepulcher.

Again there was no answer.

Morrow stepped away from the desk and went outside into the sun-dazzled street.

A little girl of about three years old toddled past. She wore a yellow dress that was grubby from play and carried a blackface rag doll in her arms. The child tripped and fell forward on her hands. She rose to her feet again and wiped her gritty palms on the yellow dress and picked up her doll.

The girl stopped and stared at Morrow with round eyes the color of hazelnuts.

Morrow ignored the child and led his horse, as tall and angular as himself, toward the sheriff's office.

To the north a golden light glimmered in the

clouds but there was no sound of thunder. The wind had picked up and the skirts of the women searching the rim flapped and fluttered around their legs, as though they'd taken a short flight around the ridge and had just landed again.

Morrow looped his horse to the hitching rail outside the sheriff's office and stepped onto the boardwalk, his big-roweled spurs ringing.

He opened the office door and went inside.

The office was a typical lawman's lair, with a desk and chair and a gun rack on one wall, wanted dodgers on the other. Morrow's rawboned likeness was not among them.

He stood in the middle of the floor for a while and listened.

From beyond a door to his right he heard a steady *thwack . . . thwack . . . thwack . . .* and recognized it for what it was—the sound of a bullwhip cutting into a naked back.

A burlap sack, rolled shut, lay on the desk. Morrow crossed the floor and opened it up.

He looked inside, grabbed a handful of jewelry and smiled. His teeth were white under a mustache as carbon black as the hair that fell to his shoulders, each strand hanging straight and lank as wet string.

Morrow shook his head and his shaggy eyebrows pinched together.

Cheap baubles, as flashy, chintzy and worthless as the tinhorn who'd stolen them.

Was this all Hank Cobb had to show for the brilliant

scheme he'd concocted to drain a town dry, squeeze it until it coughed up the last buffalo nickel?

Morrow watched the jewelry cascade through his fingers and untidily onto the table.

Thwack . . . thwack . . . thwack . . .

The sound came from behind a door at the rear of the office that probably led to cells.

Morrow's boot heel crunched a garnet-and-silver brooch underfoot as he stepped to the door and opened it. Beyond was a barred, iron gate that stood ajar. Here the air was fetid, smelling of ancient vomit, piss and the faint, but unmistakable, smoky tang of blood.

His hand dropped to his gun as he pushed the iron door wide . . . and stepped into a scene from hell.

Mink Morrow had the professional gunfighter's ability to take in a scene at a glance.

To his right stood a couple of jail cells that looked out into a large, rectangular room, lit only by a small window in the far wall that cast a wash of dusty, gray light into the murk.

But what arrested Morrow's attention was the man, naked from the waist up, who hung from a beam by his wrists.

The man's back was cut to ribbons, white bone gleaming through scarlet runnels of blood. Near the man, at a distance of ten feet, a bullwhip snaking from his right hand stood . . . Satan himself.

* * *

A few silent seconds slipped past, broken only by the soft moan of the hanging man.

Then Hank Cobb ripped off the red devil mask he wore and said, "What the hell are you doing here?"

Cobb's face gleamed with sweat and spittle gathered at the corners of his mouth. His eyebrows crawled up his forehead like black caterpillars.

"Answer me, damn you," he said.

"That's a hell of a thing to do to a man," Morrow said.

"He a friend of your'n?" Cobb said.

"Never seen him before."

"Then what is he to you?"

"It's still a hell of a thing to do to a man."

Cobb motioned with the whip.

"I killed this sumbitch before, and I'll kill him again."

"Seems to me, you're halfway there," Morrow said.

"No, I ain't. Not by a long shot. He's gonna be a long time dying and this time I'll make sure."

Cobb's big-boned face hardened. "I'll ask you again, Mink, what the hell are you doing here?"

Morrow answered the question with one of his own.

"Where's the money from the Holy Rood bank?"

"Who told you about that?"

"A feller. The figure I heard was fifty thousand, give or take."

"And you want to elbow in on a share, huh? Is that why you're here?"

"That is my intention. If the story is true."

"Oh, the story is true enough. But the money's scattered all over the ridge behind the town. If you want a share, go grab yourself a sack and join the rest of the pickers up on the slope."

"So that's what all those people are doing," Morrow said. "How did the money get up there?"

Cobb again motioned with the whip.

"He did it."

Morrow smiled. "I won't ask his motive."

"Don't. It's none of your concern."

"So I can keep what I find. Is that the deal?"

"No. You bring the money to me and I decide what you keep. How much did you have in mind? And remember, for old time's sake only goes so far. I'm not in a giving mood today."

"Ten thousand."

Cobb grinned, an ugly twist of his lips.

"In your dreams, Mink. Ride the hell on out of here and do your begging somewhere else."

Cobb couldn't see Morrow's eyes behind the shaded windows of his dark glasses, couldn't read the man, and that irritated him.

He said, "Still can't stand the light, I see."

"It's getting worse. That's why I need the money. I reckon I'll retire, maybe open an eating house."

"When I count the money, it will be in sunlight," Cobb said, his grin still in place.

"Day or night, I can still throw faster iron than you, Hank."

"Big talk from a blind man," Cobb said. "If we fight with revolvers, it will also be in sunlight, the brighter the better."

"I could drop you here, Hank," Morrow said. "Just draw and shoot. You understand?"

"But you won't, will you? Not so long as I'm your meal ticket."

Morrow's response died on his lips as a tall, lanky man wearing a worried frown and an old cavalry bandana around his neck stepped through the doorway. "Boss, we got trouble," he said.

Sudden alarm showed on Cobb's face. "On the ridge?"

"Hell no. Them folks are rabbits. It's that O'Brien ranny and another feller. They got Shannon outside, tied to his hoss." He grinned. "Ol' Shel looks all used up, like he done a day's work for the first time in his life."

It didn't take long for Cobb to think that through and guess at the implications.

"Walsh, go get Lee Dorian off the ridge and round up Ed Bowen. Then you three join me in the street," he said.

"That'll only leave Kane up there," the man called Walsh said.

"Kane can handle it. Now go do what I told you."

After Walsh left, Cobb said to Morrow, "You heading for the ridge or are you riding?"

Morrow smiled. "I'll stick with you, Hank, and

impose on your generous nature, seeing as how we were friends once."

"We were never friends," Cobb said. "Drawing gun wages from the same rancher didn't make us compadres."

"Whatever you say, Hank," Morrow said. "Whatever you say."

Cobb took a Barlow from his pocket and opened the blade. He turned his head and looked at Morrow.

"I don't want to kill you, Mink," he said. "But don't push me too hard."

"I'll bear that in mind," Morrow said.

"And don't pin your hopes of hanging up your gun and buying that eating house on me," Cobb said. "Do that and you'll starve to death, I guarantee it."

Cobb reached up and the Barlow's keen blade slashed the ropes that held Wolfden. The man tumbled in a heap. His open mouth pressed into rough pine floor and saliva trickled from his lips.

"Earn your keep, Mink," Cobb said. "Help me drag this into the office."

"I'd say he's about gone," Morrow said.

"Hell, he ain't even half dead yet," Cobb said. "If he survived the grave, he'll survive a whipping long enough to have another."

Cobb shoved Wolfden onto his back and he and Morrow hauled the unconscious man into the sheriff's office.

They left a wide, snail track of blood on the floor behind him.

Cobb let go of the man's legs and Wolfden's boots thudded onto the timber.

"Cobb! Hank Cobb!"

Shawn O'Brien's voice came from the street.

"What the hell do you want?" Cobb yelled.

"You know what we want," Shawn called back. "We want Jasper Wolfden."

Cobb stepped to the window.

Walsh and Dorian were on the boardwalk on the opposite side of the street, working themselves into a position behind Shawn and the other man, a mouse-faced runt sitting a mule.

He beamed. Both his men had rifles and they knew how to use them.

"I'm coming out, O'Brien," Cobb yelled.

He smiled, his eyes calculating.

CHAPTER THIRTY

Hank Cobb stepped through the door onto the boardwalk, followed by Mink Morrow, who'd cleared his frockcoat from his gun.

Shawn's eyes were on the slope of the ridge above town where knots of people were bent over, as though they searched for something. A single rifleman kept a wary eye on them, like a prison guard over a chain gang.

He exchanged a puzzled glance with Ford Platt, who shrugged and shook his head.

Shawn was still in the saddle, but Shel Shannon stood in front of his horse, the rope around his neck attached to Platt's saddle horn.

Cobb glanced at Shannon, and then his eyes flicked to Shawn.

"What's your deal, O'Brien?" he said.

"It should be obvious even to you, Cobb," Shawn said. "Give me Wolfden and I'll return your village idiot."

"I'm sorry, boss," Shannon said, blinking. "I was took by surprise."

"He was took by surprise at your woman's place, Cobb," Shawn said. "That was a mite careless of you, leaving her around like that."

"He took Ruby too, boss," Shannon said. His tongue touched his bottom lip. "O'Brien had the drop on me and I couldn't stop him."

"Hell, the woman means nothing to me," Cobb said. "A belly-warmer on a cold night is all. Keep her and welcome."

"Well, what's your answer to my proposition?" Shawn said.

He had a tight knot in the pit of his belly. Where were the rest of Cobb's men?

Cobb rubbed his chin and stared across the street at the white-painted storefronts that stood silent and forlorn like a flock of hobbled geese.

"I'm studying on it," he said. "I'm a slow-considering man."

"Boss!" Shannon yelled, a squawk of shocked disbelief and fear. "O'Brien plans to kill me if you don't give him Wolfden."

"I said I'm studying on it, Shel," Cobb said. He tugged on his earlobe. "I'm trying to figure how much you mean to me. So far I'm telling myself that it ain't a whole lot."

"One way or the other, don't take too long, Cobb," Shawn said. "I'm not a patient man."

Shawn's eyes flicked to Morrow.

"You must be Mink Morrow," he said.

"I must be. And you're Shawn O'Brien," Morrow said.

"My brother talked about you," Shawn said.

"Jake?"

Morrow saw Shawn nod and said, "Is he still playing the piano?"

"Last I heard."

"He should. He has a rare gift."

"You taking a hand in this, Morrow?" Shawn said.

"I don't know yet. Like Hank, I'm a man who makes slow business decisions."

"But fast draws."

Morrow smiled and his glasses caught the sunlight and glittered.

"Did Jake tell you that?" he said.

"Him and others. When you make your decision, I hope you make the right one," Shawn said.

Like Morrow, he'd cleared his Colt and the gunman knew he wasn't dealing with a pushover. No brother of Jake O'Brien's could be a bargain.

"When I do, you'll be the first to know, O'Brien," he said.

Cobb didn't want Shawn O'Brien to follow his eyes, so he bowed his head as though the low sun troubled him and stole a quick, flickering glance at the street.

Good. His men were in position.

"I've made up my mind, O'Brien," he said.

Shawn was on edge and beside him Platt tensed, sudden alarm showing tight in his face.

"Let's hear it, Cobb," Shawn said.

Cobb drew and fired.

Shel Shannon stood still for a moment, and then stared at the red rose blossoming in the middle of his chest.

"Boss . . ." he said. "Boss . . . why?"

His made a sound as though he choked down a sob, then fell to the ground, his dead eyes wide open, still unbelieving.

"No deal, O'Brien," Cobb said.

Behind Shawn Winchesters racked and he knew the game was rigged and he'd been outsmarted.

He'd staked everything on Shannon, but the man had proven to be the joker in the pack and now Cobb lay down his cards and confirmed it.

"Hell, O'Brien, did you really think I'd dicker for a piece of worthless crap like Shel Shannon?" he said. "Did you figure to play me for a fool?"

A bitter taste in his mouth, Shawn said nothing.

Cobb gave an exaggerated shake of his head.

"Damn it, man, you're an even bigger idiot than Shannon was."

He looked beyond Shawn and said, "Walsh, Dorian, relieve these gentlemen of their guns. Bowen, keep them covered."

His eyes moved to Platt. "What the hell kind of little rat are you?"

Platt smiled and seemed almost relaxed. But he went for it.

His hand streaked under his coat, but the rifle muzzle shoved under his rib cage and the grinning face of the rifleman looking up at him, froze him in place.

"You're even more stupid than O'Brien," Cobb said as the little man was relieved of his gun.

"Seems like, doesn't it?" Platt said.

"Walsh, Dorian, now assist the gentlemen from their mounts," Cobb said.

Shawn and Platt were dragged from their saddles and Cobb motioned with his gun toward the office door.

"Get inside," he said.

"Still haven't made up your mind, huh?" Shawn said to Morrow.

"I'd say that right now you boys aren't doing so great. I reckon I'll stand pat," the gunfighter said. "You must've known trying to trade with Hank Cobb was a dunghill play."

"If we didn't know it before, we surely know it now," Shawn said.

Shawn O'Brien, a rifle prodding him, stepped into the sheriff's office and the sight of Jasper Wolfden bloody and unconscious on the floor hit him like a kick in the teeth.

He swung on Cobb, who had Platt by the back of the neck, pushing him inside.

"Did you do this, you damned animal?" Shawn said.

"Yeah, I sure did, and I ain't finished with him yet," Cobb said.

He looked pleased with himself, like the man who found the hundred dollar bill in a huckster's bar of soap.

The man's smug expression enraged Shawn and he made a lunge for Cobb's throat.

But before he'd taken a step Walsh's rifle butt thudded into the back of his neck and drove him to the floor.

Cobb straddled Shawn and lifted his shoulders from the floor by his coat lapels. "O'Brien, you escaped from my jail once before," he said. "You won't do it a second time."

Shawn tried to get his blurry eyes in focus, failed, but muttered, "You go to hell."

Cobb backhanded him viciously across the face and a lace of blood and saliva spurted from Shawn's mouth.

"I love cutting hard cases like you down to size." Cobb grinned. "Now grovel on the floor where you belong."

He let go of Shawn, then Ford Platt said, "Cobb, be warned—I'll live to see you hang."

"Mister, you won't live to see the moon come up tonight," Cobb said.

He turned to his gunmen. "Put these two in a cell." Then, with a gesture of the head toward Wolf-den, "After you've done that, mix up a bucket of salt and water and throw it on his back."

"And bring him inside?"

Dorian, slack jawed and slow of wit, had asked the obvious.

"Yeah. Put him in a cell with the other two for a spell. Let them enjoy his stink before I start on him again."

"Can I watch this time, boss, huh?" Dorian said.

"Sure, Lee, and you can even take a turn with the bullwhip." Cobb grinned, showing his teeth. "Cutting a man to doll rags tires a person, don't it?"

CHAPTER THIRTY-ONE

"Something's wrong," Sally Bailey said. "They should be back with Wolfden by now."

"They say Wolfden is a shifter," Hamp Sedley said. "Maybe he turned into a bird and flew away."

"They still should be back," Ruby said. "Even if Shawn O'Brien had to ride in with a parrot named Jasper on his shoulder."

"Hamp, what do we do?" Sally said, lines of worry showing on her face.

"Wait," Sedley said. "That's all we can do."

"Or we can go after them," Sally said.

Sedley's laugh knotted in his throat and came out as a strangled snort.

"Yeah, right, like two women are gonna take on Hank Cobb and his boys."

"There's three of us, Hamp," Ruby said.

Sedley rapidly shook his head. "Count me out, ladies. I'm not a gunfighter. Hell, I can't even shoot straight."

As though she hadn't heard, Sally said, "So we have three. Ruby—"

"Two!" Sedley yelled. "I ain't going!"

"Ruby, the whole town can't be bad," Sally said. "You've lived in Holy Rood. Can you think of anyone who might help us?"

To Sally's surprise, Ruby answered immediately.

"There's one man we can trust, or I think we can," she said. "He owns the livery stable in town."

"Is he good with a gun?" Sedley said.

"I don't know. But he was with Sherman in Atlanta."

"Well, that settles it," Sedley said. "I'll have no truck with a damned Yankee, especially one who marched with that black-hearted butcher Sherman."

"The man's name is Matt Rhodes, and back in the days when I was allowed to go out riding, he told me that Hank Cobb and his boys left him the hell alone." Ruby smiled. "Or words to that effect."

"Why did Cobb stay away from him, Ruby?" Sally said.

"Matt's good with horses. Apparently, that was reason enough."

"Ruby, you said we might be able to trust him. But if Shawn and Mr. Platt are in trouble, will he help us?"

"I don't know. He's pretty old."

Sedley yelped. "Oh, great, we go up against Hank Cobb, and maybe Mink Morrow, with a Yankee Methuselah. Sally, have you any other bright ideas?"

"Yes, before we leave I'll cast a spell that will protect us."

That statement went over like a dirty joke in a nunnery.

Sally saw the stunned faces of Ruby and Sedley staring at her as though she'd suddenly grown two heads.

Then she made matters worse.

"The only real witch who ever stepped foot in Holy Rood was me," she said.

Ruby and Sedley exchanged looks, but neither could come up with words.

Sally supplied them.

"When we lived on the Kansas plains my mother practiced the Wiccan arts and she taught me," she said. "She was a white witch, who cast spells to cure people of boils, the croup, morning sickness and a host of other ailments. She also worked magic to end droughts, storms, grasshoppers, blizzards, and all the rest of the calamities that beset sodbusters."

For a few moments Sally watched a hawk describe lazy circles above the tree canopy, and then said, "Thinking back, I don't know how well those spells worked. In any case, my father was a poet and poets don't make good farmers, no matter how many spells Ma cast."

Ruby was the first to recover from her shock. "So what happened? Why are you here?"

"After a few years, the isolation and loneliness of the plains got to my mother. She missed her native Ireland so much that one day Ma walked into the prairie during a snowstorm and screamed and screamed and screamed. I was lying in bed and heard her. Pa and I went out to get her, but by then it was too late."

Sally stared down at her folded hands and said, "Ma died a week later. Of exposure, the doctor said. But it was the loneliness of the Great Plains that killed her. My father buried her and then he saddled the plow mule and left."

"Left you all alone?" Ruby said.

"When I woke one morning, there was some money on my dresser and that was it. No note. Nothing. He just . . . left."

"You poor thing," Ruby said. "When was this?"

"Two years ago when I was fifteen. I was found wandering the prairie by a cavalry patrol, and I've been wandering ever since, taking any odd jobs I can find. Surviving, I guess."

Sedley smiled. "All right, can you cast a spell that will bring us twenty U.S. marshals into camp?"

"Or bring you a spine, Hamp," Ruby said. She pulled back her hair. "Or bring me the ear that Hank Cobb took."

Disregarding the horrified look on Sedley's face, she said, "Makes it kinda personal, don't it, Hamp? Makes you want to kill the man who did that, huh? Or see him hung."

Ruby smiled at Sally. "Cast your spells, honey, but

make them fast. The longer we sit talking, the more daylight we'll lose."

"Now see here," Sedley said. "I've listened to all the nonsense about witches and ha'ants an' sich I can stand for one day. We set tight right here for a few days until O'Brien and them get back."

"He's not coming back, on his own that is," Ruby said. "We've got to help him. And besides, if we stay here, what do we do for food? Hell, you and Sally are starving as it is."

"If we're dead, we won't need food because that's what we'll be if we show face in Holy Rood," Sedley said. "We'll get gunned down in the street—and that's a natural fact as ever was."

He jabbed a finger at Ruby. "Get it through your head, lady, when Hamp Sedley says a thing he means it. And the thing he's saying right now is that he's staying put right here until O'Brien gets back. I'll wait two whole days. Then, if he don't show, I'm lighting a shuck for Silver Reef."

Sedley sat back, a smug smile on his face, as though he'd fairly stated his case and there could be no more argument.

But Ruby stared at him, blinked once or twice, and then came up with a mighty powerful argument.

She tugged open her drawstring purse, produced a Sharps .32 caliber pepperbox revolver, pointed the gun at Hamp's face and said, "Saddle the horse and get ready to leave. And be warned, Hamp—unlike you, I generally hit what I aim at."

Sedley stared into the stinger's four muzzles, as black and merciless as spider eyes, and said, "Ruby, do you know what you're doing?"

"Yes, Hamp, I do. I'm planning to save Shawn O'Brien's life if it can be done. And I'm planning to scatter your brains if you say it can't."

"All right, Ruby, I won't say it can't be done, but I can sure as hell think it."

"We have to try, Hamp," Ruby said. "If it was you, Shawn would do everything he could to save your life, even though you're a crooked gambler and probably should've been hung a long time ago."

"You sure don't take it easy on a man, Ruby. Do you?"

"Why should I? Apart from Shawn, I never met a man yet who took it easy on me."

Sally stepped out of the pines and said, "I've implored Diana, the moon goddess, for her protection. If she heard me, she will protect us day and night."

Sedley's face drained of expression and his shoulders slumped.

"Oh, good," he said. "Now I feel much better."

"Saddle the damned horse, Hamp," Ruby said.

* * *

It was midafternoon when Hamp Sedley and the two women made their way from the trees onto the wagon road.

Sally and Ruby rode double on the horse and Sedley walked, much against his will, declaring that the women should take turns walking.

But Ruby wouldn't hear of it, and Sedley trudged along the hot, dusty trail with ill grace, cursing under his breath.

For a while there was no sound but the wind in the pines and the endless squabbles of jays and squirrels that never seem to agree about anything. The sunbaked land shimmered and the back of Sedley's coat was dark with sweat.

"You know what?" he said, looking up at Ruby.

"No, but I'm sure you'll tell me," the woman said.

"I'm giving odds that we don't last an hour in Holy Rood."

"I wouldn't take any odds on that, gambling man," Ruby said.

Sedley's eyebrows drew together, signaling his worry.

"How come?" he said.

"We'll be putting a lot of trust in Matt Rhodes, and I hardly know the man," Ruby said.

"Hell, now you tell me," Sedley said. "Why did I let myself get talked into this?"

"Because you dug deep, Hamp, and found what was left of your manhood," Ruby said.

"Well, thank you," Sedley said. "I do appreciate that."

"You're welcome," Ruby said.

"You two are worse than the jays," Sally said. She closed her eyes and intoned:

> *Goddess shining bright,*
> *Protect us all by day and night.*

"I'll remember to say that when Hank Cobb's putting a rope around my neck," Sedley said.

He kicked a rock that skittered over the road ahead of him and ended up in the brush where the insects made their small music.

When they saw that the skulls had been taken from the posts and left by the side of the road, Sally declared this an excellent sign and that surely it proved that the moon goddess had heard her plea.

Ruby and Sedley stayed silent, though the woman managed a half-hearted nod and smile that seemed to please Sally, because she clapped her hands and said, "Now I have a good feeling about this."

As soon as Holy Rood appeared in the distance through the heat haze, Ruby said that they should leave the wagon road and strike out across country.

"It's just possible that Hank has a man watching the road," she said.

Sedley led the horse into a sandy, open country studded with mesquite and bunch grass. Here and there stunted juniper and piñon struggled to survive and by using the cover of the trees and a few scattered boulders, Sedley told the women that they'd manage to stay hidden from sight.

"Well, more or less," he said.

The livery stable, unlike every other building in town, was not painted white. Its warped, rough-cut timbers had weathered to a silvery gray and the entire structure showed a dramatic tilt to the left, a legacy of the prevailing winter winds that spiked across the flat.

Sally, with young sight, was the first to make out the crowd of people on the slope of the ridge above town.

Sedley removed his hat and held it up against the sun to shade his eyes.

After a while, he said, "Hell, it looks like they're picking berries."

"No berries grow on the slope, only thornbush and cactus," Ruby said. "They're up to something else, and it could have something to do with Shawn O'Brien."

"Then what are they doing?" Sedley said. "Searching for him . . . or his body?"

"No, bent over like that, I think they're looking

for something else," Sally said. "A man's body would be easy to find."

"Well, no matter what it is, we'd better get into the livery stable," Ruby said. "We're sure to be spotted if we stand around out here gawking."

They went in through the empty shacks behind the livery and Ruby led them to a back door.

It was locked.

"Then I guess we go round front," Sedley said.

"In full view of the whole town?" Ruby said.

"The whole town's up on the ridge, looks like," Sedley said.

"Maybe so, but we can't take a chance on being seen," Ruby said. "Hamp, kick the damned door down."

"Ruby . . . this is private property," Sedley said.

"We could get shot at any minute," the woman said. "Do you care?"

Sedley stared at Ruby for a moment, and then said, "I guess not."

He raised his booted foot and slammed it into the door near the lock. The door shuddered and there was a sound of splintering wood, but it remained shut.

Sedley tried again. This time the door slammed open, ripped away from its top hinge and hung ajar.

There was just enough space to allow a bearded, hard-eyed rifleman to step through.

He pointed his Winchester at Sedley, and said, "What the hell did you do that fer? I warn you, boy, there's gonna be shooting going on around here in a New York minute."

"Matt, it's me, Ruby. Surely you remember."

Rhodes peered at the woman, and then said, "Sure, I remember you, but you ain't kept a hoss here in quite a spell." He motioned to Sedley with the rifle muzzle. "Why you keepin' such low company?"

"I'm sorry about the door, Matt, but we're desperate," Ruby said. "We need your help." She wrung her hands and then said, "It's a matter of life or death."

Rhodes considered that, but judging by the pained expression on his face he obviously didn't fancy its implications.

He narrowed his eyes and said, "So, what kind of he'p?"

"I'll tell you inside, Matt," Ruby said.

"You'll tell me out here or you won't tell me at all," Rhodes said.

The grim, cranky old man was nobody's idea of a doting grandfather . . . or any kind of grandfather.

Short, shabby and gaunt, his hollow eyes and high, sunken cheekbones gave him the appearance of a skull. His voice was shrill and unpleasant, as though his every word was overgrown with thorns. When he spoke, his darting black eyes followed the movement of others like a suspicious raven.

Matt Rhodes looked exactly what he was, a dried-out, bitter husk of a man who'd fought one war too many.

"Matt," Ruby said, "this is about Hank Cobb."

Rhodes considered that for a moment, and then said, "State your intentions."

"Our intention is that you and other decent men in this town give us the help we need," Sedley said. "But if you're a frightened sheep like the rest of them, then tell us and we'll be on our way. And be damned to ye for a yellow-bellied Yankee."

"I've killed men for less than that," Rhodes said. His eyes glittered.

Sedley pushed his coat away from his holstered gun.

"You ain't marching through Georgia now, old man. So if you've a mind to get your work in, have at it."

"Hamp, let it go," Ruby said. She glared at Rhodes. "I'm sorry to have troubled you." She opened her purse. "How much to repair the door?"

"I got no liking for Hank Cobb," Rhodes said.

"Then you'll help us?" Ruby said.

"I didn't say that, but come inside," Rhodes said. He looked at Sedley with open dislike. "You can bring the Reb with you."

CHAPTER THIRTY-TWO

Mink Morrow stepped into the sheriff's office.

Hank Cobb sat at his desk and Ed Bowen, a surly gun hand out of the Nevada Territory, stood at the window drinking coffee.

Cobb looked up when Morrow entered and his expression soured.

"What the hell do you want?" he said. "There ain't no money yet."

Morrow let his eyes slowly adjust from the sunlight outside to the comparative dimness of the office. For the first time ever he'd been completely blind for a few seconds and the implication of that troubled him deeply.

"And a big howdy to you too, Hank," he said. "I've been up on the ridge, talking to the feller you have on guard up there."

"Jonas Kane ain't a talking man," Cobb said.

"He talked enough. Told me them town folks of

your'n ain't gathering much money. He reckons they're filling their own pockets."

Cobb smiled and sat back in his chair. He'd been cleaning his fingernails with a cow horn letter opener that he now tossed on the desk.

"We'll search them when they get down," he said.

"When?"

"Hell, I don't know. When it gets too dark to see, I reckon."

"You're mighty thin on the ground, Hank," Morrow said.

"What's that supposed to mean?"

"Way I figure it, you've only got four of your boys left."

"It's enough."

"Not if the fine citizens of Holy Rood decide to think otherwise."

"If that happens, you'll throw in with us, Mink. You need the money for your eating house. Blind gunfighters don't last long."

Bowen laughed. "That was funny, boss," he said. "Blind gunfighters don't last long . . . hah!"

"Yeah, Hank, you're a laugh a minute," Morrow said.

He stepped to the stove and hefted the coffeepot.

"Make a joke about this—Kane says he reckons most of the money is lost. He says it's like looking for a needle in a haystack up there."

"I'll find it. Might take another day or two, but I'll get back most of it."

"And then?"

Cobb crossed his arms and grinned. "Then we burn this burg to the ground and skedaddle."

"Who's *we*?"

"Me and the boys and maybe you. That is, if you play your cards right."

Morrow poured coffee into a cup. He took a sip and immediately steamed up his dark glasses, blurring his vision. Cobb didn't appear to have noticed and he laid down the cup on the edge of the desk.

"You're the dealer, Hank," he said. "What cards?"

"For starters, get up on the ridge with Kane here and make sure the rubes are honestly searching for my money," Cobb said. "Anybody who refuses to work or is putting coin in his pocket, shoot him." He grinned. "Or her, as the case may be."

"Anything else?" Morrow said.

Outside the wind picked up again and there was a sound of distant thunder.

Cobb rose to his feet and adjusted his gun belt.

"There will be two executions tonight," he said. "While my money is still scattered all over the ridge, I want the whole town to attend. Keep them honest, like."

"The whole town? I guess that includes me," Morrow said.

"Especially you, Mink. You'll be my assistant."

"What's the contraption outside the church?"

Morrow said. "I saw a man's body lying near the thing and he didn't have a head."

Cobb's grin and the way he lifted himself onto his toes conveyed a warped sense of pride.

"The French call it a guillotine," he said.

He waited for Morrow to speak, wanting to draw out the moment.

"What the hell does it do?" the gunfighter said.

"You saw the dead man. Do you mean you don't know?"

"I mean I don't know, otherwise I wouldn't have asked."

"It cuts heads off, of course," Cobb said. "Clean as a whistle." Then, "You'll see it in operation come dark."

"That's not my way," Morrow said.

Cobb nodded. Thunder boomed. Closer.

"Make it your way, Mink."

"And if I don't?"

Cobb smiled. "No cuttee . . . no monee. You catch my drift?"

Morrow stared into Cobb's eyes as though trying to find an answer to the question he hadn't yet asked.

"Why are you doing this, Hank?" he said finally. "Take the money you have and get out of here. Maybe you should head east, see the sights."

For a moment Morrow thought Cobb was considering that, but the man's reply crushed him.

"It ain't about money, Mink. Well, it ain't all

about money," he said. "It's about power. You any idea what it's like to have power?"

Morrow nodded and tapped his Colt. "Yeah, I cottoned onto the idea the first time I strapped on this gun."

Cobb stepped to the window and Ed Bowen moved aside.

"Thunderstorm coming," Cobb said, looking at the sky. "Blowing down from the north. Big mountains up that way."

Cobb was silent for a while, and then said, "For a time, way back when, I guess I was exactly what they said I was—a cheap tinhorn who rolled drunks for a living. Granted, now and again I'd make some extry cash on the side, like when a woman would pay me to stick the shiv into her old man or a rooster would give me fifty dollars to do the same thing to a love rival or some such."

He turned his back to the window, his head and shoulders outlined against a sky the color of rusted gunmetal.

"Pretty soon the word got around about who I was and how I made my living, and I got run out of town after town by the law the minute I stepped foot inside the city limits," Cobb said. "'We don't want your kind here,'" they'd say. 'Now you git and don't come back.'"

Cobb gave up trying to establish eye contact with Morrow, guarded behind his dark glasses and shrugged. "You see, I was pegged as a lowlife and an undesirable. Where was the power in that?"

"Count your money, Hank," Morrow said. "Money is power."

"Yeah, if you're like that Vanderbilt feller and have millions," Cobb said. "But I found real power right here in Holy Rood . . . the power over people. I'm a king, dammit, and all of a sudden I think I don't want to let it go."

"You mean you're thinking about staying here?"

"That's what I mean. I'm considering it. Remain where I'm at and continue to rule this town. I can pass laws, impose taxes, order executions. Do what any king does."

Cobb grinned. "It's like them fellers, Wild Bill Hickok was one, who smoke opium. One taste of it and you never want to let it go. Well, I've had more than a taste, of power that is, and I've begun to think that I don't want to give it up."

"The law will catch up to you sooner or later," Morrow said. "You must know that."

"The law?" Cobb snorted his amusement. "All the law cares about is that Holy Rood is a peaceful town, a burg where outlaws and low persons are not tolerated and get short shrift. The law doesn't care if a whore burns or a goldbrick artist is"—he drew his forefinger across his throat—"topped. So long as my town obeys the law, the law will leave me alone."

"But you've already made a big mistake, Hank, and you don't even know it," Morrow said.

Cobb grinned. "You're right. I'm damned if I can see it."

Morrow stepped to the desk and picked up a thin gold bracelet.

"Look at this, Hank. You've taken their valuables down to the women's wedding rings," he said. "Now you're grabbing all the money they put in the bank."

"So?" Cobb said. "What's your gripe?"

"Hank, you only have power over people when you don't take everything they have away from them. Take everything a man has, and he's free of you. It's only a matter of time until the folks up on the ridge realize this, and when they do, they'll come for you."

"Kill a few and they'll toe the line again," Cobb said. He waved a negligent hand. "They're sheep. They've proved that time and time again. Ain't that right, Ed?"

"Just like you say, boss," Bowen answered. "And sheep are bred to be fleeced. Everybody knows that."

Morrow glanced out the window where rain pattered on the panes. "Storm's almost here, Hank," he said. "It's coming down fast."

CHAPTER THIRTY-THREE

The air inside the livery stable was thick with the musky tang of horses and the wet grass smell of baled hay.

Above the door of Matt Rhodes's office hung an oval tintype of William Tecumseh Sherman in the dress uniform of a major general. A black mourning ribbon on his left arm was for Abraham Lincoln.

Hamp Sedley glanced at the image and made a face, but Ruby's warning glare kept him silent.

"If you're hungry I keep a pot of beef stew going in my office," Matt Rhodes said. "Back in the old days, drifting punchers would stop by for a bite, but it all ended when Hank Cobb took over the town."

"I could use some of that stew," Sedley said. "How about you, Sally?"

The girl nodded. "I'm sure sick of rabbit."

"Then he'p yourself, young lady," Rhodes said. "You too, Johnny Reb. Just be careful you don't choke on it."

After Sally followed Sedley into the small office, Rhodes's gaze flicked over the two dozen horses in the barn. Then, his face a grizzled blank, he said, "All right, let's hear it, Ruby."

The woman said, "A friend of mine came in to trade Shel Shannon—"

"Yeah, I know. Your friend tried to trade Shannon for Jasper Wolfden, him Cobb kilt but didn't bury deep enough," Rhodes said. "Trying to trade with Cobb was a dumb play."

Ruby opened her mouth to speak, but the old man cut her off.

"Shannon is dead," he said. "Hank Cobb gunned him. Then he took your friend prisoner, him and another feller."

"Are they still alive?" Ruby said.

"As far as I know," Rhodes said.

"Matt, you have to help us rescue them," Ruby said.

"That's a tall order, Ruby."

"You're our only hope."

A horse snorted and thumped its hoof on the timber floor. The tin rooster on the roof squeaked as the direction of the rising wind shifted and a suggestion of rain pattered on the roof.

Ruby waited for a few seconds longer than she should have for Rhodes to respond.

Finally, she said, "Matt, surely there are other men in town that'll join us to get rid of Hank Cobb," she said.

"Maybe," Rhodes said. He looked through the office window and stared at Sedley who was spooning stew into his mouth. "I don't like that feller," he said.

"Matt . . . please."

The old man nodded.

"All right, Ruby, I can think of a couple. But you got to keep in mind that Holy Rood is a town like no other. I've been in a heap o' wild cow towns, livened up by buffalo hunters, railroad construction laborers, freighters, cowboys and more riff-raff and assorted hard cases than you could shake a stick at. But the folks who lived in those towns were just as tough, just as wild as them I've mentioned, and they hired fighting lawmen to keep the peace and backed them to the hilt."

Rhodes shrugged. "Holy Rood was never like that. It's always been a gutless place. Not long before Cobb and me arrived, the town stood back and let an outlaw gang hang their sheriff, a young feller by the name of Bob Wickham. By all accounts he was a good man. I think Cobb got wind of the hanging and that's why he chose Holy Rood as his place of residence. Probably reckoned he could do anything he wanted in this town."

Sedley had finished eating and he listened intently to what the old man was saying. "And he's sure done anything he wanted," he said.

Rhodes nodded. "First sensible thing I've heard you say, Reb."

"How does a town get to be like this one?" Ruby said. "How can it exist?"

"I don't know," Rhodes said. "A bunch of gutless folks happening to congregate in one place can only be called a freak of nature."

"And such a gathering attracts predators like Hank Cobb and his ilk," Sally said.

"You got that right, young lady," Rhodes said.

Ruby gave Rhodes a pained stare.

"Is there nobody?"

Rhodes took his time to answer, and then he said, "Ruby, I'll he'p you any way I can, short of meeting Hank Cobb gun-to-gun in the street. And there's Will Granger the blacksmith. Like me, Cobb leaves him alone, though he pays him to shackle prisoners. Will is a strong man who hates what this town has become. He just might throw in with us."

"Can you bring him here, Matt?" Ruby said.

Thunder rumbled overhead and rain slanted across the open door of the livery.

Rhodes nodded. "You stay here. I'll go talk with Will."

Lightning filled the stable with shimmering light and then thunder banged again. The horses whinnied and kicked at their stalls.

Rhodes took a yellow slicker from a hook and shrugged into it.

"I can't give any guarantees," he said, picking up his rifle. "If Will says no, then there's an end to it as far as I'm concerned."

He stepped to the door and turned his head, his eyes searching the ridge.

"Cobb's up there, keeping the folks at work," he said.

The old man stepped into the street then stopped as lightning flashed, followed almost immediately by a roar of thunder.

"These summer storms can kill folks," Rhodes said, water sluicing off the brim of his hat. "It must be hell up there on the ridge."

CHAPTER THIRTY-FOUR

"He's done for, Shawn, leave him be," Ford Platt said.

"He's still breathing, and that means he isn't dead yet," Shawn O'Brien said.

"No, but he will be soon. What's left of him," Platt said.

Jasper Wolfden lay facedown on the filthy cell bunk, his back a nightmare of shredded skin, gleaming bone and dry, crusted blood. His breathing was shallow and came and went, a bad sign.

"Best think about getting out of here," Platt said. "We can't fret over a dead man."

Shawn nodded. "Last time I was here I was saved by a miracle I called Sammy. I reckon a man is allowed only one miracle in his life."

He looked at Platt, then, his voice toneless, he said, "Are we beat, Ford? Is it over?"

"Maybe not. I've got another miracle up my sleeve."

The defeat drained out of Shawn's face and he grinned from ear to ear.

"Damn right you have!" he said. "I'd forgotten about your sneaky gun."

"Two shots," Platt said. "We're not exactly an army."

"Two bullets are enough if a man can place them right."

"You want the Remington, don't you?"

"I didn't say that."

"You think maybe you can shoot better than me?"

"I didn't say that either."

Platt flexed his hand and the derringer sprang into his palm.

"I think you can," he said. "Take it."

"Putting a lot of faith in me, aren't you, Ford?" Shawn said.

"You could say that. Hell, I'm putting my life in your hands and the peashooter," Platt said.

Shawn took the Remington.

"Let's hope your faith in me and the gun is justified," he said.

"And let's hope you're within kissin' distance of Cobb when you decide to touch that thing off," Platt said.

* * *

Thunder rocked the sheriff's office and the tiny cell window glared with sizzling light that briefly seared white as iron in the gloom.

Jasper Wolfden groaned and muttered something that Shawn and Platt didn't understand.

"He's far gone," Platt said. "He isn't coming back, not after the beating he took."

"Seems like," Shawn said.

"Another whipping will kill him for sure."

Shawn nodded. He had nothing to say. Platt had stated the obvious.

"What time is it, you reckon?" the little man said.

The cell window showed only a rectangle of bruised cloud.

"Hard to say," Shawn said. "Past noon, I reckon."

"Listen to that damned rain," Platt said.

"Yeah, it's sure coming down," Shawn said.

"You think Cobb pulled his people off the ridge?"

"I doubt it. If I was him, I'd figure that the water running off the slope would wash everything down to the flat."

"Coin?"

"Why not? I reckon that by this time the ridge is shedding water like a waterfall. Everything will end up at the bottom, rocks, gravel . . . and money."

"Then this storm was lucky for Cobb, huh?" Platt said.

"That would be my guess," Shawn said.

He brought the derringer out of his coat pocket and hefted the little pistol in the palm of his hand.

"You ever shoot this piece, Ford?"

"Once. The day I bought it."

"How did it do?"

"Well, the gunsmith who made the harness for me set up a whiskey bottle at ten yards and told me to aim, then cut loose."

"And what happened?"

"For all I know the whiskey bottle is still standing there."

"Where did your shots go? Low, high, left or right?"

"I have no idea."

"Maybe ten yards was pushing it."

"Like you say, maybe. If you ask me, two yards is pushing it."

Shawn nodded. "Well, it's a belly gun right enough."

"That's what it is," Platt said. "So keep it in mind."

Shawn dropped the Remington back into his pocket.

"Wish it was a .45," he said. "With a ten-inch barrel."

"If wishes were fishes poor men would dine," Platt said. "Me, I wish it was a mountain howitzer. Then maybe we'd have a chance of shooting our way out of here."

"It's better than nothing," Shawn said.

Platt nodded. "Better than a rock anyhow."

The lightning-stabbed clouds bled a heavier, hammering rain that marched across the roof like an advancing army. The wind screamed and pounded at the walls, demanding to be let inside where it could continue its mischief.

Raising his voice above the din of the storm, Platt said, "What are you thinking about, big man?"

"Huh?" Shawn said, blinking.

"You've been staring at the window for the past ten minutes like a man in a trance," Platt said. "You thinking about tonight?"

Shawn shook his head. "No. Nothing like that."

"Then what?" Platt said. "I'm an inquisitive man."

"You'll think me strange, Ford."

"Hell, I think the whole world and everybody in it is strange," Platt said.

Shawn glanced at the window, then said, "I was remembering that a week after I laid my wife to rest, I buried her father. It was on a day like this, dark with lightning in the sky. Later, the local folks called it the thunderstorm of the century."

"Sorry about your wife, and her pa," Platt said.

"Well, his heart was weak and he'd just gone through a terrible ordeal," Shawn said. "I guess it was just too much for him."

"Man can die of a broken heart," Platt said.

Shawn nodded. "Sir James's doctor said that very thing. It didn't help much."

"I didn't mean to—"

Platt broke off his words as the iron door to the room swung open and clashed against the wall.

Two men stepped through.

One was the town blacksmith, shackles in his hands and a heavy hammer stuck into the pocket of his leather apron.

The other was Ed Bowen. He was armed with a Greener scattergun and a heavy revolver buckled around his waist.

"All right, O'Brien," Bowen said, "you know the drill. Granger here will shackle you for your execution."

"Now?" Platt said. "Early ain't it?"

"Not now," Bowen said. "You'll die later, after sunset."

The gunfighter's face hardened. "Don't ask me any more questions, bub. You may not like the answers."

He turned to the blacksmith. "Let them out." And then, "After the chains are in place, only one knee, remember. But make it real good."

Granger nodded. His face was ashen, like a man who'd just been handed down a death sentence by a hanging judge.

Shawn studied Bowen, weighing his chances.

The man was alert, as tense as a coiled spring, his hard eyes missing nothing.

Shawn knew that the gunfighter would not let him close, and at any distance a .41 caliber derringer was a mighty uncertain thing.

He could get near enough to shoot the blacksmith, of course, but what good would that do? Bowen would kill him a split second later.

Exchanging one dead blacksmith for one of Colonel Shamus O'Brien's finest sons was no kind of bargain.

"Granger, let 'em out," Bowen said. He passed the blacksmith the keys and then his eyes flicked to Shawn. "Any fancy moves from you or the runt and I'll kill you. Do you savvy that?"

"Whatever you say," Shawn said. "You're the one holding the Greener."

"And it's both wife and child to me," Bowen said.

Granger opened the cell door and Shawn and Platt stepped into the room. Thunder boomed and the racketing rain was relentless.

"What about him?" Granger said, nodding to Wolfden.

"Leave him be for now," Bowen said. "Hank will deal with him later, after these two are hung."

As the blacksmith shackled his feet, Shawn noticed that Bowen was never still. The gunfighter prowled constantly back and forth across the floor like a restless panther, his eyes never focusing on one thing for long.

He'd be a hard man to surprise. A hard man to kill.

But before the manacles clamped around his wrists, Shawn knew he'd have to try.

Then Ed Bowen's boredom saved him.

"Only the legs, leave the hands free, Granger, or we'll be here all damned day," he said.

"Then I'm done," the blacksmith said. "They're chained up good."

"All right, then use your hammer and smash a knee on each of them," Bowen said. "Hank says left or right, it doesn't matter to him."

He smiled at Shawn. "A broken knee is the price you pay for escaping the last time, O'Brien. This time you'll be thankful to stay right where you're at without moving. A busted knee pains a man something terrible."

Bowen nodded to Granger. "O'Brien first. Get him on his back and then use the hammer." He smiled. "Make sure the knee is smashed real good, Granger. Hank wants to drag these two to the gallows screaming like pigs. Folks enjoy that kind of stuff at an execution."

The big blacksmith hesitated and the muscles of his jaws bunched.

"I can't do that to a man," he said. "I won't treat him like an animal come to slaughter."

"Damn you, get it done," Bowen said, his voice rising to an enraged shriek. "If you don't, you'll die alongside of them."

Granger threw down the hammer. It skidded across the floor and thudded into Bowen's left boot.

"Do it yourself, Bowen," he said. "I'll have no truck with this."

The gunfighter's lips peeled back in a vicious snarl and he kicked the hammer back in the direction of the blacksmith.

"Damn you, pick that up and cripple O'Brien or I'll cut you in half," he said, the muzzles of the shotgun lining up on Granger's belly.

"Go to hell," the blacksmith said.

At night, a cougar scream will wake a sleeping man and still the breath in his chest. He'll bolt upright in his blankets and his eyes will reach into the darkness as he grabs for his revolver. . . .

It was such a scream that froze Ed Bowen into an immobile statue.

But only for a moment . . .

Jasper Wolfden, the terrible scream still on his lips, was almost on top of him when the gunfighter swung his shotgun and cut loose with both barrels.

The buckshot ripped into Wolfden's belly, inflicting appalling damage, but the man hardly slowed.

He reached out, grabbed Bowen in a deadly embrace, and his bared white teeth found the man's throat . . . and he bit down hard . . . like a ravenous shark.

The gunfighter's terrified shriek bubbled into bloody silence as his throat was ripped out and the dripping meat hung from Wolfden's scarlet jaws.

Ed Bowen died quickly, with no real understanding of the terrible manner of his death.

And when Wolfden opened his arms and let the man's body go, Bowen was dead when he hit the floor and would never find an answer to the mystery of how he died.

Wolfden turned to Shawn and the others. His mouth opened and Bowen's throat fell from his gory jaws.

"Jasper . . ." Shawn said. Horrified, he could find no other words.

His belly cut wide open so that the blue entrails trailed, Wolfden took a shuffling step, then another.

His bloody face so contorted that he was barely recognizable, he gasped, "Pain . . . Shawn . . ."

Wolfden stretched out his hands, pleading. His eyes were dying.

"For God's sake, Shawn," Platt said.

Like a man waking from a nightmare, Shawn looked haunted.

Then, moving like an automaton, he took the derringer from his pocket, two-handed the little pistol to eye level and fired.

Wolfden took the bullet in the middle of his forehead, yet the man had time to smile before he pitched forward onto his face and lay still.

The racketing resonance of the shot rang around the room and Shawn's hand dropped to his side, the smoking Remington still in his grasp.

CHAPTER THIRTY-FIVE

Hank Cobb stepped into the path of a gray-haired man who was fleeing the storm-torn ridge with the other townspeople.

"You, git back to work," Cobb yelled, grabbing the man's arm.

"Go to hell!" the man yelled. Thin, wet hair fell over his eyes and his hands were streaked with mud. "We can die up here!"

"Damn you, get back there," Cobb shrieked.

Lightning scrawled across the black sky like the signature of a demented god. Then thunder cracked, as though the entire world was splitting apart.

The man brushed past Cobb and hurried away, slipping and sliding on the slick slope.

Cobb, his face dark with rage, reached under his jacket, drew his gun and put a bullet into the man's back.

Hit hard, the gray-haired man threw up his arms

and fell forward. He thudded onto the muddy, rain-lashed ground and didn't move.

But the exodus from the ridge didn't stop. Dozens of people had already reached the flat and ran for their homes, heads bent against the driving wind and downpour.

Cobb fired into the air and yelled frantically at the remaining searchers to get back to work. But none heeded him, and soon the slope was deserted but for him, his remaining three gunmen and Mink Morrow.

"You can't kill 'em all, Hank," Morrow said. Rain ran off the brim of his hat and beaded on his dark glasses.

"Damn them all, I'll force them back to work once this storm passes," Cobb said.

Morrow shook his head. "It's over, Hank. After today they won't want you as king any longer."

His face stiff, Cobb turned his head and yelled, "Hey, Lee, how much you reckon we've got?"

Dorian, a vicious killer but slow of thought, called back, "I don't know, boss."

His teeth gritted, Cobb yelled, "Walsh, Kane, bring me the damned sacks!"

"Only three sacks, boss," Jonas Kane said. He and Dorian laid them at Cobb's feet. "Them folks slowed up considerable when the storm hit."

Cobb opened them up one by one, his face grimmer with each sack he inspected.

"How much, Hank?" Morrow said.

"About a tenth of it," Cobb said. "Maybe five thousand dollars in gold and silver and maybe less." He looked at Morrow and his rain-streaked face glimmered white as lighting flashed. "They were filling their own pockets, damn them."

"You forced them onto the ridge at gunpoint, Hank," Morrow said. "They weren't trying to find gold for you."

"Damn their eyes. Next time I'll drag them out of their houses and make them try." Cobb's smile was twisted and unpleasant. "Try or die, that's what I'll tell them."

He turned to his gunmen. "We'll head back to the sheriff's office until this confounded storm blows over."

"Count your money, Hank, then get the hell out of here," Morrow said.

"And what about your cut, Mink?" Cobb raised a hand. "Don't answer that, because there ain't gonna to be a cut. You're the one who should be riding."

"I don't like you, Hank," Morrow said. "And I never did."

"Well, don't that break my heart," Cobb said. He reached inside a sack, and then spun a silver dollar at Morrow. "There, you got your share, so now you can beat it."

Morrow let the dollar drop at his feet. The torrential rain fell around him.

Cobb and his three gunmen stared at Morrow, grinning, waiting for him to make his move.

His eyeglasses covered in raindrops, his gun under his slicker, Morrow knew well enough that now was not the time to make a play.

A few tense seconds passed. Cobb was ready, waiting, his Colt already in his hand.

Rain hissed like a baby dragon uncovered under a rock and thunder rumbled above the ridge.

Finally, Morrow said, "Not today, Hank."

"Now's as good a time as any Mink," Cobb said. "Why don't you—"

The flat statement of a gunshot from the street cut off Cobb in mid-sentence.

"What the hell!" Dorian said.

"O'Brien!" Cobb yelled. Then, to Morrow, "We'll settle this later."

He sprinted down the slope, his three gunmen at his heels.

Morrow hoped it was O'Brien who'd fired the shot. If it was, ol' Hank could be in a heap of trouble.

He picked up the sacks, tested their weight and grinned.

Yup, five thousand it was, enough to open a nice little restaurant with a pretty waitress. . . .

Maybe down Silver Reef way.

CHAPTER THIRTY-SIX

"Will Granger won't commit, one way or t'other," Matt Rhodes said. "He's a man who plays his cards mighty close to his chest."

Ruby looked like she'd been struck.

"Then he won't help us," she said.

"I didn't say that," Rhodes said. "I said Will wouldn't state his intentions."

The old man's words hung in silence for long moments. Then Hamp Sedley surprised everyone.

"All right, we'll do it ourselves," he said.

Ruby and Sally Bailey stared at the man in open-mouthed shock.

"Well look who just grew a backbone," Ruby said.

"Don't read too much into it," Sedley said. "I just want this damned thing over with."

"I'm with you there, Reb," Rhodes said. "So we push this thing, and there's not much time to be lost."

Three blank faces looked at the old man and he

said, "Will told me he was just about to head for the sheriff's office to shackle your friends for their execution. We'll go over there right now and see how the pickle squirts."

"It's thin," Sedley said, "mighty thin. Suppose this Granger feller won't throw in with us, what then?"

"Then we'll be no better off than we are right now," Rhodes said.

"Or we could be dead," Sedley said. "Did the blacksmith say who'll be along of him?"

"He sure did, sonny. Feller by the name of Ed Bowen, a Texas gun who's faster an' two shades meaner than the devil hisself."

Ruby's breath exhaled in a rush and she frowned her uncertainty.

"Well, Hamp, you still got that backbone you found real sudden?"

Sedley's face was strangely calm, as was his voice.

"Kiss my ass, Ruby," he said. Then to Rhodes, "Ready to take a walk in the rain, Yankee?"

"Yeah, Reb, let's get 'er done."

"We're going with you," Sally said.

"The hell you are," Sedley said.

"The hell I am," Sally said, her determined little chin jutting.

"That goes for me as well," Ruby said.

"And I say you stay here," Sedley said. "Hell, me an' the Yank could be dead a couple of minutes from now."

"Then we'll pray over your broken, bleeding bodies," Ruby said.

"Ruby, I—"

Sedley didn't finish his sentence. A single gunshot from the ridge broke it off and put a period at the end.

"That's Cobb, I reckon," Rhodes said after a while.

"Sounds like he's busy killing folks," Sedley said. "So while he's occupied, let's go."

Lightning flared and there was no letup in the hammering rain that covered the street like a coat of mail.

"Hold on just a second," Rhodes said.

He stepped into his office and came out with a handful of shells he began to feed into his rifle.

"We might be outnumbered, but I don't want to be outgunned," Rhodes said.

Sedley's jaw hardened as his impatience grew.

"Hurry it up, for God's sake," he said.

Another shot, this time from the street.

"Now I'm ready," Rhodes said, holding the Winchester across his chest.

"Let's hope we're not too late," Sedley said. "That shot could have come from the sheriff's office."

He hurried past the old man into the pelting rain . . . and the others followed.

* * *

Like two runaway trains on the same track, Sedley and Cobb collided in the street.

The gambler was the first to recover from the surprise and fired first.

Any man who uses a gun is entitled to one lucky shot in his lifetime and Hamp Sedley was awarded his.

Despite the rain, despite the ashen-gray day and the frenzied flash of lightning, Sedley's bullet ran true and crashed into Cobb's left shoulder.

Cobb had never been shot before, and he shrieked his pain and outrage and went down on one knee, the corded muscle of his neck straining against the skin.

But now his men were firing.

Ruby fell under Lee Dorian's gun and Sedley, who was now shooting wild in Cobb's general direction, took a bullet that tore a chunk out of his left bicep.

Matt Rhodes worked his rifle well and stood his ground, but with old eyes, his shooting had little effect.

He was hit hard and thumped onto the street in a sitting position, blood pumping from his chest.

Sally ran around Sedley, flung her arms into the air and yelled,

> *"Moon goddess hear me well,*
> *thrust those demons back to hell!"*

"Are you crazy!" Sedley screamed.

He grabbed Sally by the arm, dragged her onto the boardwalk and forced her to lie flat on her stomach. Sedley threw himself on top of her. Then, holding the protesting girl down with his weight, he fed cartridges into his Colt, his trembling fingers dropping more than he loaded.

Ruby crawled through the mud of the street and pulled herself onto the boardwalk, bullets kicking around her, splintering wood.

"How bad are you hurt?" Sedley yelled.

"How the hell should I know?" Ruby said.

"Then lie down and stay down," Sedley said.

"What are you doing to that girl?" Ruby said.

"Lying on top of her. Hell, she was standing in the street trying to cast spells."

"Let me up," Sally yelled.

"Hamp, you're a damned pervert," Ruby said. "Let her go."

A trickle of blood ran from the corner of her mouth and her breathing came hard and fast.

Walsh and Kane edged closer to the boardwalk, firing as they came.

Bullets split the air around Sedley and the women, and wood chips flew into the air.

Sedley raised himself up and fired at the gunmen and they retreated a few steps. Neither of them was hit.

Rhodes was down with a fatal wound, but the old soldier had sand and he wasn't out of it.

He called to Cobb by name, and then threw the Winchester to his shoulder.

Rhodes fired and clipped a half-moon of flesh out of the top of Cobb's left ear.

Cobb reacted like a man who'd just been stung by a hornet.

He clapped a hand to his ear and his eyes widened as it came away bloody.

Screaming in rage, Cobb got to his feet and charged Rhodes.

The old man tried to lever his rifle again, but it was beyond his fading strength.

Cobb staggered to the Rhodes, shoved his gun into the old man's face and triggered a shot.

Blood and bone fanning from a black wound just under his right eye, Rhodes fell onto his back and lay still.

Revolver in hand, Hank Cobb, bent over and staggering, headed for the livery. Shot for the first time in his life, his scheme to become the king of Holy Rood in ruins, his only thought was escape.

Even when Sedley took a pot at him as he went by, and missed, Cobb didn't return fire or slow his pace.

His need for a horse was greater than his desire to kill a tinhorn gambler.

Behind Cobb a volley of gunfire rattled. Angry bullets whined around him and kicked up vees of mud at his feet.

He turned his head and his eyes popped, showing the whites.

At least a dozen men, firing an assortment of contraband weapons, were spread out across the street, firing as they came.

Walsh was down on all fours, coughing up black blood.

Beside him Jonas Kane was taking hits but still getting his work in, his face grim and determined.

After a quick, terrified glance at the oncoming townsmen, Lee Dorian took to his heels and ran after Cobb.

"Hold them off, Lee," Cobb yelled over his shoulder. "I'll saddle the horses."

Dorian was showing yellow, but he fought down his fear and took up a position in the stable doorway and fired his rifle at the men in the street.

"For God's sake hurry, boss," he shrieked. "I can't hold them for long."

A few of the townsmen hesitated and looked for cover, but most stood their ground and shot back at Dorian.

The gunman yelped as a bullet burned across his thigh, drawing blood.

"Boss—"

But Cobb, riding bareback on a rangy buckskin, galloped past him.

"Get your own damned horse," he yelled.

Then he was gone, spurring the buckskin along the

wagon road. Within moments, he vanished into the sheeting rain and lighting shimmered around him.

Dorian, knowing that he'd no time to bridle a mount, stepped out of the livery, threw down his rifle and then his holstered Colt.

He glanced at Jonas Kane dead on the ground and raised his hands as the townsmen got closer.

"Don't shoot! I'm out of it!" he screamed.

Then Lee Dorian, a man killer by trade, a woman killer by inclination, looked around at the men ringing him and saw his death in their faces.

He called out to one of the men by name.

"Luke, can you make this go away?"

The man called Luke shook his head, his eyes merciless.

And a dark, wet stain appeared in Dorian's crotch and spread down his legs.

"Damn you all . . . rabbits!" he yelled.

Guns roared.

Hit by bullets and buckshot, Dorian jerked this way and that like a puppet manipulated by a child, his body almost torn apart.

He dropped to the ground, twitching, and the man called Luke put the muzzle of his rifle between Dorian's eyes and fired.

CHAPTER THIRTY-SEVEN

Shawn O'Brien stood at the sheriff's office window and looked into the street.

"Hell, Shawn, you're not one to take a hand, are you?" Ford Platt said.

"Let the men of this town redeem themselves and find their self-respect," Shawn said. "Better this was their fight."

"Pity Cobb escaped though," Platt said.

"He was badly wounded, and the only place he can find a doctor is Silver Reef," Shawn said. "I'll go after him as soon as I've settled things here."

He watched the town undertaker and his assistants lay out the bodies of six men—two townsmen, three of Cobb's gun hands and the torn, bloody corpse of Jasper Wolfden.

The undertaker was a tall thin man wearing a black claw hammer coat and a top hat. He hopped around the bodies like a crow and pushed back the gawking crowd that had gathered.

"What are you going to do with these people?" Shawn said.

"Nothing," Platt said. "I can't arrest a whole town."

A black blowfly landed on his cheek and he brushed it away.

"My job isn't done until I kill or arrest Hank Cobb," Platt said. "That's why I'll be heading to Silver Reef with you."

"Then you'll need this."

Shawn passed the derringer to Platt, who dropped it into a pocket without comment.

The door opened and Hamp Sedley, a fat bandage on his upper arm, stepped inside.

"How is she?" Shawn said.

Dark shadows pooled in the hollows of the gambler's face.

"Ruby isn't going to make it, O'Brien," he said. "She's asking for you."

"Is Sally with her? And the doctor?" Shawn said.

"Yeah, Sally is with her, but the doctor left. A couple of men stopped bullets and he's attending to them."

"That damned pill roller left Ruby to die?" Platt said.

"He's an old man who did his best," Sedley said. "He can't raise the dead."

"I'll go see her," Shawn said.

* * *

The thunderstorm had passed, but the black and mustard sky had spitefully settled into a drizzle for the rest of the day. The air smelled of wet pine, streaked with the tang of gun smoke.

Ignoring a man who yelled after him demanding to know the whereabouts of his money, Shawn crossed the street and walked into the hotel.

The surly desk clerk recognized Shawn as the man who'd rescued Sally and caused all kinds of hell. But he was smart enough to confine himself to saying. "Room fourteen. Upstairs."

"Obliged," Shawn said.

The clerk didn't answer.

Ruby lay propped up with pillows in a brass bed. The ceiling was mirrored, a relic of Holy Rood's wilder days, and a crepe-draped portrait of the gallant Custer hung on one wall.

Ruby gestured to the mirror. "Made me feel right at home, didn't they?"

Shawn smiled. "How are you, Ruby?"

The woman was very pale and the blue death shadows had gathered under her eyes.

"Dying," she said. "I'm lung-shot, and I've seen enough lung-shot cowboys to know that there's no coming back from this."

She coughed and specks of red appeared on her white lips.

"Sally cast a spell on me," she said.

"It's a healing spell, Ruby," Sally said. "It will do you good."

"Is there anything I can do for you, Ruby?" Shawn said. "Just name it."

"Yes there is, handsome," the woman said.

Shawn sat on the bed and waited.

Ruby clutched his hand, then said, "Shawn, don't let them lay my bones to rest in this town. I hated the place and all it stood for, and if I'm buried here my soul will never be at peace."

"Ruby, you'll be just fine," Shawn said, smiling as he squeezed her hand.

"You know better than that," the woman said.

Ruby turned her face to the thin glow of the lighted lamp beside her bed and looked into Shawn's eyes.

"Promise me," she said.

Shawn talked around the sudden lump in his throat.

"Where?" he said.

"You'll take me there?"

"I swear it."

Ruby smiled. "Among the pines. I want to lie in my grave and hear the wind in the branches."

Much overcome, Shawn could only nod.

"No headstone. No cross. I don't want anyone to ever find me," Ruby said.

Sally bent her head and sobbed silently.

"Swear it again, Shawn," Ruby said.

Her voice was fading, softer now, like a faint summer breeze.

"I swear it," Shawn said. "I'll do exactly as you say."

Ruby smiled.

And a moment later she closed her eyes and all the life that was in her fled.

CHAPTER THIRTY-EIGHT

"Ruby is dead," Shawn said. He still felt the ghost of her hand in his. "She died well."

"I'm sorry to hear that," Ford Platt said. "She was a fine woman."

Shawn nodded. Said nothing.

Then, after a long silence, he said, "I promised Ruby that I'd bury her far from here, among the pines."

He hesitated again, and then said, "I told the undertaker to preserve her as best he could, and lay her in a sealed coffin."

Shawn turned to Platt, who sat at the sheriff's desk.

"Hell of a thing to tell a man, any man, even an undertaker," he said.

Platt, knowing that anything he said about Ruby would be inadequate, said, "Coffee's biled."

"Smelled it as soon as I came in," Shawn said. He managed a smile. "I could sure use a cup."

"And lookee," Platt said.

He held up a full sack of tobacco and papers.

"I know you're much addicted to the Texas habit," he said.

Shawn smiled. "And the New Mexico Territory habit."

"Wherever there are cowboys, huh?" Platt said, passing over the makings.

"And vaqueros," Shawn said.

He built a cigarette, lit it and inhaled deeply.

"Ahhh . . . I'd almost forgotten how good that is," he said, blue smoke trickling from his nostrils. "Now where is the coffee?"

Shawn was on his fourth cigarette and second cup of coffee when the door swung open and four men walked inside.

"Well, gentlemen, this looks like a delegation," Platt said.

A tall, thin man with salt-and-pepper hair and a spade-shaped beard that hung halfway down his chest acted as spokesman.

"Where is our money?" he said. His tone was brusque, his eyes unfriendly. "I'm the new marshal of Holy Rood, so speak up."

"Last I heard it was scattered all over the ridge," Shawn said.

"There were sacks up there with coin in them," the man said. "They've gone. Somebody took them."

"Who took them?" Platt said.

"That's what I'm asking you," the bearded man said.

"Maybe Hank Cobb ran off with the sacks," Shawn said.

"No, he didn't. We all saw him and the only thing he had in his hand was a gun."

"Then my next suspect would be Mink Morrow," Shawn said. "If you care to go after him and call him out, you might get the money back."

The tall man's face hardened. He held a Winchester in his right hand and flexed the fingers of his left.

"There are other suspects," he said. "Maybe two of them right here in this room."

Shawn's anger flamed. The man was pushing him and he didn't like to be pushed.

"Damn you, there is no money," he said. "The only money you had was on the ridge, and by now the rain has probably washed it away to hell and gone."

Another man, short and portly with a florid face said, "Be warned, when we find those responsible for stealing our savings, we'll hang them."

That statement dangled in the air for a few seconds, then Shawn said, his voice so low it was almost a whisper, "No, you won't."

"Damn you, sir, for your impertinence," the florid man said.

Shawn rose to his feet. He wore Ed Bowen's gun rig.

"Here's what you'll do," he said. "You'll haul down the gallows and you'll do the same thing with that—"

"Obscenity," Platt offered.

"Obscenity you call a guillotine," Shawn said.

"And how do we keep law and order in this town?" the bearded man said. "What you suggest is impossible."

"I don't know how you'll keep order," Shawn said. "But you'll do it without hanging, burning and beheading people."

"There is evil in this town," the florid man said.

"I know. I see it standing right here in front of me," Shawn said.

Platt took down a shotgun from the gun rack, broke it open and loaded two bright red shells into the chambers.

He stepped beside Shawn and said, "Go do like the man said."

There was recklessness in the bearded fellow's eyes that Shawn didn't like. The new marshal of Holy Rood was an unbending man.

"The gallows and guillotine, aye, and the stake, stay, and be damned to ye," the man said.

"I'm with you, Brother Adam," the florid man said. He waved a hand to the two other townsmen. "And I'm sure these brothers think as I do."

The two men muttered their agreement, their faces hostile.

Shawn shook his head. Then, his voice toneless, he said, "You haven't learned a thing, have you? You finally got rid of Hank Cobb, and now you plan to take his place and carry on as before."

Platt said, "Listen to yourselves—you even call each other brother, like Cobb taught you."

"He was a good Christian," the man called Adam said. "When witches invaded our town, they steered Brother Cobb onto an evil path and that was his downfall."

Then, slapping the stock of his rifle for emphasis, "His legacy remains. The gallows, the stake and the guillotine will stay as long as the West is lawless. They are edifices of justice, the very cornerstones of Holy Rood."

"I wanted to save this town," Shawn said. "Tame it, as the newspapers say. But I believe that all Holy Rood can do now is die and become a ghost. The quicker the better."

He picked up the sack from the table.

"You can give the women back their rings and the men their watches," he said. "I have no need for them."

"Come, gentlemen, we're leaving," Adam said, grabbing the sack. "As for you two, you have an hour to return our money and get out of town."

"It would go better for you if you surrender the

money as you did the jewelry," the florid man said. "You'll be watched every minute by riflemen, mind."

After the four townsmen filed out the door, Platt said, "Let them destroy themselves, Shawn. My only job now is to bring Cobb to justice."

"I wonder how many more will die?" Shawn said.

"I'm not catching your drift," Platt said.

"How many more will be hanged, beheaded or burned in Holy Rood in the coming years?"

"That is no longer our concern," Platt said.

Shawn could only nod. He felt weary, like a defeated prizefighter.

"All right, we'll get Ruby's body and go," he said. "I'll round up Hamp Sedley, and then head to the hotel for Sally."

"We'll need a wagon," Platt said. He seemed a little embarrassed. "For the coffin, I mean."

"Yes, we will. And we may have to shoot our way out of this damned town."

Platt studied Shawn, the slump of his shoulders and the sad, pained expression on his face.

"Then let's get it done," he said. "I want Hank Cobb to pay for his murders and the sooner the better."

Shawn nodded.

He drained his coffee then stepped out the door.

And into an ambush . . .

CHAPTER THIRTY-NINE

The rifle bullet that zipped past Shawn O'Brien's head missed by less than half an inch, splintered into the doorjamb and drove spikes of weathered pine into Ford Platt's face.

As Platt yelped and took a step back, blood running down his cheek, Shawn spotted a man on the pillared whores' gallery of the abandoned saloon across the street.

It was the bearded man called Adam and a second rifleman stood next to him.

Shawn threw himself to his right and drew before he hit the boardwalk, bullets hitting close.

He was aware of the roar of Platt's scattergun. The buckshot must have hit close, because both men suddenly lost interest in a gunfight and scampered for the door that opened onto the gallery.

An apt student of his tutor, stern old Luther Ironside, Shawn was not a merciful man by training or inclination.

He snapped off two fast shots at the fleeing men and scored hits.

Blood staining the left side of his gray coat, Adam turned and tried to bring up his rifle. But the gallery was narrow and he overstepped and toppled headlong into the muddy street.

The second rifleman was down, and in his last agony, he slowly dragged the fingernails of his extended right hand down the harsh timber of the saloon wall, leaving behind four deep gouges.

Shawn got to his feet, his anger such a palpable thing that his snarl of rage made him look like a man-eating cougar.

It seemed that the whole town had turned out to watch him die.

Men, women and children stood in the tumbling rain, staring at him with expressionless, wooden faces, like painted dime-store dolls.

The florid-faced man was holding a Winchester. He looked at Shawn's expression, then at the rifle and quickly threw it down, as though it was suddenly red hot.

A silence stretched tight, the only sound the tick of the falling rain.

A woman stepped forward and stretched her hands out to Shawn in supplication, her face drawn with anguish.

"Lead us," she said. "Save us and save our town."

"Save yourselves, find your own redemption," Shawn said.

He was no longer in a mood to ask. Now he ordered.

"Get the undertaker back here to take care of your hurting dead," he said. "Then pull down the monstrosities from the front of the church. Holy Rood will never again have gallows."

The crowd didn't move. Just stared at him, bewildered, and Shawn's voice rose to a shout.

"Do it! Damn you, do it!"

This time the townspeople moved, the adult men toward the church, the women following, gathering their children close to their muddy skirts.

Shawn didn't wait to see if his orders were being carried out. He stepped back inside the sheriff's office. Platt moved aside for him.

After Shawn poured himself more coffee and lit a cigarette, Platt said, "I don't need to be a prophet to tell you that this town is finished."

"Seems like. Unless miracles happen."

Shawn lifted pained eyes to Platt.

"I thought I could redeem this town. All I did was destroy it."

"Some towns, some people, can't be redeemed," Platt said. "That's the way of it, the way of the world, I guess."

"Why this town, these people? Was it all down to Hank Cobb?"

"People get the government they deserve. It seems to me that Holy Rood deserved Hank Cobb."

"I don't understand that," Shawn said.

Platt smiled. "Hell, I don't either."

Restless, Shawn stepped to the window. There was no one on the street but a few of the stores were lit against the gloom of the day and the fine gray mist was creeping in from the brush flats. The sky remained a dull, iron gray with no promise of sun.

The door opened and Sedley stepped inside.

"Where is Sally?" Shawn said.

"She's over to the hotel. She's not doing so good, O'Brien. Ruby's death really affected her."

"Affected us all," Platt said.

"Hamp, Ford and I are going after Cobb," Shawn said. "Can you take care of Sally, see that she gets to wherever she's going?"

"Sure, I will," Sedley said. "I reckon the Wells Fargo stages will stop here again now that Cobb's gone."

"I wouldn't bet on it," Platt said. "Seems the folks he left behind are already missing him."

"And plan to walk in his footsteps, huh?" Sedley said.

"That's about the size of it," Platt said. "They'll follow the path of their venerated leader. Ready to puke yet?"

"I was standing outside the hotel when they tried to kill you, O'Brien," Sedley said. "Before I could move to help, it was over."

"Shawn's mighty sudden," Platt said. "Blink and you miss it."

"They didn't give me much choice," Shawn said. His shoulders slumped. "What the hell, let's get away from this place," he said. "I've lingered here long enough."

"Suits me," Platt said.

"Ford, see if you can get us some supplies for the trail," Shawn said. "Enough for a couple of days." He turned to Sedley. "Hamp, on second thoughts, I think you and Sally had better come with us. You can drive the wagon."

"I don't want to stay in this town any longer either," Sedley said. "And neither does Sally." His face framed a question. "Why the wagon?"

"We're not leaving Ruby behind," Shawn said.

"Of course," Sedley said. "Sorry I was so dim. Sure, I'll drive the wagon. Be honored to."

"We're heading for Silver Reef, going after Hank Cobb," Platt said. "When we get there, Hamp, if there's shooting to be done, leave it to us."

"We'll see," Sedley said. "I just need six feet of ground between him and me to get my work in."

"Even you can't miss at that range." Platt smiled.

"Yes, he can," Shawn said.

"Kiss my ass," Sedley said.

That made Shawn laugh and it felt good.

CHAPTER FORTY

Shawn O'Brien saddled Wolfden's white horse and hitched a grade mare to a spring wagon he'd discovered at the rear of the livery. He didn't know who owned either and he didn't much care.

Meantime, a cussing Ford Platt was still trying to convince his balky mule that a saddle was not an instrument of equine torture.

The rain had stopped and the clouds had parted. A rose-colored flush showed in the sky to the west, heralding the coming of evening. A south wind had risen and rustled around the stable like the swish of women's dresses at a grand ball.

Shawn studied Platt's struggles and said, "Why don't you pick yourself out a horse?"

"And let this creature win? That'll be the day."

"She's already won, I reckon."

"Not a chance." He raised a fist to the mule's nose. "Cooperate, or I'll punch your damned lights out."

It seemed that the mule was intimidated. She stood foursquare and lowered her head in submission.

"See, all it takes with mules is a strong hand," Platt said, grinning.

Then he jumped for his life as the animal aimed a vicious kick at his leg.

As Platt turned the air around him blue with curses, Shawn laughed.

It was the second time that afternoon and Shawn was pleased.

He'd thought he'd lost the habit of laughter and that it would never return. But just maybe he'd found it again.

After a struggle, Shawn helped Platt get the mule saddled and bridled.

"I'd better round up Hamp and Sally," Shawn said. "It's high time we were out of here."

"I smell burning," Platt said as he tied the sack of supplies he'd gathered onto his saddle. "Seems like wood."

"It's a damp day," Shawn said. "Fires being lit, I guess."

But that was not the case as Hamp Sedley made clear a few moments later.

He ran into the livery and yelled, "The church is on fire!"

"Where is Sally?" Shawn said.

"I don't know. She's not at the hotel."

"Damn it, Hamp, find her!"

Sedley hesitated, uncertainty showing in his face.

Finally, he nodded and ran to the door. There he stopped, staring to his left, his jaw dropping.

"Hell, the fire's spreading!" he yelled.

Like all western settlements on the edge of nowhere, Holy Rood's buildings were tinder dry and fire was an ever-present danger.

Despite the day's rain, the burning church showered sparks and embers onto roofs that readily caught fire, urged on by the strong south wind.

When Shawn ran out into the street, he knew in an instant that Holy Rood was in mortal danger.

Beside him, Ford Platt stared at the church and whispered, "Oh, my God."

Then Shawn saw what Platt saw.

Sally stood in front of the church with her arms upraised. Her hair was undone and streamed wild in the firestorm and she yelled something over and over that Shawn could not hear.

Behind the girl the church was a scarlet and orange rectangle of soaring flame and a column of smoke rose into the air, only to be bent into a black bow by the rising wind.

"Sally!" Shawn shouted. "Get away from there!"

Then he was running toward the blaze.

Frantic people jostled past him in the street, fleeing toward open ground as building after building erupted in fire. A dry goods store burned, only a dress shop away from the rod and gun premises that was sure to have a supply of gunpowder and dynamite.

Shawn knew that if the sporting goods store went up, the town was doomed. But there was nothing to be done. Driven by the remorseless wind, fires on both sides of the street raged out of control. The inferno tinged the early evening sky blood red and the air was thick with acrid smoke and glowing cinders.

Shawn burst free of a panicked knot of people and sprinted faster in the direction of the church.

"Sally!" he yelled. "Sally!"

Then, above the roar of the firestorm, he heard her.

> *"Goddess of the eternal moon.*
> *Let this town meet its doom. . . ."*

"No, Sally!" Shawn yelled. "Get the hell out of there."

The girl saw him, her face shimmering scarlet in the glow of the flames.

"I burned them out, Shawn!" she shouted, her mouth stretched on an O of glee. "They'll never send another witch to the stake in this double-damned town."

The heat was intense as billows of flame consumed the church like crimson waves breaking on a rock.

His arm raised to protect his face, Shawn stepped

closer to Sally. Sparks scorched his hands and he smelled burning broadcloth as windblown cinders stuck to his coat.

But the girl stepped back when she saw Shawn get closer.

Her hair was on fire.

His eyes smarting from smoke, Shawn lunged, reaching out for her.

Too late. Too late by moments.

Shawn heard a tremendous *craaack!* Then the church roof caved in, erupting serpent tongues of flame and sparks. A moment later, the front of the building collapsed and instantly Sally was buried under a mass of blazing beams and timbers . . . her funeral pyre.

Shawn retreated, the heat now unbearable.

He stood at a distance and the only sounds he heard were the feral snarl of the fire and the crackle of burning wood.

"She's gone, O'Brien. Sally is dead."

Hamp Sedley stepped beside Shawn. His skin bunched around his eyes and he looked as though he'd aged a decade in just a few moments.

"Seems like," Shawn said. He didn't trust his emotions should he try to utter anything more.

"You look like a Georgia minstrel," Sedley said. It was the kind of unthinking thing a man in deep shock says. "Your face is black."

"I guess so," Shawn said.

The street was streaked with smoke and flying embers and fire cartwheeled through the buildings on both sides of the street, like a foretaste of hell.

"I think she must have taken the oil lamp from her hotel room and snuck into the rear of the church," Sedley said. "Doesn't need much to start a fire."

"No. No it doesn't."

"I can't believe Sally's gone, O'Brien," Sedley said again. "But if we stand here much longer we'll join her."

A moment later the rod and gun shop exploded.

CHAPTER FORTY-ONE

The fire had leapfrogged across the New York Dress & Hat Shoppe and left it relatively unscathed, but for a few embers that quickly burned themselves out on its timber roof.

But the store's luck ran out less than five minutes later.

Flames engulfed the rod and gun shop and quickly found stacked barrels of gunpowder and a wooden crate that held sticks of dynamite.

The resulting blast boomed like a thunderclap.

The entire building lifted itself off its foundations and blew apart in the air, scattering jagged metal chunks and lethal shards of timber that swept the street like grapeshot from a battery of cannon.

It was unfortunate that the florid-faced man had chosen that spot to try to rally a group of terrified stragglers, demanding that they battle the fire and save the town—both now impossibilities.

When the rod and gun store detonated, shrapnel

whiffed across the street and half a dozen people went down, their bodies torn to pieces so that they sprawled in the mud like bloody rag dolls.

Among them was the florid man, his head gone, neatly severed by a gyrating length of hoop iron from a ten-penny nail barrel.

Shawn O'Brien and Hamp Sedley had been far enough away from the blast that they were unhurt, though Shawn's ears rang and a flying piece of wood cut a furrow across Sedley's cheek.

The survivors of the explosion had already fled in panic when Shawn and Sedley ran to the scene of the carnage.

Flames fluttered like scarlet moths to the charred beams that stuck up above the black ruins of the gun store. Shawn thought he could make out the twisted, carbonized shape of a man's body in the wreckage, but he couldn't be sure.

The bodies on the street told a clearer story.

Three men—one headless—and two women were dead, their bodies so torn it looked as though they'd been savaged by a pack of ravenous wolves.

Another woman was unconscious, but bleeding so badly from a terrible, gaping gash in her neck that the remainder of her life could be measured in minutes.

Now the whole town was on fire, including the large gingerbread houses and most of the tarpaper shacks behind the street.

It was impossible for Shawn and Sedley to stay

where they were, and the dying woman, her breath now coming in short, feeble gasps, could not be saved.

But to leave her to die alone . . .

It was Sedley who made the decision for both of them.

"O'Brien, the horses!" he yelled.

Like a man waking from sleep, Shawn stared at Sedley for a few moments, stunned . . . then he sprinted toward the livery.

The stable was set at a distance from the rest of the town structures, but even so smoke lifted from its roof, so thick that the tin rooster was hidden behind a curling white pall.

Shawn's eyes were wild, his smoke-streaked handsome face showing strain.

"I'll get the horses out," he yelled to Sedley. Then, a single word that summed up all his fears, "Ruby."

"Too late," Sedley said. "The funeral parlor is burning like all the rest. We'll never get her out of there, not now."

There was no time for discussion. Shawn and Sedley rushed into the stable. The roof was on fire and hay smoldered in the loft.

But the horses were gone and so was the spring wagon.

"Platt," Sedley said. "It could only be Ford Platt."

Shawn nodded. "Let's go find him."

He walked out of the livery and looked out at the burning town of Holy Rood. He heard a distant *clang!* as the guillotine blade dropped free of its blazing scaffold and hit the ground.

It seemed to Shawn that the noise put a period at the end of the last sentence of the last chapter of the town's history.

He'd hoped to tame Holy Rood, make it a decent place to live, but he'd helped annihilate it.

Then so be it. As Platt had told him, like some people, there are towns that don't deserve to exist.

Sedley, thinking that Shawn was grieving over his promise to Ruby that he could no longer fulfill, stepped beside him.

"You know what's going to happen, O'Brien, don't you?" he said.

Then, without waiting for an answer, he said, "In years to come, the only visitor to Holy Rood will be the wind. It will blow strong and lift Ruby's ashes and carry them away from here and scatter them among the pines, maybe on the slopes of the high mountains where the spruce grow."

Sedley put his hand on Shawn's shoulder.

"By and by, Ruby will be gone from here and her soul will be at rest."

"And Sally and Jasper Wolfden? What about them?" Shawn said.

"They'll be with Ruby," Selden said. "They'll be carried to the pines by the same wind."

Shawn nodded. "I'll say a rosary for them, and for Sammy, remember him? I'll pray that they all rest in peace."

Sedley nodded. "And I'll say their names aloud whenever I can. I recollect my ma telling me that if you say a dead person's name, he or she will never be forgotten."

"A good thing to remember," Shawn said.

The roof of the livery collapsed with a roar and the fire flourished.

Shawn and Sedley turned their backs on the burning, smoking town of Holy Rood and walked onto the wagon road in search of Ford Platt.

They didn't look back.

CHAPTER FORTY-TWO

The exodus from Holy Rood halted on a flat within view of Black Ridge, a rugged parapet of red rock cut through by vast and mysterious canyons. Here and there the summer thunderstorm had created waterfalls that fell from the tops of mesas and looked like glistening glass rods in the distance.

Like a lost tribe, the numbed citizens camped on muddy ground among piñon and juniper, surrounded by the few belongings they'd managed to carry from their blazing town.

They looked at each other with harrowed faces and ignored their crying children, too shocked by the destruction of their town to speak.

Shawn O'Brien could not find it in his heart to pity them.

In their blind obedience to an evil man and his wicked philosophy, they'd reaped what they'd sowed and there was an end to it.

Shawn and Sedley met up with Ford Platt and they made camp apart from the others.

They agreed that they'd pull out at first light and head for Silver Reef and a showdown with Hank Cobb.

"If it comes down to it, O'Brien, can you shade him?" Sedley asked. "Cobb is good with a gun."

Shawn smiled. "If it comes down to it, I'll learn the answer to that question pretty damn quick."

"I hope you're alive to let us know," Sedley said. He looked at Platt. "Cat got your tongue?"

The little man shook his head, as though clearing his thoughts.

"Ruby's death was hard to take," he said. "Sally's was even harder. She was young and beautiful and I liked her a lot."

"Her mother went crazy," Sedley said. "Maybe it ran in the family."

"Maybe so," Platt said. "But I didn't realize how much she hated the town. If I'd known that maybe I could have saved her."

"She was a witch, and Holy Rood burned witches," Sedley said. His eyes lifted to the sky where the stars were out. "She wanted to get even, I guess."

Platt said, "Shawn, can you make any sense out of it?"

"Sally's death? No, I can't. I can't make any sense out of Ruby's death either or Jasper's or Sammy's. I do know that the man who is ultimately responsible

for it all, including what just befell Holy Rood, is
Hank Cobb."

Shawn poured coffee into a tin cup. "That's why
I aim to kill him."

He started to build a cigarette, then stopped as a
woman's voice, thin, reedy, trembling with emotion, rose from the darkness into the night air. . . .

"*Abide with me, fast falls the eventide.*
The darkness deepens, Lord with me abide.
When other comforts fail and comforts flee,
Help of the helpless, O abide with me."

One by one, other voices, male and female, took
up the hymn. . . .

"*Swift to its close ebbs out life's little day.*
Earth's joys grow dim, its glories pass away.
Change and decay in all around I see.
Oh thou who changest not, abide with me."

Shawn and the others sat silent as the singing
rose in volume and intensity as it reached the last
verse.

"*Hold thou thy cross before my closing eyes.*
Shine through the gloom and point me to the skies.
Heaven's morning breaks, and earth's vain
      shadows flee.
In life, in death, O Lord abide with me."

Platt was the first to speak.

"People survive," he said. "Maybe they'll change for the better and rebuild their town."

"They'll never rebuild their town," Shawn said. "But maybe they can rebuild their lives."

"You think there's a chance for them, O'Brien?" Sedley said.

"They've turned to their god," Shawn said. "It's a hopeful sign."

Platt nodded. "And let us hope so. Then maybe all the lives were not lost in vain."

Despite the mud and the water ticking from the trees, fires flickered in the refugee encampment.

The darkness hid the smoke rising from their burned town, but sparks continued to rise into the night sky . . . like tiny, scarlet stars.

CHAPTER FORTY-THREE

When Shawn O'Brien rode into Silver Reef with Sedley and Platt, the town's boom years were almost over.

A hundred businesses still stretched out along its mile-long main street, and the town still boasted six saloons, nine grocery stores, eight dry goods stores, a bank, a Wells Fargo stage depot, a hospital, hotels and boardinghouses and five restaurants.

But the silver mines were all but played out and the population had dropped to a thousand people, and dozens of miners were leaving every day.

The signs of decay were everywhere and in a few years, when the last mine closed, Silver Reef would become a ghost town.

The town marshal was a Texan by the name of John Payton. He was fast on the draw and shoot and he didn't take any sass.

Or so the bartender at the Silver Dollar saloon

told Shawn and the others as they stood at the bar eating soda crackers and cheese and drinking beer from the local brewery that was still cool from the remaining winter ice.

The bartender was an exquisite creature with glossy, pomaded hair and a waxed mustache. He wore a brocade vest and a large diamond stickpin glittered in his cravat. Like most mixologists of the time, he was a talking man.

You boys looking for work?" he said, wiping the bar in front of Shawn with a yellow cloth. "If you are, you'd better ride on. The mines are closing and nobody's hiring. Hell, just the other day I'd seven men apply for the job of swamper. A couple of years ago, I wouldn't have had a single applicant."

The bartender smiled, revealing a shiny gold tooth.

"I guess you boys are catching my drift, huh?"

"We're not looking for a job, we're looking for a man," Shawn said.

The bartender was taken aback and his shoulders stiffened.

"Here, you're not the law are you?" he said. "Marshal Payton was once engaged in the bank-robbing profession, and he don't take kindly to lawmen of any kind."

"We're not the law," Shawn said. He brushed a cracker crumb from his mustache. "We're looking for a . . . friend of ours. Seems his ma is keeping poorly and wants him to home."

"We got folks passing through all the time—drovers, drummers and fancy women and the like. What does your friend look like?"

"He's easy to spot," Shawn said. "He got shot in the shoulder a few days back."

The bartender's eyebrows rose.

"You sure you aren't the law, mister?" he said.

"I didn't shoot him," Shawn said. "And no, I'm not the law."

"It was an accident, like," Sedley said.

"Cleaning his gun," Platt said. His face was solemn, as though he was the soul of integrity.

"Well, I haven't seen a gunshot man in town," the bartender said. "Well, not recently. Used to see plenty back in the old days."

Then, his face brightened, as though he'd just remembered something.

"Here, you know who's in town? You'll never guess in a million years."

The bartender stood back, grinning, waiting for an answer.

"Well, we don't have a million years, so tell," Platt said.

"Mink Morrow, as large as life and as ever was."

Shawn pretended surprise and mimed a rube's jaw drop.

"You mean the famous gunfighter?" he said.

The bartender nodded. "Yup, as bold as brass.

They say he's killed more men than John Wesley or that Bill Bonney kid, and I believe it. Yes, sir, he's a mean one all right and looks it, wears them dark glasses that take away a man's eyes."

"But how is the Marshal Payton handling this?" Shawn said. "I don't imagine he's keen to see a man like Mink Morrow in his town."

"So long as Morrow keeps his nose clean in this town, Payton don't much mind," the bartender said. "When it comes to outlaws an' sich, on account that a lot of them were his friends, he's inclined to live and let live. If they're just passing through, that is."

"And Morrow, is he just passing through?" Shawn said.

"As far as I was told, he saw how things are in Silver Reef, with the mines closing an' all, and said he plans to light a shuck for Texas. Said something about opening an eating house, but I don't know if that's true or not."

"Geez, I'd love to shake his hand," Sedley said. "Wouldn't you, O'Brien?"

"I sure would," Shawn said. "I've never met a real gunfighter in the flesh before."

The bartender grinned. "Well, you boys are in luck. Morrow's been hanging out at Elmer Brown's Last Chance saloon at t'other side of town." He glanced at the railroad clock on the wall. "It's just past ten and Mink always eats breakfast about this time. Elmer sells the best sowbelly and eggs in Silver Reef."

"What a lark," Shawn said, still playing the wide-eyed hayseed. Then to the others, "Let's go meet him."

"You didn't fool that bartender for one minute, Shawn," Platt said.

"What do you mean?" Shawn said, genuinely puzzled.

"It's mud-stained and getting a tad ragged, but you're still wearing a forty-dollar English coat and no rube ever owned the gun rig you've got strapped around your waist," Platt said.

"So how did he peg me?" Shawn said.

"A gun. Just like Morrow."

Shawn and the others led their mounts down the main street, rubbing shoulders with miners, cowboys in from the neighboring ranches, a few Chinese and the occasional woman.

It was still early in the morning and the town's sporting crowd, gamblers, whores, dance hall loungers and the like, wouldn't surface until sundown.

"He was real obliging," Shawn said, as he led his horse around a loaded brewery dray and then a pile of dung in the street. "A talking man and disposed to be friendly."

"Sure, he was friendly," Platt said. "Look around you, Shawn. This town has lost its snap. A gunfight between you and Morrow would liven things up and give a talking man something to talk about."

"I've got no problem with Morrow," Shawn said. "But I reckon he knows where we can find Hank Cobb."

"Yeah, but will he tell you?"

"Why not? He's got no love for Cobb."

"Sedley and me will come with you," Platt said.

"Just let me handle Morrow alone," Shawn said.

"Then we'll watch your back," Platt said.

"Damn right," Sedley said.

Shawn looped his mount to the hitching rail and smiled at Sedley.

"Hamp, if it comes to shooting, let Ford handle it," he said. "All of a sudden the Last Chance saloon could become a mighty dangerous place if you cut loose."

"Kiss my ass," Sedley said.

CHAPTER FORTY-FOUR

A relic of Silver Reef's booming past, the saloon's door was a single sheet of frosted glass adorned with a bucolic scene of naked nymphs feeding bunches of grapes to stalwart silver miners with impressive beards.

When Shawn opened the door, a brass bell jangled above his head, and every eye turned in his direction.

There were a dozen patrons in the saloon, mostly business types drinking coffee and brandy in a blue haze of cigar smoke.

The Last Chance was no frontier gin mill, but a dark-paneled men's club with overstuffed chairs, polished tables, a stage at the rear and a long mahogany bar that at one time accommodated eight bartenders.

The saloon looked tired and faded, like an aging belle, and there was dust on the crystal chandelier and in the corners of the windows, a sure sign of neglect.

Mink Morrow sat with his back to the wall beside the stage, the crockery-littered table in front of him dominated by a silver coffeepot that, like the saloon, showed signs of tarnish.

Armed men were not rare in Silver Reef, but Shawn's height and handsome features attracted the attention of saloon patrons as he walked toward Morrow's table and stopped, looking down at the man.

"Howdy, Mink," he said. "Long time no see."

The gunfighter said nothing, but with a nod of his head he indicated the chair opposite his.

Then, "Coffee?" he said.

"Don't mind if I do," Shawn said.

Morrow turned his head and called out to the man behind the bar, "Hey, Elmer, bring us a cup, will you?"

The man gave Shawn a wary glance as he placed a white cup and saucer with blue pictures of Chinese people on the table.

"I regret that I can't offer you breakfast," Morrow said.

"I already ate," Shawn said.

After a few moments of silence, his eyes unreadable behind his glasses, he said, "You're here about the money I took, huh?"

Shawn shook his head. "No, Mink, that's not why I'm here."

But for some reason Morrow didn't want to let it go.

"I won't give it back," he said.

"There's no one to give the money back to, Mink. Holy Rood burned to the ground and as far as I know, all the people are scattered to hell and gone."

Morrow poured coffee into Shawn's cup with his left hand.

Shawn saw that and knew what it implied.

"I'm looking for Hank Cobb," he said.

"He's around."

"He hasn't braced you?"

"Cobb is a man who doesn't want to die. I saw him, just once in the street, and he ignored me."

"I figured he'd want his money back."

"I think he's got something bigger in mind. He'd hooked up with a hard case that goes by the name of Simon Badeaux. Him I don't know much about. But I'm told he has some kind of reputation as a man killer."

"Where is Cobb, Mink?"

"Chinatown." Morrow nodded to the south. "About a mile that way."

"Why there?" Shawn began to build a cigarette.

"I don't know, but here's a clue: The Chinese

don't trust banks so there's said to be a lot of silver money in Chinatown."

Morrow thumbed a match into flame and lit Shawn's cigarette.

"According to John Payton, ol' Hank already established his bona fides by killing a man. Self-defense, he claimed."

"And Payton believed him?"

"Had to. No jury of Silver Reef miners is going to convict a man for shooting a Chinese who helped undercut their wages."

Morrow lifted his head and his glasses silvered in the morning sunlight that streamed through a window.

He sat forward in his chair. "Are those your compadres I see with you, O'Brien?"

Shawn smiled. "Yeah, they're watching my back."

"I wouldn't shoot you in the back, or the front, you being brother to Jake, an' all."

"That's mighty white of you, Mink."

"I'm pulling out tomorrow, heading for Texas."

"Good luck with that."

"I sure thought you'd come here for the money."

"Like I told you, I wouldn't know who to give it to."

Morrow smiled. "Give it to Hank Cobb, maybe."

"I'll pay him off all right, but in lead, not gold."

"He's fast, O'Brien. As fast as they come. Step real careful."

"As fast as you?"

"I don't know. I no longer see too good anymore if the light is bright." Morrow smiled faintly. "Hell, I don't see too good if the light ain't bright. You understand? A doctor told me I'm going to be blind in a year, maybe less." He shook his head. "Hell of a thing to tell a man."

"It is, and I'm sorry to hear it."

"Well, that's why I need the money I took from Holy Rood. I plan to open a restaurant and tell big windies to the customers about my gun-fighting days."

"I wish you well, Mink."

Shawn drained his coffee cup and looked up when Morrow spoke again.

"Maybe Hank isn't as fast as you, O'Brien, I don't know. But he's sneaky. If he throws down his gun and tells you he's out of it, you can bet your bottom dollar he has a hide-out on him somewhere."

Shawn nodded. "I'll keep that in mind."

"When I saw him, he had his left arm in a sling," Morrow said. "That's where he'll stash a sneaky gun."

"Thanks for the advice and the coffee, Mink," Shawn said.

He rose to his feet.

"Wait," Morrow said.

Suddenly, his Colt was in his hand, and Shawn,

caught flatfooted, could only stand and marvel at the speed of the man's draw.

Morrow grinned, reversed the revolver in his hand, and held it out to Shawn.

"Take this," he said. "It might give you an edge."

Shawn was about to refuse, but Morrow held up a silencing hand.

"This here Colt shoots true to the point of aim and the trigger breaks like a glass rod," he said. "There's none better in the Utah Territory or anywhere else."

The revolver was a plain blue .45 colt with a hard rubber handle, the barrel cut back to five inches.

When Shawn took it in his hand the balance of the revolver was superb, and when he tested the action, it cycled as smooth as polished ivory.

"I can't take your gun, Mink," he said.

"Yes, you can. I've got no further use for it. No matter how fine the weapon, it isn't much use to a blind man."

Shawn hesitated and Morrow said, "Take the Colt, O'Brien."

After a few moments, Shawn relented. He shoved the revolver into his waistband and said, "I'm beholden to you, Mink."

"Empty chamber under the hammer, remember," Morrow said. He waved a hand. "I think you should go now."

Morrow looked weary, used up; a man walking the ragged edge of exhaustion or perhaps despair.

"Good luck, O'Brien," Morrow said. "Next time you see Jake, tell him I asked after him."

"I surely will," Shawn said.

Morrow looked pained for a moment. Then, as though he had to force out the words, he said, "I got to say it straight out, O'Brien, but I'd feel a lot better about things if it was Jake and not you going after Hank Cobb."

Shawn smiled. "Me too, Mink. Me too."

CHAPTER FORTY-FIVE

After Shawn O'Brien recounted his conversation with Morrow, Ford Platt said, "So how do we play it?"

"That's easy to answer," Shawn said. "We head for Chinatown and open the ball."

He paused with a foot in the stirrup and said, "Ford, you ever heard of this Simon Badeaux feller?"

Platt shook his head.

"How about you, Hamp?"

"Draws a blank with me," Sedley said. "Morrow said he's a gun, huh?"

"Yeah, something like that."

"We'll take care of . . . whatever the hell he's called," Platt said. "You concentrate on Cobb."

Shawn swung into the saddle and looked down at the little man.

"I think Morrow believes that I can't shade him," he said.

"We can always get the marshal involved," Sedley said.

"And tell him what? That we need his help to kill a man?"

"I can arrest him," Platt said. "I have the power."

Shawn smiled. "Something tells me that Hank Cobb won't care to be arrested today."

Platt's face was deeply lined by conflicting emotions.

"Shawn, if you want to ride away from this, there isn't anyone here going to blame you," he said.

"I appreciate that, Ford," Shawn said. "But the man who was responsible for Holy Rood and the deaths of so many still walks the earth. So long as his shadow falls on the ground, I can't step away from it."

Platt nodded. A fly buzzed around his head. "Well, you got sand, Shawn."

"No, I don't. I'm scared to death. Now mount up and let's ride."

The main street of Silver Reef was busy with people, but they walked slowly in the building heat as though they'd lost their sense of purpose.

The rapid closing of the silver mines had gutted the town and everyone but the most hopeful or unintelligent knew it was headed for oblivion.*

---

*By 1890 Silver Reef was a ghost town. In the early 1900s, most of its buildings were demolished and a fire in 1908 destroyed what was left. Many attempts were made to resurrect the town, the last in 1950, but all failed.

A pretty woman wearing a green silk morning dress, a lacy white parasol shading her porcelain skin, gave Shawn a bold look from under the black fans of her eyelashes as he rode past.

But he didn't notice her. His mind was focused on Hank Cobb.

Chinatown was a collection of shacks sprawled hit or miss across a sandy flat, hemmed in to the west by rolling hills, to the east by the timbered breaks of the Hurricane Cliffs.

It was in the heart of silver country, a vast area where glittering fortunes had been made and lost for a decade.

The Chinese, most of them former railroad construction laborers, had lived south of Silver Reef since 1879. They'd found work in the mines and now many were packing up and getting ready to move on, some of them back to China.

When Shawn and the others rode into the dusty settlement, about two hundred people still remained but the only stores in town, a grocery and a dry goods, were as yet open for business.

The sun was bright, the sky blue with only a few cotton ball clouds, yet a pall seemed to hang over the town, and Shawn knew that the cause could only be Hank Cobb.

A few men and woman, slender as reeds, walked around, but they did not raise their heads or show any interest when the three white men dismounted outside the grocery store and stepped inside.

The store smelled sharply of spices and of the dried ducks that hung like little brown soldiers in an orderly row above the counter.

Behind the counter stood a young, pretty girl with coal-black hair pulled back in a severe bun. Her huge brown eyes moved to Shawn's guns and she breathed rapidly, her small breasts rising and falling under the pink silk shirt she wore.

Without a sound, the girl reached under the counter and dropped a small, white coffee sack on the counter that clinked in the silence.

"That is all there is," she said. "My grandfather has no more."

Shawn picked up the sack and hefted it in his hand. When he opened it up, he saw a dozen gold and silver coins.

"Why did you give us this?" Shawn said.

The girl looked frightened.

"My grandfather has no more. It's all been taken."

"Who took your grandfather's money?" Shawn said.

"The white man who killed Qiang Cheung, our mayor." The girl's eyes flashed. "As if you did not know this."

"The man who killed your mayor, is he called Hank Cobb?" Shawn said.

The girl shook her head and looked lost.

"I do not know what he's called."

Shawn laid his left arm across his chest.

"Does he carry his arm like this?"

This time the girl nodded. "Yes, it hangs from his shoulder in a cloth."

"That's our man," Ford Platt said.

"Where is he, this man?" Shawn said.

The girl opened her mouth, but the words died on her lips.

"Don't be afraid," Shawn said. He pushed the sack across the counter. "We don't want your grandfather's money."

"The man you seek lives in the house of Qiang Cheung."

An old Chinese man walked through a bead curtain that swayed back into place when he stepped behind the counter.

He had a wispy white beard that hung from the pointed chin of a wrinkled face the color of parchment. He wore a plain white shirt over a black, floor-length robe of some kind and a round cap balanced on the crown of his tiny, well-formed head.

"Is he there now?" Platt said.

Beside him, Sedley made a show of studying the dried ducks, but his hands were clutched in front of him, betraying his growing anxiety.

"He is there," the old man said. "The people bring him tribute."

He shrugged thin shoulders. "All the young men have gone to find other work, and only the women and the old like me are left. Who is to tell this man Cobb no?"

"I will," Shawn said.

"He will kill you if he can."

"I know."

The old man reached behind his neck and untied a jade medallion, carved with the symbol of an eagle perched on a rock amid a turbulent sea.

"If you were my own son I would give you this," he said, extending the talisman to Shawn. "It is reserved for heroes and it will give you strength and protect you in battle."

"I am honored," Shawn said. He tied the string around his neck and the medallion hung on his chest.

"Warrior," the old man said, smiling as he stepped back. "I have offered sacrifices to the great goddess Mazu to send me a man such as you and she has answered my prayers."

"Well, let's hope so, mister . . . ah . . ." Shawn said, slightly embarrassed.

"My name is Tian," the old man said.

Shawn touched the medallion. "Thank you for this, Tian."

"Yeah, thank you, Tian," Hamp Sedley said. "Something tells me we're gonna need it."

CHAPTER FORTY-SIX

Tian's granddaughter pointed out the mayor's house, a low, timber building that didn't look even vaguely Chinese. A hastily built pole corral at one end of the cabin held two horses, a long-legged buckskin and a paint mustang.

The place seemed deserted, but thin smoke trailed from the chimney and the smell of coffee hung in the air.

"So what do we do, O'Brien?" Sedley said after they'd stopped at a distance from the cabin. "Knock on the door and wait until they ask us in for tea?"

"I'm calling him out," Shawn said.

"Suppose he doesn't want to come out?" Sedley said.

"Then I'll kill him at a distance," Shawn said.

"No, Shawn, I'll call him out," Ford Platt said. "I'm here in my official capacity as a representative of Wells Fargo. It's my sworn duty."

"Hell, it don't matter a damn who calls him out,"

Sedley said. "It's what happens when he comes out that's the problem."

"Sedley, is that the first or second sensible thing I've ever heard you say?" Platt said.

"Second, I think."

"Good, then you're improving."

Platt stepped toward the cabin, Shawn and Sedley behind him.

The afternoon was hot and near the cabin the branches of a dead, overturned piñon gleamed like scattered white bones in the sun glare. Crickets rasped in the bunch grass and, a ways off, a solitary buzzard flapped to an untidy landing and regarded the three men with a cold, merciless eye.

Platt stood in front of the cabin, spread his legs and filled his chest with air.

"Hank Cobb!" he yelled. "Do you hear me, Hank Cobb? I'm calling you out!"

There was no answer.

A dust devil spun around Platt's legs and tugged the bottom of his pants.

"Oh, well, there's nobody to home, O'Brien," Sedley said. "Better luck next time, huh?"

"They're to home," Shawn said. "Their horses are in the corral and they sure didn't go anywhere on foot."

"Hank Cobb!" Platt yelled again, leaning heavily on his cane. "Get out here and take your medicine like a man."

Shawn saw a curtain twitch in a window to the

front of the cabin and then from somewhere inside a man's voice droned followed by a laugh.

Then, "Who the hell is out there?"

Hank Cobb's voice . . .

"My name is Ford J. Platt, and I've been deputized to arrest you for complicity in the murder of a Wells Fargo passenger on the Silver Reef to Cedar City stage. What is your reply?"

Cobb made no answer, and Platt raised his voice even louder. "Do you hear me, Hank Cobb?"

"I hear you," Cobb yelled.

"Then state your intentions."

"I'm a wounded man who's feeling right poorly, but I'm coming out."

Shawn stepped closer to Platt and Sedley did the same.

But the gambler swallowed hard and he looked pale and Shawn wondered if he'd stand.

He didn't blame Sedley. The man wasn't a gunfighter and this would be close and sudden work, calling for quick hands and steady nerves.

Concerned for the man, Shawn said, "You all right, Hamp?"

Sedley's face settled into a scowl.

"Don't worry about me, O'Brien," he said. "I'll stand."

"I never thought otherwise," Shawn said.

"Yes, you did."

"Well, maybe I did."

Sedley face cleared and he managed a smile.

"And so did I," he said.

The cabin door opened and Hank Cobb stepped outside. With him was a lean, hawk-faced man with careful eyes, wearing a two-gun rig, a rarity on the frontier at that time.

"I see you cut yourself shaving, Hank," Platt said.

Cobb's fingers strayed to the bloodstained triangle of newspaper on his left cheek.

"I enjoy a shave before I kill a man," he said.

Cobb's eyes crawled over Shawn and Sedley like snails and his thin mouth widened in a smile.

"Well, well, well, all my dear friends are here, just like old times," he said. He adjusted the hang of the sling on his left arm.

"Cobb, you're a piece of human garbage," Shawn said. "And I'm not your friend."

"No, I guess you're not at that," Cobb said.

His gaze dropped to the Colt in Shawn's waistband.

"The hell if that's not Mink Morrow's gun. Did you kill him, O'Brien?"

"No. He gave it to me as a gift."

"Generous of him."

"I thought so."

Platt spoke slowly as though he was deliberately choosing his words.

"Well, Cobb, will you come quietly?" He read the scorn on the other man's face and said, "I can promise you a fair trial."

"And a first-class hanging, huh?"

"If that is the jury's decision, then yes."

Cobb turned his head to Simon Badeaux.

"What do you think?"

"I think you tell him to go to hell."

Badeaux had a heavy French accent that would have been at home in a café shaded by the horse-chestnut trees along the Champs-Elysees, and he had a tightness around his mouth that Shawn didn't like.

Cobb stared at Platt. "You heard the man. He said go to hell. So cut loose your wolf!"

And he went for his gun.

Cobb's draw was fast and smooth and he targeted Shawn, having long before pegged him as gun slick.

In that, he was right.

Shawn drew from the waist and had a bullet into Cobb's chest an instant before the man fired. Shawn took the hit on the top of his left shoulder. Cobb's bullet burned across his skin like a red-hot iron.

Cobb's eyes were wild, shocked. He knew he was hit hard, but couldn't believe it had happened to him.

He staggered back a step, his face grim and worked his Colt.

He fired.

A miss.

Shawn, past and present angers driving him, was relentless.

He fired, fired again.

Hit in the belly and again in the chest, Cobb screamed his rage and dropped to his knees. Scarlet blood and saliva ran from his mouth and his eyes were murderous.

He tried to bring up his Colt. . . .

Then something happened that Shawn, Cobb . . . no one could have anticipated.

The old Chinese man named Tian darted from the corner of the cabin, running at a speed that belied his age.

A moment later, with tremendous strength, he swung a flat, wide-bladed sword, a red tassel hanging from the hilt, and the honed steel bit into the right side of Cobb's neck . . . and kept on going.

Cobb's head seemed to jump a foot from his shoulders. It rolled in the dirt and came to a stop close to Shawn, who kicked it aside.

He turned and caught the last moments of the gunfight between Badeaux and Ford Platt.

Platt, pulling a gun from the pocket of his coat, had been slower than Badeaux. But he'd taken his hits, remained on his feet, and gamely got his work in.

But now he was down on one knee, his chest splashed with blood.

Hit, Badeaux had staggered to the cabin and shoved his back against the wall.

Now he shouldered himself off, steadied his stance, and took deliberate aim at Platt.

Shawn and Sedley fired at the same time.

Hit twice, Badeaux fell against the cabin and slowly slid down the wall to a sitting position.

His eyes were wide open . . . but he saw nothing.

Cobb's eyes were also open . . . but God alone knew what they were seeing. . . .

CHAPTER FORTY-SEVEN

Shawn O'Brien glanced at Tian.

The old man wiped his bloody sword on Cobb's back and then looked at Shawn and grinned.

"Warrior," he said.

Shawn put a hand on Tian's shoulder and nodded. "Warrior."

He stepped to Ford Platt and took a knee beside him.

The little man's lips were bloodless and he was obviously trying hard to conceal the pain that nonetheless showed in his eyes.

"How badly are you hit?" Shawn said, looking for a wound.

"Bad enough," Platt said. "I reckon I'm all shot to pieces. I think one bullet went clean through me and the other . . ."

He glared at Sedley. "Hit me up the ass."

Hamp Sedley was gracious enough to look guilty.

"I'm not used to this fast draw stuff," he said. "Damn gun went off by itself."

"Next time stand in front of me, preferably bending over," Platt said. "Maybe my gun will go off by itself."

"There won't be a next time," Sedley said. He tossed his Colt into the dirt. "I'm finished with that. Seems like I always miss my enemies and shoot my friends."

"You got a bullet in Badeaux, Hamp," Shawn said. "I'd say you did all right, apart from shooting Ford that is."

Ignoring Sedley's groan of remorse, Shawn examined Platt's wounds.

After a couple of minutes, he said, "You're right, Ford, Badeaux's bullet hit you high in the chest and exited just above your right shoulder blade."

Shawn, his face empty, said, "The second bullet is still lodged in your left butt cheek."

"Then I'm done for," Platt said. "It's all up for me."

He angled Sedley a look that would have shriveled a thornbush.

"No, I don't think so," Shawn said. "But you need a doctor real quick. Can you handle the ride back to Silver Reef?" Shawn put his fingers to his mouth. "Oh, sorry, I forgot."

"My ass didn't let me forget," Platt said, irritated.

Tian, the sword hanging by his side, looked down

at Platt and said, "We have a doctor who can treat your wounds."

Platt narrowed his eyes. When he spoke his voice was barely a whisper.

"Is he a good Christian? I will not submit myself to heathen pokings and potions."

Tian shook his head. "Not Christian, but Dr. Chang is a fine physician."

"Then I'll pass," Platt said.

"If you don't see a doc, you'll pass away, Platt," Sedley said.

"Advice from my murderer," Platt said. "That's all I need."

"Hamp is right. You need those bullet wounds treated, Chinese doctor or not," Shawn said. Then to Tian, "Where is he located?"

"I will show you the way. Can the patient walk?"

"Hell no, I can't walk," Platt said.

"Then we'll carry you," Shawn said. "Hamp, help me."

He and Sedley cradled Platt, each holding a leg, and followed Tian. A crowd of excited Chinese gathered to watch, while others busily ransacked Hank Cobb's cabin.

Buzzards, as elegant in flight as fallen angels, quartered the sky above the town and a north wind carried the smell of pine and sage from far places.

"You two are delivering me into the hands of the heathen," Platt protested in a thin whine.

"Lucky for you, huh?" Shawn said.

Sedley, still wracked by guilt, bit his lip and said nothing.

Dr. Chang's cabin looked no more Chinese than the others.

But inside told a different story.

The doctor himself was a small, frail bag-of-bones with an impossibly yellow skin networked by wrinkles. His eyes were black, as bright and alert as a bird's, and he could have been any age upward of a hundred. He wore traditional Chinese dress: a crimson silk robe decorated with a dragon motif and a mandarin hat with a red tassel. He wore a wispy mustache and beard and a plaited pigtail hung down his back.

Shelves of jars and bottles filled with various dried herbs lined the walls and more plants hung from the ceiling. Incense burned in a shallow, jade dish.

The only furnishings were a chair and a couch, the latter covered by a purple cloth decorated with the signs of the zodiac embroidered in gold thread.

When Platt was helped inside, he looked around with wide eyes and immediately panicked, demanding to be taken to Silver Reef, shot butt or no.

But Dr. Chang would have none of it.

"Please place patient on couch on right side," he said to Shawn and Sedley.

They did as they were told as Platt begged loudly for mercy.

"Now leave us, please," the doctor said. "I have assistant who will help."

Shawn reached over Platt and deftly removed his Colt from the holster.

"Just so you don't get any ideas, Ford," he said.

"Damn you, Shawn, I'll never forgive you for this," Platt said. "You're leaving me to my doom."

Sedley, who obviously felt he'd been contrite long enough, said, "You know, Platt, for a man who just stood his ground against a professional killer, you sure are a crybaby."

Platt stared hard at Sedley, then said, his voice very low and quiet, "Shawn, let me have my gun for just a moment."

Shawn smiled. "Dr. Chang, we'll leave you to your patient. If he gives you any trouble, hit him over the head with something hard."

As he stepped out of the dark cabin into sunlight, Shawn heard Platt yell, "As long as I live, I'll never forget this!"

This was followed by a yowl of pain, and Sedley said, "I guess my bullet went in deep. I did shoot him at close range, you know."

Shawn nodded, only half-aware of what Sedley had said. His eyes were fixed on Cobb's cabin.

The man's head scowled at him from atop a tall

stake, driven into the ground a few feet in front of the cabin.

Tian's granddaughter stood at the door, distributing gold and silver coins from a burlap sack to a crowd of people who patiently stood in line.

How she knew who got what, Shawn didn't know. Perhaps the inherent honesty of the Chinese made her job easier.

Sedley stopped in his tracks, staring at the head.

Finally, he said, "Ol' Hank got what he handed out."

Shane nodded. "I believe it's called poetic justice."

"I prefer to call it gun justice, O'Brien," Sedley said. "Your gun, your justice."

"Yeah, and it's the only thing I've done right since the day our stage overturned in Holy Rood," Shawn said.

CHAPTER FORTY-EIGHT

Shawn O'Brien and Hamp Sedley sat at the rear of Tian's store, eating an excellent chicken soup with Chinese noodles, when the beaded curtain parted and Dr. Chang stepped inside.

The physician's report was concise and to the point.

Mr. Platt's surgery had been a great success. The wound in his shoulder and back had been cauterized, then treated with healing herbs and would mend nicely. The bullet had been removed from his buttock and that too would heal.

In short, the patient was doing as well as could be expected.

But at the moment he was deeply sedated and would not be fit for travel for at least two weeks.

Then, with a flourish, Dr. Chang presented his bill, itemized under the heading:

FOR MOST EXCELLENT AND
HUMANE MEDICAL SERVICES

The total came to ten dollars that Shawn paid out of his dwindling supply of money and then he thanked the doctor for his fine work.

After Dr. Chang bowed and left, Sedley said, "So what do we do, O'Brien? Stay here until Platt is fit to ride?"

"No, I don't think he'd expect that," Shawn said. "We can spend the night here and return to Silver Reef in the morning."

"Do you think he'll be all right?" Sedley said.

"The doctor seems to think so."

"He's Chinese."

"So what? The Chinese had fine doctors when our ancestors were still living in mud huts and wearing goatskins."

"Itchy," Sedley said.

"What?"

"Goatskins."

Shawn shook his head. "Eat your soup."

But no sooner had Sedley picked up his spoon when Tian's granddaughter clicked through the bead curtain. She looked concerned, almost frightened.

"There's a man waiting to see you gentlemen," she said.

"Did he give a name?" Shawn said.

"Yes. He says he's Marshal John Payton. He has a silver star on his shirt."

Ignoring Sedley's startled glance, Shawn said, "Show him in."

He rose to his feet, adjusted the hang of his Colt and waited.

"Judging by Mink Morrow's description, you must be Shawn O'Brien," Marshal John Payton said.

"I must be," Shawn said. "What can I do for you, marshal?"

"Well, you can tell me why Hank Cobb's head is stuck on a pole out there."

Shawn opened his mouth to speak, but Payton held up a hand.

"Later. A badass like Cobb is only worth a later. First, I've got some news for you."

John Payton was a tall, hard-eyed man with iron gray hair and a head as big as a nail keg. There was a stillness about him, a lack of any fidget that Shawn had seen before in men who lived by the gun. A great Texas mustache, as bristly as a horse brush, covered his top lip.

"Good news or bad?" Shawn said.

"That depends. Mink a friend of yours?"

"He was a friend of my brother's," Shawn said.

"Then my news might be bad only for your brother. Mink Morrow is dead."

Shawn flinched. "Dead? How?"

"He hung himself in his hotel room."

"Mink was going blind," Shawn said.

"I know that," Payton said. "For a man in his line of work it was the end of the trail."

Payton reached into his shirt pocket and produced a crumpled paper.

"Morrow wrote this and it don't say much," he said, passing the note to Shawn.

It took only a few moments to read the words Mink had left for posterity.

> *To whom it may concern—*
>
> *Money on the dressser. Use $2 to bury me and give the rest to poor folks.*
>
> *Yours Respectfully,*
> *Miles Morrow, Esq.*

Shawn dropped the note onto the table.

"Not much of an epitaph for a man," he said.

"I guess that was all the epitaph he wanted," Payton said.

The lawman glanced at the table. "Finish your soup," he said. "And while you're doing that, tell me about Hank Cobb."

"It's a long story, marshal," Sedley said.

"I got nothing but time," Payton said.

His eyes were diamond hard.

* * *

After Shawn recounted what had happened in Holy Rood from the time of the stage wreck to the death of Hank Cobb, Payton sat in silence.

He waited until Shawn poured himself coffee and built and lit a cigarette until he spoke.

"Hell of a story," he said finally.

"You heard it," Shawn said. "What's your opinion?"

"Maybe it's a pack of lies. Maybe Holy Rood was a fine town with good people and Hank Cobb was an upstanding lawman who tried his best to make his town safe for families to prosper in peace and safety."

"That's one way of looking at it," Shawn said. "But you'd be derailing the truth."

"Your brother is Jacob O'Brien, the gunfighter, and your pa's range covers about half of the New Mexico Territory, ain't that so?"

"Close enough," Shawn said.

"Jacob would've handled the affair better."

"Jake marches to a different drum than the rest of us," Shawn said. Then, after a moment, he added, "Yeah, I reckon he would have done it better."

The brown, sun-ravaged skin of the marshal's face was taut against the bone.

"You did all right," he said. "Maybe I think that."

"Yes, maybe you do, but that cock won't fight. I messed it up right from the git-go. I wanted to tame the town and I ended up destroying it."

"You had help," Payton said. "I heard that Jasper

Wolfden was good with a gun, and something about how the Navajo had made him a shape-shifter."

"He was an actor, that's all," Shawn said. "And yes, I got help from Jasper. And in the end I got him killed."

"Sometimes for a lawman, that's the cost of doing business," Payton said.

Hamp Sedley frowned his irritation. "All right, marshal, you've been tippy-toeing around this thing like a saloon girl on a miners' dance floor," he said. "If you don't believe us, say it straight out and then state your intentions."

Payton smiled. "I believe every word O'Brien said. Only one of them dime novel writers could make up a story like that."

He reached out, took the makings from Shawn's shirt pocket, and built a cigarette.

"Got a light, O'Brien?" he said. Then, "I'm trying to quit these things, but as you see, it ain't going too well."

Shawn lit the lawman's smoke. Payton inhaled deeply, and then said, "Why would white folks do that? Hell, would Americans do that, sell their souls to the devil?"

"I've asked myself that question many times, marshal, and I still can't come up with a good answer," Shawn said. He stared intently into Payton's flinty eyes. "Why didn't the law stop it?"

"I guess you don't fix what ain't broke," Payton said. "Holy Rood seemed to be a peaceful, law-abiding town. Sure, they hung undesirables now and then, but what town doesn't?"

Speaking behind a cloud of smoke, Payton said, "A year before I became marshal, Silver Reef hung a man and his two sons for being chicken thieves and damned nuisances. The whole town turned out to see the hangings, and not one voice was raised in protest."

"Holy Rood was worse, marshal, a whole lot worse," Shawn said.

"Not in the eyes of the law. And those were the only eyes that mattered."

"Would you have hung the chicken thieves?" Shawn said.

"Sure, if a judge and jury found them guilty," Payton said.

"Then are you any different from Hank Cobb?"

The marshal took that question in stride.

"The difference is that I wouldn't have tried to make a profit out of the hanging," Payton said. "I keep the peace for sixty dollars a month."

He dropped the butt of his cigarette into the dregs of Shawn's coffee cup.

"What's next for you, O'Brien?" he said.

"That depends on you," Shawn said.

"You didn't commit any crimes in Silver Reef that I'm aware of, so you and Sedley are free to go. Since he's one of their own, Wells Fargo will come collect Ford Platt."

"Well, I guess I'll move on," Shawn said. "I don't want to go back home to Dromore, at least not yet."

Payton nodded. "I wanted to hear something like that."

"Why?"

"I have a proposition for you."

Shawn opened his mouth to object, but Payton said, "Hear me out, me being so willing to let bygones be bygones and all that."

"All right, I'm listening," Shawn said.

CHAPTER FORTY-NINE

Marshal John Payton leaned back in his chair.

"Well, O'Brien, what's your answer?" he said.

Shawn shook his head. "It's thin, marshal."

"I know it is," Payton said. "But Connall Tone sent me a wire, not a letter, and it wasn't much to go on."

"Why don't you head to Cedar City yourself?" Hamp Sedley said. "You say you owe this Tone feller a favor."

"He saved my life one time," Payton said. "So yes, I owe him a favor, but I can't leave Silver Reef. I'm the only law in town."

"And all Tone told you is that his son's a lawman in a town north of the Sweetwater in the Wyoming Territory and needs help," Shawn said.

"Yes, that was all. His son's name is Garvan and the last I heard he'd gone to college back East somewhere. What a college boy is doing as sheriff of a Wyoming cow town, I have no idea."

"And you want me to go in your place, is that it?" Shawn said.

"That sums it up, O'Brien," Payton said. "My feeling is that young Garvan needs a fast gun at his side, and you fit the bill."

"My brother Jake could do it better."

"Maybe, but he's not here. You are."

"Payton, you know my town-taming record. So far it's not so grand."

"Who said anything about town taming? Young Garvan needs help." Payton shook his head. "Hell, for all I know the kid has an ingrown toenail and needs somebody to walk his rounds for him."

"But you don't believe that," Shawn said.

"No. No, I don't. Connall Tone is a proud man and he wouldn't ask my help if it wasn't serious."

"In Irish history, Tone is a noble name," Shawn said.

"Yeah, well, Connall is an Irishman, so that would figure," Payton said.

"Hell, O'Brien, head for Santa Fe and have some fun," Sedley said. "Haven't you had enough of guns and gunfighting for a spell?"

"Sedley has a point, so it's up to you," Payton said.

"Ask your rich pa for some money and enjoy a year of wine, women and song," Sedley said. "It will help you forget what you badly need to forget."

"Your compadre makes sense, O'Brien," Payton

said. "Why stick your neck out for somebody you don't know?"

Shawn smiled. "I thought you wanted my help, marshal. Now you're trying to talk me out of it."

"Like I already said, it's up to you. It will be your life on the line, so it's not for me to influence you one way or t'other."

Shawn thought it through, and then said, "I'm not promising anything, Payton, but I'll go to Cedar City and talk to Connall Tone. Like my father, he's an Irishman who's heir to a proud name and as such he deserves a hearing."

"Glad to hear that, O'Brien," Payton said. "You can take the noon stage from Silver Reef tomorrow."

"You're not hurrying me or anything like that, marshal, huh?" Shawn said, smiling.

"If Tone's wire is anything to go by, I don't think there's much time to be lost."

Sedley said, "O'Brien, you're crazy."

"Nobody ever said otherwise about the O'Briens of Dromore," Shawn said.

"Then I must be crazy as well, because I'd like to tag along and keep you out of trouble," Sedley said. "Hell, I was heading for Cedar City anyway before all the trouble started."

"Because I ran you out of town, Sedley," Payton said. He grinned. "Names, yes, but I never forget a face."

"You got some sore losers in your town, marshal," Sedley said.

"I'd be sore too if I caught you dealing from the bottom of the deck," Payton said.

Sedley shrugged. "It was all a misunderstanding."

"A misunderstanding that could have gotten you lynched if I hadn't put you on the stage."

Shawn grinned. "Glad to have your company, Hamp. Maybe if I decide to head for Wyoming, I'll find time to teach you how to shoot straight."

"Good luck with that," Sedley said.

Before sunup the next morning, Shawn and Sedley took their leave of Ford Platt.

Despite the early hour, the little man was in good spirits, going so far as to swear that if he ever had a misery again the only doctor he'd allow to treat him would be Chinese.

"Hell, Shawn, Dr. Chang says that once I recover from my wounds, he'll fix my leg," Platt said. "The man's a miracle worker. That's what I reckon anyhow."

To show that he harbored no ill will toward Sedley, he presented, with exquisite ceremony, his masonic watch fob to the gambler and urged him to join the craft at his earliest opportunity.

"Make a man of you, Sedley," he said.

To Shawn, he gave his sleeve rig and the Remington derringer.

"You're a man much given to adventure and the

paths of danger," he said. "This outfit may one day stand you in good stead."

Shawn's thanks were interrupted by Dr. Chang, who insisted that it was time for his patient's medications and that the gentlemen should withdraw, "instanter."

But Sedley, much moved by Platt's forgiveness and handsome gift, remained long enough to shed a few tears and give Platt a ferocious hug before the doctor shooed them out of his house and into the dawning morning.

The Wells Fargo stage driver slowed the mule team to a walk when he reached the blackened wreckage of Holy Rood.

He leaned from the box and yelled to the passengers, "This whole damned place went up in flames. That's why all you can see around are ruins."

The grizzled rancher who sat opposite Shawn, a sporting rifle between his knees, said, "Looks like everybody's gone."

"Not much to stay for, I reckon," Shawn said.

The rancher leaned forward. His breath smelled of whiskey.

"They say this was the most law-abiding town in the West," he said. "And I heard there's a fortune in gold hidden on the slope of the ridge you see there. The story is that the townsfolk buried all the money from their bank to save it from the fire and it's still up there. They never could find it again."

"Too bad," Sedley said."

· The rancher tapped a forefinger against his nose.

"One day I'll come back and look for what folks are calling The Lost Treasure of Holy Rood Ridge," he said. Then, grinning, "Make myself a rich man."

"Well, good luck," Shawn said.

The stage was due west of the tall pine country surrounding Timber Top Mountain, when a large gray wolf appeared from the trees and loped alongside.

"Well, lookee here," the rancher said. "I could use a wolf pelt."

He raised his rifle, but Shawn pushed down the barrel, his eyes on the big lobo that was staring at him with amber eyes.

"Leave the wolf be," he said. "He could be an old friend of mine. . . ."

J. A. Johnstone on William W. Johnstone
"When the Truth Becomes Legend"

William W. Johnstone was born in southern Missouri, the youngest of four children. He was raised with strong moral and family values by his minister father, and tutored by his schoolteacher mother. Despite this, he quit school at age fifteen.

"I have the highest respect for education," he says, "but such is the folly of youth, and wanting to see the world beyond the four walls and the blackboard."

True to this vow, Bill attempted to enlist in the French Foreign Legion ("I saw Gary Cooper in *Beau Geste* when I was a kid and I thought the French Foreign Legion would be fun") but was rejected, thankfully, for being underage. Instead, he joined a traveling carnival and did all kinds of odd jobs. It was listening to the veteran carny folk, some of whom had been on the circuit since the late 1800s, telling amazing tales about their experiences, which planted the storytelling seed in Bill's imagination.

"They were mostly honest people, despite the

bad reputation traveling carny shows had back then," Bill remembers. "Of course, there were exceptions. There was one guy named Picky, who got that name because he was a master pickpocket. He could steal a man's socks right off his feet without him knowing. Believe me, Picky got us chased out of more than a few towns."

After a few months of this grueling existence, Bill returned home and finished high school. Next came stints as a deputy sheriff in the Tallulah, Louisiana, Sheriff's Department, followed by a hitch in the U.S. Army. Then he began a career in radio broadcasting at KTLD in Tallulah, which would last sixteen years. It was there that he fine-tuned his storytelling skills. He turned to writing in 1970, but it wouldn't be until 1979 that his first novel, *The Devil's Kiss*, was published. Thus began the full-time writing career of William W. Johnstone. He wrote horror (*The Uninvited*), thrillers (*The Last of the Dog Team*), even a romance novel or two. Then, in February 1983, *Out of the Ashes* was published. Searching for his missing family in the aftermath of a post-apocalyptic America, rebel mercenary and patriot Ben Raines is united with the civilians of the Resistance forces and moves to the forefront of a revolution for the nation's future.

Out of the Ashes was a smash. The series would continue for the next twenty years, winning Bill three generations of fans all over the world. The series was often imitated but never duplicated. "We all tried to copy the Ashes series," said one publishing executive, "but Bill's uncanny ability, both then and now, to predict in which direction the political winds were blowing brought a certain immediacy to the table no one else could capture." The Ashes series would end its run with more than thirty-four books and twenty million copies in print, making it one of the most successful men's action series in American book publishing. (The Ashes series also, Bill notes with a touch of pride, got him on the FBI's Watch List for its less than flattering portrayal of spineless politicians and the growing power of big government over our lives, among other things. In that respect, I often find myself saying, "Bill was years ahead of his time.")

Always steps ahead of the political curve, Bill's recent thrillers, written with myself, include *Vengeance Is Mine, Invasion USA, Border War, Jackknife, Remember the Alamo, Home Invasion, Phoenix Rising, The Blood of Patriots, The Bleeding Edge,* and the upcoming *Suicide Mission.*

It is with the western, though, that Bill found his greatest success and propelled him onto both the *USA Today* and the *New York Times* bestseller lists.

Bill's western series include *The Mountain Man, Matt Jensen, the Last Mountain Man, Preacher, The Family Jensen, Luke Jensen, Bounty Hunter, Eagles, MacCallister* (an Eagles spin-off), *Sidewinders, The Brothers O'Brien, Sixkiller, Blood Bond, The Last Gunfighter,* and the upcoming new series *Flintlock* and *The Trail West*. May 2013 saw the hardcover western *Butch Cassidy, The Lost Years*.

"The Western," Bill says, "is one of the few true art forms that is one hundred percent American. I liken the Western as America's version of England's Arthurian legends, like the Knights of the Round Table, or Robin Hood and his Merry Men. Starting with the 1902 publication of *The Virginian* by Owen Wister, and followed by the greats like Zane Grey, Max Brand, Ernest Haycox, and of course Louis L'Amour, the Western has helped to shape the cultural landscape of America.

"I'm no goggle-eyed college academic, so when my fans ask me why the Western is as popular now as it was a century ago, I don't offer a 200-page thesis. Instead, I can only offer this: The Western is honest. In this great country, which is suffering under the yoke of political correctness, the Western harks back to an era when justice was sure and swift. Steal a man's horse, rustle his cattle, rob a bank, a stagecoach, or a train, you were hunted down and fitted with a hangman's noose. One size fit all.

"Sure, we westerners are prone to a little embellishment and exaggeration and, I admit it, occasionally play a little fast and loose with the facts. But we do so for a very good reason—to enhance the enjoyment of readers.

"It was Owen Wister, in *The Virginian* who first coined the phrase *'When you call me that, smile.'* Legend has it that Wister actually heard those words spoken by a deputy sheriff in Medicine Bow, Wyoming, when another poker player called him a son-of-a-bitch.

"Did it really happen, or is it one of those myths that have passed down from one generation to the next? I honestly don't know. But there's a line in one of my favorite Westerns of all time, *The Man Who Shot Liberty Valance,* where the newspaper editor tells the young reporter, 'When the truth becomes legend, print the legend.'

"These are the words I live by."

Turn the page for an exciting preview!

Born to a family of hard-fighting Scotsmen. Sworn to a legacy of blood and honor. Duff MacCallister brings his own brand of justice to the new American frontier— in this explosive western saga from bestselling authors William W. Johnstone and J. A. Johnstone.

SHOOTING IS THE ONLY WAY OUT

In a town like Chugwater, Wyoming, you know who your friends are, who your enemies are, and who your kill-crazy maniacs are. For Duff MacCallister, the last category belongs to Johnny Taylor and his gang. Duff has wrestled with this polecat before, and knows that his bite is worse than his smell. But when Taylor's gang tries to rob a bank—and Duff manages to shoot one and arrest Taylor's brother— the outraged outlaw raises a stink straight out of hell. First, he begins to randomly slaughter innocent townsfolk one by one. Then, he leaves a note on the bodies warning: *"We will kill more of your citizens if you do not let my brother go."* Now, he's kidnapped a woman as bait—lighting a fuse under Duff MacCallister that's bound to ignite the biggest, bloodiest showdown in Chugwater history. . . .

FIRST TIME IN PRINT!

MACCALLISTER, THE EAGLES LEGACY: DEADLOCK

by William W. Johnstone
with J. A. Johnstone

CHAPTER ONE

The sound of a shot rolled down through the gulch, picked up resonance, then echoed back from the surrounding walls. Emile Taylor, who was holding a smoking pistol, turned to the others with a smile on his face. He had just broken a tossed whiskey bottle with his marksmanship.

"I'd like to see somebody else here who can do that," he snarled.

Emile was one of six men who had made a temporary camp in an arroyo that was about five miles west of the town of Chugwater.

"Emile, there ain't nobody said you wasn't good with a gun, so there is no need for you to be provin' yourself to us," Johnny said. Johnny was Emile's brother. "Anyhow, that don't really matter all that much."

"What do you mean it don't matter?"

"Hopefully, we ain't goin' to be gettin' into no gunfights. The only thing we're goin' to do is ride into town, rob the bank, then hightail it out of there before anyone knows what hit them. And if we pull this off right, there won't be no shootin'."

"What if someone tries to shoot at us?" Emile asked.

"Then you can shoot. But I don't want no shootin' unless we absolutely have to."

Emile was about five feet four inches tall, with ash-blond hair and a hard face. Johnny was two inches taller, with darker hair. Johnny was missing the earlobe of his left ear, having had it bitten off in a fight the last time he was in prison. Although the two men were brothers, they didn't look anything alike until one happened to look into their eyes. Their eyes were exact duplicates: gray, flat, and soulless.

"After we do the job I think we ought to split up . . . ever' man for hisself," Al Short said. "That way, if they put a posse together they won't know which one to follow."

"No, but they might choose to follow just one of us," Julius Jackson pointed out. "And whoever the one is they choose to follow is goin' to be in a heap of trouble."

"Besides which, if we do that, where at will we divide up the money amongst us?" Bart Evans asked.

"I don't know," Short said. "I didn't think about that."

Evans chuckled. "You didn't think about it? Hell,

man, the money is what this all about. How can you not think about it?"

"What we ought to do is, once we leave town, just wait behind a rock and shoot 'em down," Clay Calhoun suggested.

"You mean you'd shoot them from ambush?" Emile asked. "That ain't a very sportin' thing to do."

"Hell, yes. I ain't like you, Emile. I ain't tryin' to build myself no reputation. If someone is comin' after me, I don't need to kill the son of a bitch fair and square. . . . I just want to kill him."

"Clay has a point," Evans said. "The best way to handle a posse would be to set up an ambush. Besides which, most of 'em will be nothin' but store clerks and handy men anyway. Prob'ly ain't none of 'em ever used a gun more 'n once or twice in their life anyway, so even you faced 'em down, there wouldn't be nothin' you could call sportin' about it."

"Well then, if we're goin' to do that, ambush 'em I mean, maybe it would be better for us to all stick together," Jackson said.

"No," Short replied. "I still think it would be best if we split up. I think we'll have a better chance that way."

"All right," Calhoun said. "How about this? Instead of all of us separatin', what if we was to break into two groups? That way the posse will still have to make a choice as to who to follow. And if they decide to split and follow each group, it will cut their numbers in half, which means we would have a better chance."

"Yeah, that sounds like a pretty good idea," Short said.

"No need for any of that," Johnny said. "I've got an idea that will throw them off our trail, once and for all, so that we all get away clean. Only we're going to need different horses."

"What do you mean we are going to need different horses?" Jackson asked. "We got horses already. We got good horses."

A big smile spread across Johnny's face. "Yeah," he said. "But these ain't the horses we're goin' to use when we hold up the bank. These horses ain't even goin' to get close to town."

"That don't make no sense to me a' tall," Evans said.

"Then let me explain it to you," Johnny said. "The way I got it planned out, we're goin' to steal us some horses from several different places. Then, just before we go into town to hold up the bank, we'll hobble our horses in some place out of the way, and when we go into town to rob the bank, we'll be ridin' the stolen horses."

"I don't understand," Jackson said. "Why would we take a chance on ridin' stole'd horses when the ones we got is perfectly good? What if we have to leave town at a gallop? We won't know nothin' a' tall 'bout the mounts we'll be stealin'."

"All they have to do is get us into town and out again, and any healthy horse can do that," Johnny said. "Then when we get to a place that we will have picked out, we'll dismount, take off our saddle and harness, then send the stolen horses on their way."

"Why would we do that?" Short asked. "I mean, if we go to all the trouble to steal 'em, why would we just turn 'em a' loose?"

"You said it yourself, Al. Like as not after we rob the bank, the marshal will be rounding up a posse," Johnny said.

"I reckon he will, but what does that have to do with stole'd horses?"

"The posse will be trailin' us by followin' the tracks and such we leave when we ride away from the bank, right?"

"Yeah."

"All right, now follow me while I try to explain. When we turn them horses loose, where do you think they will go?" Johnny asked.

"Well, I reckon they would—" Short started, and then he stopped in mid-sentence as a huge smile spread across his face. "Son of a bitch! They'll more 'n likely go back wherever it was we stole 'em from."

"Yes," Johnny agreed. "And if we steal each horse from a different place, then the horses will lead the posse all over hell's half-acre. And while the posse is followin' them, we'll be takin' off on our own horses."

"Yeah!" Short said. "Yeah, that's real smart. Did you come up with that all by yourself?"

"Ha!" Emile said, hitting his fist in his hand. "I may be the best shot in the family, but there can't nobody say Johnny ain't the smartest. And that's why he is in charge."

"You need to get on into town now, little brother," Johnny said. "Look around, see what you can see. But don't get into no trouble."

"I'll have a drink for all you boys," Emile said as he started toward his horse. "One for each one of you."

"Just don't get drunk and foolish," Johnny cautioned.

Duff MacCallister's ranch, Sky Meadow, was fifteen miles south and slightly east of where Johnny Taylor and the others were plotting to hold up the Chugwater bank. Duff MacCallister left Scotland four years earlier, and shortly after arriving in the United States, he moved to Wyoming. Here by homesteading and purchase of adjacent land, he started his ranch. Since that time he had been exceptionally successful, and Sky Meadow now spread out across some 30,000 acres of prime range land lying between the Little Bear and Big Bear creeks.

Little and Big Bear creeks were year-round sources

of water, and that, plus the good natural grazing land, allowed Duff to try an experiment. The experiment was to introduce Black Angus cattle. He was well familiar with the breed, for he had worked with them in Scotland. His experiment was successful, and he now had 10,000 head of Black Angus cattle, making his ranch one of the most profitable in all of Wyoming.

Duff's operation was large enough to employ fourteen men, principle of whom was Elmer Gleason, his ranch foreman. In addition to Elmer, who had been with Duff from the very beginning, there were three other cowboys who had been with him for a very long time. These three men: Al Woodward, Case Martin, and Brax Walker, not only worked for him, they were extremely loyal and top hands, occupying positions of responsibility just under Elmer Gleason.

Though the relationship between Duff and the three men was solid now, it had not gotten off to a very good start. Their first encounter had been at a community dance which was held in the ball room of the Antlers Hotel. The hotel was on the corner of Bowie Avenue and First Street in the nearby town of Chugwater.

On that night, Duff had escorted Meagan Parker to the dance, but Woodward, Martin, and Walker had shown up without women. Given the general disproportionate number of single men to single women in the West, it was not all that unusual for young cowboys to come alone. But Woodward,

Martin, and Walker spent the first half-hour getting drunk on the heavily spiked punch.

"I got me an idea," Woodward said. "Martin, let's me 'n you join one o' them squares."

"We can't, we ain't got no woman to dance with us."

"That don't matter none," Woodward explained. "Once we start the dancin' and the do-si-do 'n and all that, why, we'll be swingin' around with all the other women in the square."

"Yeah, Martin said. "That's right, ain't it?"

"No, it ain't right," Walker said.

"What are you talkin' about? What do you mean it ain't right?" Woodward asked.

"Well, think about it. Whichever one of you takes the woman's part will be do-si-do 'n with all the other men when you get to swingin' around."

"Yeah, I hadn't thought about that," Martin said.

"Hell, that ain't nothin' to be worryin' about," Woodward said. "Next dance, why, we'll just switch around. Martin, you'll be the woman on the first dance, then I'll set the next one out, and Walker, you can come in and let Martin be the man. Then on the third dance, why, I'll come back in and be the woman. That way, all three of us can do-si-do with the other women."

"All right," Martin said. "But let's pick us a dance with some good-lookin' women in it."

When the next sets of squares were formed,

Woodward and Martin joined the same square as Duff MacCallister and Meagan Parker.

"Well, lookie here, Martin," Woodward said, pointing toward Duff. "Looks to me like you won't have to do-si-do with all men. You'll get one man that's wearin' a dress. That ought to count for somethin'."

The "man in a dress" remark was prompted by the fact that Duff MacCallister had arrived at the dance wearing kilts. But it wasn't just any kilts; it was the green-and-blue plaid, complete with Victoria Cross, of a captain of the 42nd Regiment of Foot, better known as the Black Watch, the most storied regiment in the British Army.

"Man in a dress," Martin said derisively, laughing just as the music started.

As the couples broke apart to swing with the others, Martin made a round with the men, including Duff. But on the next round, he rebelled. Pushing one of the men aside, he started swinging around with all the women until he got to Meagan. That was when Duff stepped out into the middle of the square and grabbed him by the arm.

"Get out of my way, girlie," Case Martin said to Duff. He reached for Meagan, but as he did so, Duff, using his thumb and forefinger, squeezed the spot where Martin's neck joined his shoulder. The squeeze was so painful that Martin sunk to his knees with his face screwed up in agony. The other squares, seeing what was happening in this one, interrupted their dancing. Then the caller stopped, as did the band—the music breaking off in discordant chords.

"If you gentlemen are going to dance in our square, you'll be for doing it correctly," Duff said, talking quietly to the man who was on his knees in pain.

"Missy, you done started somethin' you can't finish," Al Woodward said, throwing a punch at Duff.

As gracefully as if he were performing a dance move, Duff bent back at his waist and allowed Woodward's fist to fly harmlessly by his chin. Duff counterpunched with one blow to Woodward's jaw, and Woodward went down to join Martin, who was still on the floor.

Walker, who had been sitting this dance out, pulled his pistol and leveled it at Duff.

"No!" Meagan shouted.

Duff reacted before anyone else did. Pulling the *sgian dubh,* or ceremonial knife, from its position in the right kilt stocking, he threw it in a quick, underhanded snap, toward Walker. As he had intended, the knife rotated in air so that the butt, and not the blade, hit Walker right between the eyes, doing so with sufficient force to knock him down.

Marshal Ferrell and his deputies took charge then, escorting all three of the troublemakers out of the dance hall and down to the jail.

CHAPTER TWO

Within three months of that unpromising beginning, Woodward, Martin, and Walker began working at Sky Meadow. On this day, almost two years after the three had been hired, they were working the south range of the ranch. They weren't herding, they were just making certain that the cattle, which had a tendency to wander about as they were grazing, stayed within the confines of the ranch. As they were riding up a long, low hill, they heard a cow bawling.

"Listen to that," Woodward said.

"Listen to what? It ain't nothing but a bawlin' cow," Martin replied.

"That ain't no ordinary bawlin'. That's a scared bawlin'," Woodward insisted.

The three cowboys urged their horses into a rapid lope up the rest of the rise, and when they crested the ridge, saw that a pack of wolves had brought down one of the animals.

"The sons of bitches! Look at that!" Martin said. He pulled his rifle from the sheath.

"No," Woodward said holding his hand out to stop Martin. "You can't hit the wolves from here. We need to get closer."

Thinking the newly killed cow would keep the attention of the wolves, the three men rode down the hill as fast as they dared across the uneven ground, hoping to close the distance so they could come within range of the wolves.

Just before they got into range though, the wolves sensed their presence and darted off.

"The bastards are getting away!" Martin said, angrily. Pulling his rifle, he began shooting, though the range was too great and the bullets did nothing but kick up little dust clouds where they hit. The wolves escaped easily.

Dismounting, the three cowboys walked over to the steer. It was lying on the ground now, still alive, even though the wolves had already begun to eat him. Too weak to make any sound, the animal looked up at the three men with big, brown, pain-filled eyes.

"Damn," Woodward said. "Look at the poor bastard." Pulling his pistol, he shot the animal in the head, putting it out of its misery.

"This is the third one we've found like this," Walker said.

"Yeah, well, now we know for sure what's causing

it, 'cause we actual seen the wolves while they was doin' it," Martin said.

Woodward chuckled. "What did you think was doin' it, Case? Prairie dogs, maybe?"

"No, but I thought it maybe could have been a cougar or somethin'."

"Yeah, I guess it could have been. All right, come on, let's see if we can find them wolves before they get 'em another one."

The three cowboys hunted the wolves for the next two hours, but without success.

"What do we do now?" Martin asked.

"We need to tell Elmer," Woodward said.

"I ain't lookin' forward to tellin' him about a problem that we ain't took care of yet," Walker said.

"I know what you mean, but it's got to be done."

Back at the ranch, Elmer was supervising the half dozen or so men whose duties this day had not taken them out on the range. Cowboys, as Elmer explained patiently, almost patronizingly, anytime he hired a new hand, had to be jacks of all trades.

"You got to be part carpenter so's you can keep the buildings up, and part wheelwright so as to keep the wagons repaired. You need to be some veterinarian too, so's you can take care of the animals, and even a little bit of a doctor to take care of wounds and such, seein' as we're so far from town that it ain't always that easy to get to a real doc."

At the moment, a couple of the cowboys, Ben and Dale had one of the ranch wagons jacked up with the left rear wheel off. They were packing the hubs with grease, a job that was so dirty and unpleasant that it was passed around among the men so that one person didn't have to do it all the time. Elmer approached the two men, carrying two glasses of lemonade.

"I thought you boys might like this," he said, offering a glass to each of them.

"A cold beer would have been better," Ben said. "But this will certainly do. Thanks, Elmer."

The two men wiped as much grease from their hands as they could before they took the glasses.

"How is it goin'?" Elmer asked.

"This here is the last wheel on the last wagon," Ben replied. "What you got in mind for us after this?"

"I don't have nothin' more in particular for you, today. Why don't you boys just look around and see if you can find somethin' that you know needs doin'. If you do find something needs done, just go ahead and take care of it."

"All right. Hey, Elmer, after we're done for the day, you don't mind if we run into town, do you? They say there's a new girl at Fiddler's Green," Ben said.

"I don't mind, if all your work is done," Elmer said. "New girl, huh?"

"Yeah, and they say she's really a looker," Dale added.

"She'll just be one more way Biff has of getting money from you boys," Elmer said. "By the way, have either of you seen Simon Reid?"

"Reid? Ain't he mucking stalls today?" Dale asked.

"He is supposed to be. But he ain't there."

"He ain't? You mean he's left Earl to muck the stalls all by his ownself?"

"It sure looks like that," Elmer said.

"I don't like to tell tales on others," Dale said. "But if you got three men workin' and one loafin' on a job, you can bet the one loafin' will be Reid."

"I tell you what," Ben added. "If that son of a bitch run out on me like he did to Earl, I'd near 'bout lay an axe handle up alongside his head next time me 'n him seen each other."

"And I'd hand you the axe handle," Ben added.

"If you see him, tell him I'm lookin' for him," Elmer said.

"Will do," Dale promised.

Elmer left the two men, mumbling to himself as he started back toward the ranch office. The ranch office was a relatively new addition to the Sky Meadow compound, a small building that sat between the "big house" as the cowboys called Duff MacCallister's residence, and the bunkhouse. Duff was in the office tallying the latest numbers, compiled by the almost daily count given him by the cowboys.

"Elmer, you're looking a bit peeved," Duff said when Elmer came into the office and sat down at his own desk with a disgusted sigh. "Would you be for tellin' me what has you in such a state?"

"It's Simon Reid, again," Elmer replied. "That son of a bitch is as worthless as tits on a bull. I thought I was a better judge of men than that. I should 'a' known from the time I hired him that he wasn't worth a cup of warm piss."

Duff laughed. "Elmer, 'tis no one I know with a more colorful grasp of the English language than you. Sure 'n' sometimes I wonder if 'tis English at all that you speak."

"Damn it all to hell, Duff, I'm tryin' not to cuss, I really am. But Reid absolutely makes my ass knit barbed wire."

Duff laughed again. "Och, mon, now your language has gone from colorful to incomprehensible. How does one's arse knit barbed wire? Never mind, I know the answer to my own question. One's arse would knit barbed wire very painfully."

At that moment there was a knock on the door.

"Maybe that's Reid," Elmer said, getting up to answer the door.

It was Woodward, Martin, and Walker.

"We need to talk," Woodward said.

"Duff is cipherin' an' such. Let's talk outside, so's not to disturb him," Elmer responded, stepping out of the office, and then shutting the door behind him.

"We've got problems, Elmer," Woodward said. "Big problems."

"What kind of problems?"

"Losing beeves kind of problems," Woodward said. "We found three of 'em down half eaten."

"Half eaten?" Elmer replied, confused by the comment.

"By wolves," Walker added.

"You're sure its wolves?"

"Yeah, hell they was still workin' on one of the beeves when we seen them," Woodward said. "Five of the critters they was."

"Why didn't you shoot 'em?"

"We tried to shoot 'em, but we can't get close enough to the bastards to hit 'em," Martin said.

"They're too damn smart—they either see us or hear us or somethin'. But we can't get no closer 'n about two or three hunnert yards from 'em before they start runnin'. And you can't hit no wolf from three hunnert yards away. Hell, you can barely see the sons of bitches from that far," Walker said.

"The bastards started eatin' on that last poor critter even before it died. We had to put it out of its misery," Woodward said.

"Good, that was the right thing to do," Elmer said. He sighed. "All right, thanks for tellin' me about it. I'll let Duff know."

"I agree, Duff needs to know," Woodward said. "But for the life of me, I don't know what he will be able to do about it."

"This is Duff MacCallister we're talking about, remember?"

Woodward laughed. "Yeah," he said. "Now that I think about it, I have no doubt but that he will take care of it."

"Listen, you boys haven't seen Simon Reid, have you?"

"Reid? No, not since this mornin'," Woodward said. "Didn't you toll him out for workin' in the barn today?"

"Yeah, I did. But he ain't there, and accordin' to Earl, he ain't seen hide nor hair of him since just after lunch."

As Elmer, Woodward, Martin, and Walker were having their impromptu conference, Simon Reid, the subject of their conversation and the man who had been the cause of Elmer's earlier agitation, was having a business meeting with three men. The meeting was being conducted five miles away from the ranch compound. It was at the extreme west end of Sky Meadow, and its remote location was by design, for the business at hand was cattle rustling. The cattle being rustled belonged to Duff MacCallister.

"As you can see, I've cut out ten of 'em," Reid said, referring to the cattle that stood stoically nearby. "They're Black Angus, which is the finest and most expensive cow in the country. Do you have any idea how much these here cows is bringin' at the Kansas market?"

The three men Reid was making his pitch to weren't Sky Meadow cowboys. They weren't even local men. Creech, Phelps, and a third who called himself Kid Dingo, were from Bordaux, a town that lay twelve miles north of Chugwater.

When none of the three answered him, Reid continued his pitch. "Right now, these cows, at the Kansas City market, is bringin' forty dollars a head."

"Yeah, well that's interestin' an' all, but you may have noticed that we ain't exactly the Kansas market," Creech replied.

"And I ain't askin' for no forty dollars, neither," Reid said. "I'm just tellin' you that so's that you know what a good deal I'm givin' you. I'm only askin' twenty dollars a head."

"We'll give you five dollars."

"Five dollars?" Reid replied, reacting sharply in response to the low offer. "What do you mean five dollars? Come on, Creech, are you out of your mind? I'm takin' a hell of a risk by sellin' these cows to you in the first place. I stole these here cows from Duff MacCallister's herd, and if you don't know much about him, well, let me tell you, he ain't somebody you cross. Besides which, I know you're goin' to get at least thirty dollars a head for 'em, when you get 'em back to Bordaux."

"What we sell 'em for ain't no concern of your'n," Phelps said.

"Come on, fellers, me 'n' you've know'd each other a long time," Reid said, continuing to plead his case. "You ain't got no call to try and cheat me like that."

Creech, Phelps, and Kid Dingo moved away a few feet so they could talk privately. They consulted for a moment, then, nodding, Creech turned back to Reid.

"All right, we'll give you ten dollars a head for 'em, but that is as high as we are goin' to go. That's a hunnert dollars for you, and we'll take it from here. All you got to do is put the money in your pocket and ride away," Creech said.

"A hunnert dollars," Phelps added, with a smile. "Think of the whiskey and the whores you can buy with a hunnert dollars."

"All right," Reid said. "Give me the hunnert dollars and the cows is yours."

The transaction made, Reid pocketed the money and started back toward the barn. He was supposed to be mucking out the stalls. That was a job he hated, but he smiled as he thought of the one hundred dollars riding in his pocket right now. Having that much money would make the job bearable.

CHAPTER THREE

At the butte where Woodward and the others told him they had seen the wolves, Duff MacCallister reined up his horse, Sky, then sat in the saddle for a moment as he perused the range before him. Except for roundup, and cattle drives, such as when he would drive a herd down to the loading pens and rail head in Cheyenne, the cattle were never in one large herd. Rather, they tended to break off into smaller groups, bound to each other within those groups as if they were family units.

Duff saw one such group now, gathered near the water and standing together under the shade of a cottonwood tree.

With a pair of binoculars hanging around his neck, Duff dismounted, and then walked out onto a flat rock overhang. Lifting the binoculars to his eyes, he studied the open range below him. That was when he spotted them: at least eight wolves, sneaking up on the cattle.

Duff walked back to his horse, then pulled a Remington Creedmore Rifle from his saddle sheath. The rifle, a recent purchase, had been developed especially for the Creedmore Marksmanship Club. It had a well-deserved reputation for accuracy, featuring a telescopic sight as well as a device that would allow the shooter to compensate for range and wind.

Woodward had reported that when anyone tried to get close enough to the wolves to shoot them that the crafty creatures would see, smell, or hear them, then dart quickly out of the way. That meant that the only way the wolves could be eliminated would be if someone could shoot them from a standoff position that was so far away that the wolves would not even realize they were in danger.

Such a feat would take a rifle with extreme range, as well as a marksman who was skilled enough to take advantage of that superior range. The scoped Creedmore was that rifle and Duff MacCallister was that marksman.

Lying down on his stomach, Duff took up a prone firing position on the rock. He cranked in the range, then, picking up a few grains of grass dropped them to estimate the windage. That done, he sighted in on the wolves. The wolves were at least five hundred yards away, so distant that without the magnification of the scope, they could barely be seen.

Because of the great distance the wolves were totally unaware of Duff's presence. They approached their prey with the extreme confidence of a predator who knew that, collectively, they were superior to any creature that might be near.

But Duff was not near, and they were not superior to him.

Duff squeezed the trigger, and the gun boomed and kicked back against his shoulder. One and a half seconds later the lead wolf was sent sprawling by the impact of the heavy bullet. A tenth of a second after the strike of the bullet, the sound of the shot reached the remaining pack, but it was so far away that they were unable to connect that sound to what happened to the leader of the pack.

A second shot killed a second wolf, and within less than a minute, Duff had killed every one of them. His work done, he picked up the remaining shells, returned to his horse, replaced the rifle in its boot, mounted Sky, and started back home.

When Duff returned to the compound, he could hear the blacksmith's hammer ringing, and outside the machine shed he saw Ben and Dale painting a wagon. He could also hear his foreman's voice coming from the barn. The voice was loud and angry, and Duff heard Reid's name being spoken.

"I gather Elmer has found the errant Mr. Reid," Duff said to the two men who were painting.

"It ain't as much Elmer findin' him, as it is Reid

just come ridin' back in without so much as a by-your-leave," Ben said.

"He told Elmer he thought he was finished with the work he was give to do," Dale added.

"And Elmer took issue with that, did he?"

"Yes, sir, he sure did, an' ole Elmer's been givin' Reid hell ever since."

"Keep the damn stalls clean!" Elmer's voice said loudly. "You wouldn't want to be sleeping, ankle deep in horseshit, would you?"

"They're horses," a voice replied. "This is only natural for them. Horses is supposed to live in shit."

"It ain't natural at all," Elmer said. "If we was doin' things natural, the horses wouldn't be in stalls in the first place. They'd all be runnin' free. We're the ones that's got 'em all cooped up, so the least we can do is give 'em a clean place to be. Now get it done."

"I didn't sign on to clean horse shit out of a stall," Reid said. "You want the shit cleaned, you clean it yourself."

"I've had about enough of you, Mr. Reid," Elmer said. "You've been slacking off way too much here, lately. You lollygagged around all mornin' long, and after lunch you wasn't nowhere to be found. You left Earl to do the work all by himself."

"I told Earl where I was goin'. Yesterday, my rain slicker fell offen my saddle, and I went back to look for it. Then, while I was lookin' for it, I seen some cows drifting off the ranch. I figured savin' them cows was more important than cleanin' up horse shit."

"Did you now? Well, here is the thing, Reid, how do I know you was actually roundin' up wanderin' away strays? Or even lookin' for your rain slicker, for that matter. I mean, you lied about greasing the wheel on the hay wagon last week, and because it didn't get no grease, the axle got so wore down that it's out of round and we're goin' to have to put on another one."

"Then why don't you have me doin' somethin' important like that, instead of shovelin' shit out of a stall?"

"I tell you what, Reid. You don't have to worry about cleaning out no more shit because you ain't a' goin' to be working here no more. Get your tack and get out of here. You're fired."

"You can't fire me, old man. The only one who can fire me is the man that owns this place."

Duff had been just outside, listening in on the discussion, and he chose that moment to walk into the barn.

"That is where you are wrong, Mr. Reid," Duff said. "Elmer Gleason is the executive administrator of this operation, and as such, has full authority to fire anyone he deems needing fired."

"He's the what?" Reid asked.

"I'm the ramrod," Elmer said. "Now, get."

"Someday you are goin' to regret this," Reid said.

"That wouldn't be a threat now, would it, Reid?"

Elmer asked. "Because if it is, well by God, me 'n' you can just settle this out here and now."

"I'll leave, but I ain't goin' nowhere without drawin' my pay," Reid said.

"How much are you owed?" Duff asked.

"I'm drawin' forty dollars a month."

"Reid, you do know that Mr. MacCallister is payin' more than any other rancher in the valley, don't you? Most anyone else is paying is thirty dollars and found."

"Here's twenty dollars," Duff said.

"You're bein' awful generous, Mr. MacCallister," Elmer said. "The most we owe him right now is ten dollars, and we don't even have to settle up with him for that, until the end of the month."

"If I am for understanding the way you feel about him, Elmer, the more distant he is from Sky Meadow, the better things will be."

"I guess that's true, all right."

Duff smiled. "Then let's just say he can get farther away on twenty dollars, than he can on ten."

Reid took the twenty-dollar bill, and then glared for a moment at both Elmer and Duff.

"You got your money, Reid. Now get," Elmer ordered.

Reid walked outside where his horse, still saddled, stood tied to a hitching rail.

About half the cowboys employed by Duff owned their own horses, while half rode horses that belong to Sky Meadow. Reid was one of the cowboys who owned his own horse, and from the very first day that had given him an attitude of superiority over those who did not. Now, as he rode away from the compound, a few of the other cowboys turned out to watch him leave.

Reid's air of superiority, his lack of cooperation with the others who worked on the ranch, as well as his general laziness, had not engendered strong friendships. As a result, those who had turned out to watch him leave did so with a sense of satisfaction that he was gone. A few even called insults out to him.

"Ha! I'll bet this here is the first time anyone ever seen a bag o' shit ridin' a horse before," one of the cowboys called.

"Look there, boys, that's somethin' you don't see all that often," another said. "Two horse's asses at the same time, one at the horse rear end, and the other sittin' in the horse's saddle."

There were other insults and derisive comments shouted until Reid, who urged his horse into a gallop, moved out of range.

"It looks as if your decision to fire Mr. Reid is being well received by the others," Duff said.

"It looks like it, don't it?" Elmer replied. "It turns out there didn't nobody like the son of a bitch. So tell me, Duff, did you see any wolves?" he asked.

"Aye, eight of the creatures I saw," Duff said.

"Good. I'll get someone out there to bury them."

"Sure now, 'n' how is it that you know I killed them?" Duff asked.

"How do I know? Because you seen 'em, that's

how I know. You ain't a'goin' to tell me they run off now, are you?"

"They're dead," Duff said.

"Uh-huh. Like I said, I'll get someone out there to bury 'em. If we leave 'em to lay around and rot, next thing you know the water could get bad."

"I'm going into town this afternoon to check the mail and collect a few items at the store," Duff said. "Would you be for wanting me to pick something up for you?"

"Better get some coffee," Duff said. "You bein' an Englishman, you always remember tea, but don't always remember coffee."

"Och, 'tis a Scotsman I am, and nae an Englishman," Duff corrected him. He smiled. "Sure now, and have you nae corrected me anytime I refer to you as a Yank?"

"Lord, no, don't do that," Elmer said with a wince. "You know damn well I ain't no Yankee."

"Aye, I know well, Elmer Gleason. 'Tis a pair of rebels we both be, but in differing ways."

When Elmer walked back out to the barn, he saw the wagons painted and glistening, with the wheels greased and reattached.

"Good job, men," he said.

"Al, Case, and Brax are goin' into town. Since all the work you give us to do is done, can we have the rest of the afternoon off to go into town with them?"

"I reckon so," Elmer said.

Ben smiled, broadly. "Come on, Dale, let's get washed up, some."

Ben, Dale, Woodward, Martin, and Walker lived in the bunkhouse. A long, relatively narrow building, the bunkhouse was one of several buildings that now occupied the compound. It had seven beds on either side. The individual beds, and the area immediately around the bed, became the personal domain of the cowboy who slept there, his space as inviolate as if it were his home. And in fact, it was his home.

The cowboys used different forms of expression to personalize their "homes," which not only established it as their private area, but gave them a sense of belonging and identity.

Dale had a picture of a fancy saddle that he had cut from a Sears and Roebuck Catalogue pinned to the wall above his bed. Ben had a blue ribbon he had won in a foot race in Cheyenne the year before. There were other pictures and bits of memorabilia tacked to the wall above other bunks, from a calendar featuring a picture of a passenger train roaring through the night, to more than one "lucky" horse shoe.

Ben and Dale filled a Number Two washtub with water, and then flipped a coin to see who got to use the water first.

Ben won the coin toss and was now sitting in the

tub in the middle of the floor, scrubbing his back with a long-handled brush.

"Dale, you ever been to a big city?" Ben asked.

"I been to Cheyenne."

"No, I mean a big city, like maybe Denver, or San Francisco, or St. Louis, or someplace like that."

"Well, I was borned in St. Louis, but I don't remember it."

"I ain't never been to no big city either, but I'd dearly love to go someday."

"Why?"

"I've heard tell that in San Francisco they got a whore standin' on near 'bout ever' corner."

"They got whores in Chugwater."

"Yeah, but most of the whores in Chugwater are so ugly they'd make a train take five miles of dirt road. The ones in the city is all real pretty, and 'cause they got so many, it don't cost you hardly nothin' at all to go to bed with 'em."

"Maybe someday me 'n' you can go to San Francisco," Dale suggested.

Ben climbed out of the tub then and started toward his bunk.

"The water is all your'n now," he said.

Dale walked over to look down into the tub. "What water?" he asked. "Looks to me like I'm about to climb into one of them bog holes we sometimes got to pull the cows out of."